ACCL...

THE FALA -FACTOR-

AND
Stuart M. Kaminsky

humor to produce entertainment

at its best."

—*Chicago Sun-Times*

★

"Packed with realistic historical detail,
topsy-turvy action, and wisecracks."

—*Booklist*

W9-DFV-300

more . . .

The Toby Peters Mysteries

THE MELTING CLOCK★
POOR BUTTERFLY★
BURIED CAESARS★
THINK FAST, MR. PETERS
SMART MOVES
THE MAN WHO SHOT LEWIS VANCE★
DOWN FOR THE COUNT★
THE FALA FACTOR★
HE DONE HER WRONG
CATCH A FALLING CLOWN
HIGH MIDNIGHT
NEVER CROSS A VAMPIRE
THE HOWARD HUGHES AFFAIR
YOU BET YOUR LIFE
MURDER ON THE YELLOW BRICK ROAD
BULLET FOR A STAR★

★Published by
THE MYSTERIOUS PRESS

STUART M. KAMINSKY

THE FALA FACTOR

THE MYSTERIOUS PRESS

Published by Warner Books

A Time Warner Company

MYSTERIOUS PRESS EDITION

Cover design and illustration by Tom McKeveney

This Mysterious Press Edition is published by arrangement with St. Martin's Press, 175 Fifth Avenue, New York, NY 10010.

The Mysterious Press name and logo are trademarks of Warner Books, Inc.

Mysterious Press books are published by
Warner Books, Inc.
1271 Avenue of the Americas
New York, NY 10020

 A Time Warner Company

Printed in the United States of America

First Mysterious Press Printing: October, 1993
10 9 8 7 6 5 4 3 2 1

For Carol and Al Slingo

Once in 1945, when General Eisenhower came to lay a wreath on Franklin's grave, the gates of the regular driveway were opened and his automobile approached the house accompanied by the wailing of the sirens of a police escort. When Fala heard the sirens, his legs straightened out, his ears pricked up and I knew that he expected to see his master coming down the drive as he had come so many times.

—Eleanor Roosevelt, *On My Own*

1

The little black dog on my desk wanted to play, but with a corpse sitting in the corner and a murderer on the way up to my office on the elevator I just wasn't in the mood. I patted his head, tried not to smell his breath, and said, "Maybe later."

This didn't please him. The Scottie lay down, covering the letter telling me where I was to pick up my sugar ration stamp book, put his head on his front paws, and looked up at me sadly. I checked my .38 automatic to be sure it was loaded, aimed it tentatively at the door to my office and hoped that I wouldn't have to use it, and, if I did, that it would work. It had never proved particularly reliable in the past.

Somewhere far below, the elevator of the Farraday Building ground its way upward. When I was a cop in Glendale back in 1933 or '34, I'd been on a call with my partner, a guy named John Thompson, who was short, dark, like a floor model Philco radio. He had a few months to go before retirement when we saw a couple of guys running out of a cigar store looking a little excited. We would have paid no attention if one of them hadn't been holding a shotgun.

Thompson had sighed, "Oh shit," pulled our car over, shuffled out, and, with me backing him up, stepped in front of the two guys, who were so busy looking back at the cigar store they didn't see us till we were no more than a ten-foot pole apart.

2 STUART M. KAMINSKY

"What seems to be the discrepancy?" Thompson had said in his beer-grated voice. One of the two stopped and turned to us with his mouth open. He was about thirty and needed a shave and a good dentist. The other guy, the one with the shotgun, was older, maybe forty, and apparently slow of mind and body. His shotgun came up in an arc that would have brought its barrel in line with my stomach in the time between two heartbeats. I didn't, couldn't move. Next to me I heard Thompson let out the start of a weary little puff of air, but I didn't hear the end of it. It was covered by the shot that John took at the shotgun holder. My left ear went temporarily deaf but my right ear caught the sound of the shotgun clattering to the sidewalk.

The gun skittered toward us, sending up sparks. The sound went down my back like false teeth on a wet blackboard. That was the sound that the Farraday Building elevator always reminded me of, but that wasn't the reason I seldom took the elevator. The elevator was just too damned slow for transportation. If it weren't for the noise, it would have been great for thinking, but I couldn't think of anything but that shotgun when I rode in the Farraday elevator.

So, there I was, May 1942, a little black dog on my desk, a Tuesday night when I was supposed to have been with Carmen watching Henry Armstrong take on two guys in an exhibition at the Ocean Park Arena. If the dog and I made it through the next hour, I might still be able to pick Carmen up and catch the match. I knew I had at least four bucks left. So, with a buck for the tickets I could . . . The dog whined. He either needed a walk, sensed my fear, or had some moment of dog magic that told him something was about to happen.

The elevator ground up past the first floor. My office, really a closet inside the offices of Sheldon Minck, D.D.S., was on the fourth floor. So, considering the speed of the elevator and the way things seemed to be slowing down, I had plenty of time. I glanced over at the corpse in the corner. He looked like a guy who just fell asleep waiting in Union Station for the next train to Anaheim. His hands were folded in his lap and his chin was resting on his chest. His eyes were closed. I had closed them. A whisp of hair dangled over his forehead and down past his nose. If he were a cartoon character, he'd have blown the wisp of hair away while still asleep and the audience would have laughed. But he wasn't blowing and he wasn't funny.

The dog whined again and I looked down at him. His brown eyes looked up at my face. What he saw was a private detective named Toby Peters who was closer to fifty than forty-five, had more than a few gray hairs in his sideburns, sweated too easily, and lived with an always sore back and memories bought with hard time. Standing up, which I seemed to be doing less and less, I was close to five nine. My face was dark and most notable for the piece of flesh in its center, which could only charitably be called a nose. God began to remold my nose when I was about thirteen. God used my older brother Phil as his instrument and my brother used a baseball. Later God, without too much creativity, remolded the nose some more with an automobile windshield. Still not content, he let my brother put the final touches to the job with his fist.

That God/sculpture explanation isn't mine. It was given to me a few years back by my landlord at the Farraday, Jeremy Butler, ex-pro wrestler, present poet. I didn't see the work of God in my nose when I looked in the mirror or at my reflection in a store window on Main Street. I saw a tough-looking, surprisingly amused man who needed a new suit and a shave.

"Dog," I said aloud, "why am I happy?"

The dog whined again, but it wasn't heightened animal awareness. I was now sure he needed a walk. I looked around and decided that he couldn't relieve himself anywhere in my office. I could let him out into Shelly's office and pretend I didn't know what he was doing. Given the recently scrubbed state of Shelly's lair, even Shelly might notice.

"Dog," I whispered, patting his head, "you'll just have to hold it. Think about something else."

The dog had no intention of thinking of something else. He stood up again on his stumpy legs and looked toward the window and downtown Los Angeles. There was an alley out there but it was four stories down.

The elevator ground past the second floor and the corpse

slumped a little further in his chair, probably from the vibrations of the approaching elevator. Maybe it was a warning. Whatever it was, it scared the dog, which stood up on the desk and proved that he couldn't think about something else. I jumped up and back, but my office is just big enough for my desk, my chair, and one other chair jammed behind the door. There was no place to escape but out the window. His leg was up and he was aiming at the telephone.

"No," I said calmly. "Don't. Wait. For Chrissake, is a little bladder retention too much to ask after all I've done for you?"

I didn't expect him to understand me, at least not the words. When I was a kid, I had had a dog named Murphy. I used to talk to Murphy a lot, and he always pretended that he understood, which is what dogs learn to do early when they discover that they're really too stupid to understand. Sometimes you can fool a dog that way. The dog in my office was smarter than the average dog. He put his paw down and whined.

I reached over to the desk and into the bag of Fritos I'd picked up earlier at Safeway and offered a handful to the dog. He sniffed at them, forgot his problem for a second, licked a Frito, took one in his mouth, and sat down to chew on it.

I had lost track of time. Maybe it was the grinding of Fritos in dog teeth that had covered the sound, but I suddenly realized that the elevator had stopped. I tried to listen but the dog had gone for the Frito bag and was pushing paper and grinding, his black nose turning Frito orange. The door to the outside office opened, and then the inner door. All that was left for the killer was to take six or seven steps across the room and open my office door. Above the sound of the distracted dog on my desk I counted the steps and watched as the shadow fell across the pebbled glass of my door.

A hand reached for the door, hesitated, and turned the knob. I reached for my gun on the desk, but it wasn't where I had just put it. The dog had probably kicked it to the floor, where it lay somewhere in darkness.

The door began to open, and I had no time to come up with a plan that didn't include a gun in my hand. I sat back as the door pushed cautiously forward and did my best to look like a dangerous man who has aces full. I said, "We've been waiting for you. Sorry I can't offer you a chair but the only one I've got is occupied by a corpse."

The killer, whose gun I was trying not to look at, stepped in and with a smile said, "Then both chairs will soon be occupied by corpses."

"I don't think so," I said, grinning and reaching slowly to pat the damned dog that might be responsible for getting me permanently punctured. "I've got a few things to tell you."

"Have you?" said the killer with some amusement, closing the door and stepping in. The gun was now leveled at my belly, about where the shotgun would have pointed a decade earlier if Thompson hadn't put a not-too-neat hole in that robber in Glendale. But Thompson couldn't help me now. He had retired to a hardware store in Fresno.

"I have," I said, hoping to catch a glimpse of that damned gun from the corner of my eye.

"Then tell them. I've always liked *The Arabian Nights*, Mr. Peters," said the killer with smart-ass amusement, leaning back against the wall. "You, like Scheherazade, will live as long as your tales amuse me and are relevant to our present situation."

"What I have to say you'll find interesting," I said with a lopsided grin.

"Begin," said the killer, and since I had no idea what I was going to say, I cursed the moment one week earlier on a May day when I had entered the Farraday Building feeling sorry for myself but expecting more than a week of time left on earth.

2

Normally, I parked my '38 Ford coupe behind the Farraday. But "normally" didn't exist any longer. There was a war on and car parts were hard to get, especially tires. The best source for fenders, running boards, bumpers, and tires was your friendly neighborhood garage mechanic, who might have a deal with some enterprising youngsters or oldsters who could strip a defenseless car in three minutes. If the war went on more than a few years, I suggested to No-Neck Arnie, the mechanic who had sold me the car, we'd get to the point where there would be only a few cars left, each one a monster combination of Fords, DeSotos, Caddies, and whatever.

"You're a philosopher," Arnie had said, shifting his body around to look at me, since he had no neck. "Like that guy on the radio, what's his name, Fred Allen."

I had a deal with Arnie. I parked my car in his garage, where he stopped his people from taking it apart. He also kept it running. In exchange for this, he charged me more than the usual war budget, which, considering the times, was quite fair. I looked back at the Ford, whose bumper sagged and whose right headlight looked bloodshot.

"A beauty, Arn," I said before going out through the open garage door. I was in no hurry. I had nothing waiting for me in the office besides a list of phone calls to make to see if I could pick up some fill-in for hotel detectives who might be going on vacation. I also had a lead on some guard work at Grumman's. A guy I had once worked with at Warner Brothers told me they were beefing up their night staff now that they had government contracts, and maybe I could get on part-time.

That was going to be the last call on my list. The Grumman lead was desperation, a confession that I was up against it. I had told myself five years earlier that I was not going to put on a uniform again, not no time, not never. I'd made my vow after wearing the Glendale cop uniform and the uniform of the security staff at Warners. There was no way I was going to put on a uniform again unless there was nothing else to do. Not never comes sooner than you think when you have to come up with the rent and enough cereal and eggs to stay alive.

I took in the late morning sun heading down Main Street toward the Farraday, which is on Hoover and Ninth. I went past the row of Mexican *tiendas* at the Plaza end of Main. Some guys were arguing in Spanish in a barber shop. One of the guys was the barber, who held a scissors in his hand. In any other part of town, you could be sure the barber would win the argument, but there's no one more stubborn than a Mexican who knows he's right, even if the other guy is holding a sharp scissors and has him pinned in a chair. Some tinny music blared out of a phonograph shop as I crossed over and passed the new city hall that looked like one of those Egyptian obelisks with windows.

Now I was in my neighborhood, crowds passing dark working men's clothing stores, storefront burlesque houses, and nickel movie theaters. Before the war the crowds moved slowly, people from other neighborhoods looking for bargains, and people from this neighborhood just looking at the ground and shuffling along. The war had changed that. Now people were hurrying and the faces were those of kids in soldier and sailor uniforms with little bird chests, looking scared or trying with little success to look tough. The street smelled of the stuff they cleaned the uniforms with.

The crowd thinned out when I hit Hoover. The smell of the lobby of the Farraday was one of the things I could count on. Not many people love the smell of Lysol. I love it. The Farraday Building perspired Lysol, which Jeremy Butler used generously to try to fight off mildew and decay. Lysol was the dominant smell, but there were others beyond it in the dark echoing hall as I paused in front of the lobby directory to be sure my name was still there. Seeping through the Lysol was the smell of drunks who kept finding places to sleep in the nooks and crevices of the Farraday until they were routed gently but firmly by the giant landlord, Jeremy, who lived in a comfortable apartment there, the only apartment in the building, maintained only so he could be near the trenches for his constant battle with dirt, grime, and humanity. Jeremy never complained. He simply swept, polished, cleaned, and carried on with the knowledge that the process never ended. The other smells of the Farraday vied for my attention when I got past the lobby and headed for the wide stairs, listening to the echo of my own footsteps. I smelled sweat, bacon, oil, glue, paper from the four floors of cubbyhole offices that housed bookies, doctors who might not be doctors, companies that did not do business that anyone could identify, and photographers whose sample photos in the hall dated back to the days of silent movie stars.

I whistled as I went up, ignoring the tug inside my body that reminded me that a sore back was never more than a trauma away. By the fourth floor I wasn't feeling quite so loving about the Farraday, and when I paused in front of the door to Shelly Minck's office, my good mood had disappeared. I was getting close to that uniform, and the sound of Shelly's drill didn't help.

Shelly was constantly changing the sign on the glass outside our office. He had a deal with one of the tenants in the Farraday, Kevin Potnow the photographer, who also did a bit of signpainting. Shelly took care of Kevin's teeth and Kevin did photographs of Shelly and his wife Mildred and changed the lettering on our door when a new idea struck Shelly for drawing in clientele who happened to be passing by the darkened door on the fourth floor of the building on their way to oblivion.

The current lettering, in gold, read:

S. DAVID MINCK, D.D.S., L.L.D., O.S., B.R., PH.B.
DENTIST AND ORAL SURGEON

In small, black letters below this was written:

TOBY PETERS, INVESTIGATIONS

The *t* in Peters was almost gone. I went in, ignored the filthy anteroom, and went through the next door into Shelly's suite. The dishes were still piled high in the sink in the corner, with various dental tools peeking up out of pots in which at some unremembered point in time chili had been burned. The coffee was bubbling black in the pot on the hot plate and Shelly, short, bald, and glaring myopically through his thick, slipping glasses, was chewing on his cigar butt and drilling away at the mouth of someone who looked familiar.

Shelly paused to wipe his sweaty hands on his dirty smock as his voice hummed "The Man I Love."

"Seidman," I said, looking at the cadaverous man in the dental chair, "what the hell are you doing here?"

Seidman refused the not-too-clean cup of water handed to him by Shelly for rinsing and spat into the white porcelain bowl.

"You're a detective. Figure it out," Shelly said, searching for some instrument beneath the pile of metal on the table nearby. "We don't need William Powell for this one." He chuckled. "A man is in a dental chair." Shelly looked up grinning, the blunt instrument he had been seeking now in his hand. "A dentist," he went on, pointing the instrument at his own chest, "is standing over him and a white cloth covers the man from the neck down."

"A nearly white cloth," I said.

"As you will," Shelly said, grandly removing his cigar so that he could cough and adjust his glasses. "But one might conclude that the said Seidman is having his dental health looked after."

"I'm not sure that would be a reasonable conclusion, Shelly," I said.

"You can't insult me, Toby," Shelly said, turning again to his patient and indicating that he wanted Seidman to open his mouth.

"Oh, I can insult you, Shel. It just doesn't have any effect," I said, stepping closer and looking at Seidman.

"I dropped by to see you," Seidman said, arresting Shelly's hand in midflight, blunt instrument poised. "Minck said he saw something wrong with my front tooth. So . . ."

"Right, Shelly's hypnotic," I agreed. "He reeks of confidence."

"Can't insult me," Shelly sing-songed, moving his head from side to side to get a better look at Seidman's offending tooth.

"Phil wants to see you. This afternoon," Seidman managed to say before Shelly inserted the drill and looked back at me through thick lenses to let me know who was in charge here. Sergeant Steve Seidman was my brother's partner. My brother was Lieutenant Phil Pevsner, Los Angeles Police Department, Wilshire District. Maybe he just wanted to give me the semiannual name lecture. Phil was never quite sure whether he was pleased that I used the name Peters instead of Pevsner. On the one hand, it kept people from associating us with each other. On the other hand, he didn't like the idea that I didn't use the name I'd been born with. Hell, I didn't even use the brains I had been born with. Some wild thing had been born with and in me, a banshee or a dybbuk. I was strange, wonderful, with new worlds to conquer every day, like the lobby of a fleabag hotel on Broadway or the dark night corridors of a defense plant while wearing a gray uniform two sizes too big.

"I'll drop by," I told Seidman, but I didn't think he heard me over the drill. So I shouted to Shelly, "Any messages, Shel? Anything new?"

"Sugar rationing books are ready," he shouted back around his cigar as Seidman's tooth gave way.

"That's not what I had in mind," I shouted. "Have I had any calls?"

"No calls," bleated Shelly.

"Thanks," I said, reaching for the coffee and trying to catch sight of Seidman's face. I had never seen any expression on Seidman's pale face, but I was sure that if anything could bring some life to it, it would be Shelly at work. Seidman seemed to be as calm as usual. He was the perfect partner for my brother, whose emotions tingled on the surface of his face and in his fists like one of No-Neck Arnie's overheated batteries.

The coffee was hot and awful, just the way Shelly liked

it. I had my own cup, a ceramic job that had WELCOME TO JUAREZ hand painted on it along with a little picture of a sombrero. No one was supposed to touch the cup but me, though I suspected Shelly sometimes went for it when nothing clean was left.

Cup in hand, I reached for the knob to my office door.

"Almost forgot," Shelly said, looking at me over his shoulder. "Lady came in about ten minutes ago, just before Sergeant Seidman. She's in your office waiting for you. Between you and me and the OPA, she could use some dental work on that overbite. You might suggest she stop and see me."

Since my office is not soundproof or Shellyproof, there was no doubt the woman inside had heard him, especially since at that point I had the door partly open.

In the hope of finding a new client who could save me from the darkness of hotel corridors or worse, I regretted that I hadn't tightened my tie, set my face in a serious frown, and stepped into my office . . . where I found myself face to face with Eleanor Roosevelt.

"You're Eleanor Roosevelt," I said.

"I know," she answered, looking over her glasses with an amused smile. "I'm afraid you will have to do a bit better than that if you are to convince me of your skills."

I closed the door to cut out some of Shelly's humming and drilling, and stood there looking at her. She had cocked her head back to examine me from the single chair in front of my desk. Her hair, cut short, was dark with gray creeping in. She looked her age, which was fifty-eight, but there was something there that I had never seen in photographs. Sure, she was homely, not much in the way of a chin, an overbite, though not nearly as much as people joked about, and a body without moments. She wore a black dress with little flowers on it and a thin dark coat. But it was her eyes that made the difference, that gave something a newspaper or newsreel picture couldn't catch. They were dark and deep and always looking right at you. From that moment on, every time I talked to her, she gave me all of her attention. She sat now with her hands neatly folded in her lap like an obedient schoolgirl.

"Would you like some coffee?" I said, holding out my Juarez cup to show her what coffee was.

She examined the cup seriously and then said, "No thank you," as she removed her glasses and put them in a dark case that she pulled out of the May Company shopping bag at her side.

"Is it all right if I sit down?" I said.

"It *is* your office," she answered, the smile back, her voice slightly high-pitched, with a back-East accent that reminded me of tea parties and bad jokes about the rich, the kind they have in *The New Yorker*.

I sat and looked at her to the somewhat muffled sound of the drill and of Shelly now singing "Ain't We Got Fun."

"Did you get my letter?" she asked, leaning forward slightly.

"Letter," I repeated, cleverly wondering if I should open my top drawer and sweep into it the garbage on my desk, which included the remnants of two day-old tacos from Manny's down the street, a handball, and an almost empty emergency box of Kellogg's All-Bran.

"Right," I said, trying to wake up. "I got a letter a few weeks back from the White House, a note from some woman named Francis something, said somebody would be in touch with me about a personal matter and . . . that was you?"

She nodded and opened her eyes wider. "What did you think it was?"

"I don't know," I said with a shrug. "I thought it was something millions of people were getting. Maybe I wasn't going to get a sugar or gas ration book. Maybe a new law was going into effect to draft fifty year olds."

She reached into her shopping bag and came out with a small notebook, which she opened after putting on her glasses again. She glanced down at it and returned the notebook to the bag. I wondered what she had bought at the May Company and how they had reacted at the dinnerware counter when Eleanor Roosevelt asked for two hundred juice glasses on sale for the White House.

"You are," she said, "forty-seven years old, not fifty,

and even if the draft age were raised substantially, I doubt that with your back you would be considered an asset to our war effort.''

"I'm not sure what brought you here," I said, sipping coffee and stopping myself from straightening my tie, "but you must have the wrong Toby Peters."

Her mouth twitched slightly and her right cheek puffed out. A sound of air slipped between her lips as behind us Shelly launched into "Josephine Please Don't Lean on the Bell," complete with his famous Eddie Cantor imitation.

"You want me to try to shut him up?" I said, nodding toward the door.

"He sounds irrepressible to me," she said.

"He is," I agreed, guessing she meant that nothing short of mayhem would stop Shelly.

"You had a dog when you were a boy," she said, looking into my eyes for an answer that suddenly seemed very important. For a moment I speculated that Eleanor Roosevelt had wandered away from her keepers, who were frantically searching the streets for her. I had, perhaps, stumbled onto a great White House mystery: The First Lady was nuts.

"I had a dog," I agreed, putting down my Juarez cup and adjusting my tie.

"The one in the picture on the wall behind me?" she said without turning to the photograph.

"Right," I agreed. "But that was a long time ago. He's dead now."

"Almost everyone is," she agreed brightly. "Who are the others in the picture?"

"The younger kid is me before my nose got flattened for the first time," I explained, looking up at the picture over her shoulder. There was a crack in the glass that I should have fixed at some point, but that had never really bothered me till I knew that Eleanor Roosevelt had been looking at it. "The older kid is my brother Phil—"

"Who is a police officer," she added.

"Right," I said. "Do you know how he voted in the last election?"

"Democrat," she said without a smile. "He is a registered Democrat and no doubt voted for Franklin. I have no idea of how you voted."

"I voted for Willkie," I said, meeting her eyes.

"May I ask why?" she said.

"Is it important?" I shot back.

She brought her clasped hands up to her mouth and touched her larger lower lip with her knuckles. "It may be, Mr. Peters. Your political feelings may affect the matter we may soon be discussing."

Shelly shouted, "When you neck please no breaka da bell," and I held back the violent urge to go out and strangle him.

"I thought Roo . . . your husband looked tired," I said. "I thought he looked like a man who'd had enough, been through enough, a man who deserved a rest. And besides, I liked Willkie."

"So," she said, "did I and so did Franklin. After the election Mr. Willkie came to the White House to visit. I had an appointment, but I cancelled it just to get a look at the man. I think he would have made a good president, not as good as Franklin, but quite good. And Franklin was quite prepared to lose and take that rest. And what do you think about your choice now?"

"I'm glad your husband is president," I said. "Mostly because of the war, but I want to get this straight right now, I'm not much on politics. I read the bad headlines and go for the sports section. Once in a while I read your column, but only once in a while because I'm an L.A. *Times* reader."

I was having a nice friendly chat with an apparently insane Eleanor Roosevelt. Shelly had paused and Seidman was choking. I thought of the possibility of Secret Service men bursting through the door with guns drawn and putting a few holes through me on the chance that I had kidnapped the First Lady.

"The man," Mrs. Roosevelt said, returning her hands to her lap.

"Man?"

"The one in the photograph on the wall," she explained.

"My father," I said, looking up at him standing between me and Phil. "He died when I was a kid."

"As did my father," she said. "And like yours, my mother died even before him."

"You know a lot about me."

"And the dog's name?" she said gently.

"Murphy, when that picture was taken," I humored her. "Later, when Phil was in the army during the last war, I renamed him Kaiser Wilhelm . . . a kind of family joke."

"I see," she said. "My sources say that you are a man who can be relied upon for discretion. Is that true?"

"It has made my fortune," I said with a sad grin, looking around the small office and up at the ceiling where a fascinating crack looked like a wacky river across a dry desert.

"You have a fondness for dogs," she went on. "I mean by that, you can understand the sentiment of one who invests a great deal of affection in an animal."

I nodded.

"Have you looked at the newspaper or heard the news this morning?" she went on. "What do you remember of it?"

Behind her Shelly had turned off the drill and was humming something I hoped he created.

"Dolph Camilli hit two home runs, one in the ninth, to give Brooklyn an eleven-eight win over Cinci," I recalled. "Sugar rationing books can be picked up at elementary schools. There's a big sale of Lucky Lager beer, and twenty-nine of the toughest inmates on Alcatraz were taken from the island in a secret evacuation because they can't black out the island and the warden was afraid of a break if the island had to be blacked out during a Jap raid. I was interested in that because at least one of that twenty-nine is probably a guy I helped send there and would not like to see—"

"And you didn't read the war news?" she jumped in, her head on the side like a scolding teacher.

"I read it," I said with a shrug.

"You needn't work so hard to convince me of the narrowness of your interest," said Mrs. Roosevelt.

"Sorry," I said.

"That is all right," she forgave me, and went on. "The Japanese, as I believe you know, are on the Burma Road. The war in Europe is going a bit better but not appreciably. In his May Day address, Premier Joseph Stalin pledged that Russia has no territorial ambitions upon foreign countries and declared that the Soviets' sole aim is to liberate its lands from the, and I quote, 'German Fascist blackguards.' Franklin and others are concerned about Mr. Stalin's true intention. In short, Mr. Peters, the pressures on my husband are as great as they have been on any man in history."

"I'm sorry," I said, "but what—"

"I have good reason to believe that the president's dog has been taken," she said softly, her eyes on mine. "I am not sure of the word in this context. For a child it is kidnapping. I suppose we could say Fala has been dognapped."

"I'm listening," I said, leaning forward and pulling out the small, spiral-bound notebook I carried in my pocket. Spiral-bound notebooks were the ancient enemies, like organized society. Within seconds after I purchased one it would creep out a tiny metal finger from the spiral and go to work tearing the lining of my jacket or my pants. The current one was no different. I found a pencil piece that I had to scrape with my thumbnail to get at the lead, and tried to ignore Mrs. Roosevelt's eyes.

She told her story quickly and more efficiently than a twenty-year homicide squad veteran who wants to get home for a couple of beers and an Italian beef sandwich.

The dog's full name was Murray the Outlaw of Fala Hill. He had been given to FDR by Margaret Suckley in 1940. Margaret was a close friend of the family. The family had many dogs, including a German shepherd who had recently taken a chunk out of the prime minister of Canada, but Fala was the president's dog and had proven to be the only dog in the family that really liked the White House. That Roosevelt loved the dog was without question. It was also evident that the dog returned the affection. Things, she said, could be pretty tense at the White House. Public visits had stopped, everyone who entered had to be fingerprinted and issued a pass, and, most unsettling, gun crews were now posted in the wings of the residence. There was, in fact, a dog—supposedly Fala—in the White House at the moment. The president had noticed a number of changes in the dog, but meetings and war planning had kept him from questioning its identity. Mrs. Roosevelt had gradually become convinced that the dog was not Fala at all but a strikingly similar animal with a radically different temperament. She had kept her observations to herself for several reasons. First, she did not want to upset the president, and second, she didn't want to appear demented. The press, she said, took every opportunity to attack her and she did not wish to be an embarrassment to the president. Meanwhile, she had been occupied with moving their New York address from East Sixty-fifth to a seven-room apartment in Washington Square. So, aside from a few inquiries, she had not pushed her suspicion further. The slightest suggestion of her concern, she said, might be used by the press, the Republicans, the Japanese, or the Germans against the president.

There were two things that made Mrs. Roosevelt believe that the kidnapped dog was in Los Angeles. First, a veterinarian, Roy Olson, who had treated Fala, had suddenly packed up and moved from Washington to Los Angeles. Mrs. Roosevelt had initiated a discreet inquiry in Los Angeles through a sympathetic Secret Service operative. The inquiry had turned up nothing but some eccentric characters. However, after the inquiry, among the many crank letters that came to the White House each day, there began to appear ones specifically mentioning the loss of Fala. The Secret Service, as it did with all threats, checked the signed letter from Los Angeles and concluded that the writer, a Jane Poslik who had worked for Roy Olson and had been contacted during the inquiry, was mentally disturbed and that her letter had not been a threat at all but the voicing of a paranoid fear suggested by the investigation. My job, if I took it, was to find enough information, if it existed, to make a formal investigation reasonable.

"One week from today," she concluded, standing up, "on the eighth of May, I must be back in Washington for our first state dinner since Pearl Harbor. We will be entertaining the president of Peru. For a week I will remain in the Los Angeles area, where I do have some things to do, including gathering material for my column, and though I have resigned from the Office of Civil Defense, I have agreed to prepare a discreet report on California defense. May I assume you will accept the task?''

I stood up with her, thinking for the first time since I had seen her in my office that this would give me a week or two before I had to go back to checking out the Grumman job. Besides, it was my patriotic duty. I was thinking about how to bring up the question of money when I took the hand she offered me.

When she released my hand, she went into her shopping bag and pulled out an envelope, which she handed me.

"There is three hundred dollars in the envelope," she said, pulling her coat around her shoulders and picking up the shopping bag. "It is my own personal money and I will provide more if it is needed. I cannot give you a check because I do not want my name on any document associated with this. I will, however, expect an itemization of your expenditures. My secretary knows your name and will take a message if I am not there when you call. Have you any questions?"

"None," I said. "I'll get right on it."

Eleanor Roosevelt turned to look at the photograph of my father, Phil, me, and the dog. She paused for a second, looked at the picture, and then looked back at me and said, "Be careful Tobias, and keep me informed."

With that, she was gone. I opened the envelope, found the pile of twenties, which I folded into my well-worn *hecho-a-mano* Mexican wallet, and memorized the phone number. I repeated it twenty times, imagined it written on the wall, and then tore it into small pieces, which I dropped into my empty wastebasket. Jeremy kept the floors clean and the wastebaskets empty.

There wasn't much question about where I would begin. Finding Jane Poslik and Roy Olson didn't even require my going to the phone book. Mrs. Roosevelt had provided both of their addresses. The only choice was which one to start with and that was easy, the woman who had written the letters.

I swept off the top of my desk, shoved the notebook and pencil into my pocket, took the final handful of All-Bran, washed it down with the cool remnants of Juarez coffee, and went into Shelly's office. Seidman was gone, and I made a note to get in touch with my brother Phil before the day ended. I didn't want him coming for me. It was never pleasant when Phil wound up coming for me, even when he started off reasonably friendly.

Shelly was sitting in his dental chair squinting at a pad of paper on his lap. He puffed away at his cigar and tapped his pencil on the pad. He heard me come back into the room and looked up.

"I'm working on an ad," he explained. "How about 'Good tooth care is vital for victory'?"

"Catchy," I said.

"Sorta like the Rinso Jingle," he mused. "You know, 'Rinso White, Rinso White, happy little washday song.' That's the kind of thing I'm looking for, you know what I mean?"

"Sort of," I said. "Look, I've got to go out. I've got a client. Will you—"

"You mean the one with the shopping bags?" he said, returning to his pad. "You should have her see me about those teeth. I can do all sorts of things with them."

"I'm sure you could, Shel, but she's from out of town, and I'm sure she's got her own dentist," I said.

"He isn't doing much for her," he went on, tapping his pencil. "You know she reminds me of someone. I just figured out who. You know that little lady in *The Lady Vanishes*, The English cookie, what's her name, Lady something or Dame something."

"I know who you mean," I said. "I'll check back in later."

"Sure, sure," Shelly told his pad. "Toby, I could use your advice before you go."

"Go ahead," I said. In situations like this I had for some time said "Shoot," but since someone had taken me literally in Chicago a few years before and shot me, I had gone for the simple though less colorful "Go ahead."

"Promised Mildred we'd go out this weekend," Shelly said, taking his cigar from his mouth and dropping a fat ash on his smock, where he failed to notice it. "I could suggest Volez and Yolanda at the Philharmonic Hall. *Life* magazine says they're the world's greatest dancing couple. That might cost as much as four bucks for the good seats. Or we could go to the Musart and see *She Lost It at Campeche*. Even the best seats are only a buck each. The show's been going on for almost a year and the ad in the paper says it's 'hot as a firebomb.' What do you think?"

"Shel," I said, reaching for the door. "Go for the culture even if it costs a few bucks extra. Mildred will appreciate it."

I was through the door and standing in the anteroom when I heard Shelly say to himself, "Hot as a fire bomb," and I knew where Mildred Minck would be on Saturday night.

I made my way back to No-Neck Arnie's garage and told him to fill up the Ford with gas. He tilted his body to the side to look at me, and I proved my good faith and financial standing by showing him a twenty-dollar bill. Arnie filled her up.

"Took almost a full tank," he said as we stood near the pump amidst the aroma of gasoline.

"Great," I said. The best way to handle things was to keep the tank full since the gas gauge didn't work. It had broken within minutes of my buying the car from Arnie. Arnie had advised me not to have it fixed because it wasn't worth the expense. Fundless, I had agreed. I had learned since then that you can get used to almost anything, a wife leaving you, a war, various beatings, back pain, but the tension of never knowing if your gas tank is full or empty is too much for a reasonable human to have to bear.

"Arnie, I want the gauge fixed," I said, getting into the car.

"Suit yourself," he said with a shrug as he rubbed his always greasy palms on his greasy overalls. "It'll cost."

"How much?"

"Maybe five, maybe more. Maybe even ten."

He leaned on the car, foot on the running board, and

examined the vehicle as if he had never seen it before. "Maybe ten."

"Then let's get it fixed," I said, starting the engine.

"Came into a bundle, huh?" he said with a grin of wonderfully uneven teeth.

"Got a new client," I explained. "Eleanor Roosevelt. I'm getting a nice fee for finding out who kidnapped the president's dog."

Arnie gave me a sour look as I pulled slowly away. "Come on," he said wearily. "Never kid a kidder. You know what I mean?"

I knew what he meant, but I had never known Arnie to be a kidder. As far as I could see, he had no sense of humor except when it came to repairs, and then he was laughable. I stuck my head out of the window and called back, "I wouldn't kid an old friend like you, Arn."

Then I shot forward into the street, almost hitting a Plymouth driven by a gray man who looked like a broom handle. I gave him my best grin, turned on the car radio for a little music, found Fred Waring and His Pennsylvanians, smiled up at the morning sun, and headed for Burbank and Jane Poslik.

Fred Waring kept me company down Hollywood Boulevard, and through the hills. I listened to "Rosemary" and was about to get the news when I found the street where Jane Poslik lived. It was about two blocks off Burbank Boulevard on a residential street. Hers was one of the two-story brick apartment buildings nestled together for protection on a block of single-family frame houses. It was the kind of street where nothing happens during the day because everyone is working or the families are too old to have little kids.

Jane Poslik lived in the second floor apartment, but she didn't answer her bell or my knock. I tried to look through the thin curtain on the window near the door, but nothing seemed to be moving inside. So I went downstairs and knocked at the door of a Molly Garnett. There was no answer but I could hear something moving inside, so I ham-fisted the door.

"Molly Garnett?" I shouted.

"Shut up out there," came a shrill woman's voice. "Shut up. Shut up. I'm not opening up for you, Leonard."

"My name's not Leonard," I shouted. "It's Peters. I'm looking for Jane Poslik. I've got to talk to her."

"You're not Leonard?" came the shrill voice.

"I'm not Leonard."

"You're not from Leonard?" she tried.

"I'm from Hollywood," I said patiently. "I'm looking for Jane Poslik. She's not home."

"You're telling me?" cackled Molly Garnett.

"Where is she?" I tried.

"She's a cuckoo," came a cackle, which I think was a laugh.

"I'm interested more in where she is than what she is," I shouted.

"She thinks someone is after her," came the cackle voice. "You seen her? No one would be after crazy Jane, I can tell you. Men used to be after me though."

"I'm sure," I said to the door. "You have any idea where I might find her?"

"You sure you're not Leonard?"

"Cross my heart," I said. "Jane Poslik, where might I find her?"

Molly Garnett went silent and I turned from the door. Jane Poslik would wait. It was on to Dr. Olson, but first I'd make that trip to see Phil and find out what he wanted.

3

The second-floor squadroom of the Wilshire District police station was unusually quiet for a Friday afternoon. On the way there I had stopped for a Taco and Pepsi Victory Special at Paco's On Pico. Sergeant Veldu, the old guy on the front desk, had waved me in with a beefy hand and told me to look out for Cawelti, who was in and in a bad mood. I had known Sergeant John Cawelti for two years, since he first came to the Wilshire with his hair parted down the middle like a barkeep and his fists permanently clenched. We had not hit it off well. A clash of personalities. Two spirits destined to ignite. I had once suggested, in his presence, that the Los Angeles police trade him to the Germans for an old pair of Goering's underwear. It had not pleased my enemy.

So I pushed open the door of the squadroom on the second floor feeling the itch of a good insult creeping into my mind. I approached the desk where Cawelti was hissing through his teeth at a Mexican guy covered with dark hair and two days of beard. The Mexican guy was nodding yes to everything. He was so skinny that each nod of his head threatened to knock him off balance. I considered pausing to warn him about the floor of the squadroom. One could get lost on that floor in the generations of accumulated food, tobacco, and human body fluids ranging from blood to urine. Some of the former was mine. Cleaning up amounted to nothing more than keeping the dirt-black wooden floor from becoming un-passable.

"Top of the morning, John," I heard myself say as I passed Cawelti's desk.

Cawelti's answer was a low grunt and the sudden swing of the bound notebook in his hand, which banged against the cheek of the Mexican, who crumpled in front of me on the filthy floor.

"Hey," I said, jumping out of the way. "I can make a citizen's arrest on this one. Littering, illegal use of a con-cealed Mexican junkie, assault with a deadly alien."

Cawelti stood up, his suit dark and neat, his face turning a pocked red. There were a few other detectives and one uniformed guy making coffee in the corner. They didn't bother to watch our little drama. Neither did the Negro kid handcuffed to the waiting bench about ten feet away from us.

He was doing his best to pretend that he hadn't seen the whole thing and hoping that he wasn't going to be questioned by Cawelti.

I faced Cawelti as I knelt down to help the Mexican guy up. The Mexican smelled like vomit, and Cawelti was grinning.

"*Gracias*," the Mexican said dizzily.

"I'd stay down there if I were you," I said, grinning back at Cawelti. "He's only going to do it again when I leave."

"Peters, Peters," said Cawelti, "we're coming to that time. Things are changing around here, and you and me are going to dance in the moonlight." The last had been punctuated with a finger jabbed at me for "you" and a thumb at himself for "me."

"Poetry will get you nowhere, John-John," I said, propping the Mexican back up in the chair while trying not to let any of him rub off on me.

"Hey," a voice, deep and dark, called across the babble of the room. I turned, and beyond the bulk of a mountainous sergeant drinking a cup of coffee, I saw Steve Seidman waving at me. Without another word to Cawelti, I skipped past an overturned basket that had something wet and red in it, hopped over the Negro kid on the bench, who pulled back into a protective ball, and weaved around the mountain of a cop whose name was Slaughter and whose disposition was known to match his name. He almost spilled his coffee as he made way for me to get past him. I gave a half-second prayer that the coffee didn't spill and put Slaughter into a worse-than-normal mood.

"Been making friends in the squadroom again?" Seidman said, sitting back against the edge of his desk in a corner. There were two small fruit crates on top of the desk. One had once been filled with Napa Sweetheart artichokes and was now piled high with papers, notes, and assorted junk.

"Early spring cleaning?" I asked, nodding at the desk.

"Moving day," he answered, pushing away from the desk and starting forward. I followed him.

"How's the tooth?" I said as we angled past the semiclear space near the filthy windows that tried but failed to keep out all of the sunlight. Seidman's right cheek was definitely puffy.

"The man," Seidman said over his shoulder, "is a butcher, an incompetent unclean quack."

"And those are Shelly's good traits," I said as he opened the door marked LT. PHILIP PEVSNER.

"You're a class act, Toby," Seidman said emotionlessly as I moved past him. Then he whispered, "Be careful, Phil's in a good mood."

I stepped in and Seidman stepped out, closing the door behind me but not before I caught a glimpse of his hand reaching for his cheek. Phil was standing behind his small desk in the office, which was about the same size as my own. His bulky back was to me. He was in his rumpled gray suit looking out the grim window at the blank wall. A cup of coffee was in his hand. He didn't turn when the door closed but I caught a movement of the shoulders that led me to believe that he wasn't lost in some form of meditation.

"Happy birthday," I said, resisting the temptation to sit in the chair across from his desk. I'd been trapped in that chair more than once and wound up with books in my face, a kick in the leg that led to orthopedic therapy, and a variety of lesser but equally interesting injuries, each of which was good enough for at least a fifteen-yard penalty.

Phil grunted and took another sip of coffee. He was just too fascinated by that brick wall to turn around. I couldn't blame him. More than ten years of looking at it could not dim the fascination of its potential mysteries.

"What are you looking at?" I heard myself say, knowing that it was exactly what I shouldn't say, at least what I shouldn't say unless I wanted my brother to turn in murderous rage, which is probably what I did want. Old habits die hard. I had once said that to my friend Jeremy Butler. He had said, "Old habits never die. They are only repressed and come back to haunt us in disguise." So, I had decided it was better to make friends with my bad habits than to hide them away. The result had been a lost marriage, a bad back, no money in the bank, a diet that would destroy the average Russian soldier, a brother whose fists clenched when I was within smelling range, and a few interesting encounters.

Phil did not turn around murderously. He didn't turn

around at all but answered calmly, "You know how old I'll be at the end of this week?"

"Fifty," I said, leaning back against the wall as far from him as I could get.

"Fifty," he agreed, taking another sip. "Half a century. And you're only a few years behind."

"Physically," I agreed.

"Physically you're over the century mark," he grunted. "How many times you been shot?"

"Three," I said. "And you?"

"Four, counting the war," he answered.

"Well," I sighed, "it's been nice talking about the good old days, but I've got a client, and some groceries to pick up. I'll needle you once or twice about Ruth and the boys. You throw something at me, tell me what you want, and I'll be going."

That should have gotten him, but it didn't. What was worse was that he turned around with a sad near-smile on his face and his scarred sausage fingers engulfing his cup. His hair was steel gray and cut short as always. His cop gut hung over his belt and his tie was loose around the collar of his size-sixteen-and-a-half neck.

"I got the word Monday," Phil said, looking down at the dregs in his cup and shaking it around a little. "I made captain. I'm moving down the hall this afternoon."

Four wisecracks came like shadows into my mind but I let them keep going and said, "That's great Phil. You deserve it."

Phil nodded in agreement. "I paid for it," he said. "I paid."

And so, I thought, did a stadium-load of criminals and people who just got in Phil's way. For the first ten years of being a cop, Phil had tried to single-handedly and double-footedly smash every lawbreaker unlucky enough to come within his smell. He kicked, bent, broke, twisted bodies and the law, and gained a reputation for violence I could have told Jimmy Fiddler about when I was ten. The second ten years, after he made lieutenant, had been like the first decade but sour. Crime hadn't stopped. It had gotten bigger and worse. If Phil had paid attention to the books our old man had given him from time to time, he would have known all this from Jaubert or the cop in *Crime and Punishment*, but Phil was a dreamer with a pencil-thin, overworked wife, three kids, one of whom was sick most of the time, and a mortgage.

"Seidman's moving in here," he went on. "He's up for lieutenant next month. Your pal Cawelti might move up too."

"That will make me feel safer at nights," I said.

"Enough shit," Phil said, putting down his coffee cup and pulling his tie off. "I'm never going higher than captain. There's no place higher for me to go. So, no more damned ties. No more fooling around."

"You've been fooling around all these years?" I said, looking into a grin I didn't like, a grin that made me feel a twinge of sympathy for the unknown offender who next came within the grasp of my brother.

"Eleanor Roosevelt," he said, throwing the tie on the desk. I think it was a tie I had once given him, picked up as a partial payment from Hy of Hy's Clothes For Him for finding Hy's nephew, who had departed with Hy's weekly cashbox and was spending it freely in a San Bernardino bar when I found him. Hy had a bad habit of losing his relatives and a worse habit of paying me off in unwanted clothes when I found them.

"Eleanor Roosevelt," I repeated sagely.

"That's what I want to talk to you about," Phil said, leaning forward, his fists on the desk. The pose was decidedly simian, I noted, an observance I managed to keep from sharing with him.

"Seidman was following her this morning," he went on. "That's what he was doing in that nearsighted geek's office."

"I'll tell Shelly you send him your best," I said sincerely.

Phil didn't answer. He just stared at me with brown, wet eyes, his lower lip pushing out.

"The Secret Service doesn't tell us anything. The FBI doesn't tell us anything," he continued. "It came to us from the mayor's office, straight in here. I'm responsible. I'm on the line. I don't think they can take captain away from me, but they can make me the captain of canned shit if this gets screwed up.''

"Well put," I said.

"So," he said, evenly bouncing his fists on the desk, "I'm going to ask you some questions. You are going to answer the questions. You are not going to play games because you know what I can do to people who play games. You remember Italian Mack?''

I didn't want to remember what Phil had done to Italian Mack. What he had done to Italian Mack had probably kept him a lieutenant for an extra three years.

"Ask," I said, back to the wall.

"What the hell is the president's wife doing coming to your office?''

I couldn't stop it. It came out of the little kid who lives inside me and doesn't give a final damn about my bruised and broken body. "Looking for campaign contributions from leading citizens," I said. But I overcame the kid and before Phil could get out from behind the desk. I soothed, "Wait, wait, hold on. She had a job for me."

He stopped halfway around the desk. From beyond his door, a single voice shrieked out in Spanish, "*No lo hice, por Dios.*" Phil didn't seem to notice.

"What kind of job could you do for her that the FBI, the Secret Service, and the L.A. police couldn't do?" he asked. It was a reasonable question.

"Find a dog," I said. "I swear, find a dog. A friend of hers in Los Angeles, Jack Warner's wife, lost her dog. Mrs. Roosevelt promised to help her find it but she can't go to you or the FBI on a personal thing like this. She's had enough crap in the papers and on the radio without having people say she's using the government's time and money to find lost pets for big campaign donors.''

It sounded kind of reasonable and was a little bit true at the same time. I don't know where it came from, but I heard it coming out of me when I needed it. It was usually like that. I was one hell of an on-the-spot liar. It was what every good private detective had to be in a world of liars. Phil, on the other hand, was a lousy liar. He didn't have to lie. He had a cop's badge and the gun that went with it.

"Why you?" he asked, pausing, his head cocked to the side.

"You know I used to work for Warner's. They throw me business once in a while."

"Warner would have had the gulls going for your liver if he had his way," Phil said. "He hates your face."

"We have an understanding," I lied. "I did some work for him a few years back and—"

"Toby, how much of this is horseshit?" His hand slammed down on the desk sending a spray of pencils flying from the clay cup his son Nate had made for him five years ago. Beyond the closed door the Mexican guy seemed to be whimpering in sympathy for me.

"About half," I said honestly, which was a lie. "Phil, it's nothing, a missing dog, a two-bit case. No scandal, no politics, no danger for the First Lady, just a lost dog. I said I'd keep it quiet, but, okay, call Mrs. Warner, check it out. I promised I wouldn't tell, but the hell with it. Check it out. I need the few bucks. It's either look for a lost pooch or do the night guard shift at a defense plant, and you know how I hate uniforms."

Phil pulled his pouting lip back in and looked at me for about half a minute while I tried on the wide-open, sincere, and slightly pathetic face I had come near perfecting by looking into the mirror on humid summer nights.

Finally he sighed, a sigh to take in all of his troubles and those of the Allies. "Get out," he said, turning his back again. This time he put his hands behind him. "If anything happens on this, anything, I'll come for you, Toby. I'll come and all the bad times in the past will be Mother Goose compared to it."

"Thanks Phil," I said, inching for the door. "Give my best to Ruth and the kids."

"Ruth wants you to come for dinner, Sunday," he said gruffly.

"I'll be there," I said, my hand on the door knob. "And Phil, you deserved to make captain."

Something like a laugh came from him. I couldn't see the face that matched it, but the voice had a touch of gravel in it. "The war got me this promotion," he said softly. "Younger guys are gone, younger lieutenants. Tojo and Hitler got this promotion for me. Without them I'd go out a lieutenant. Funny, huh?"

"You're selling yourself short, brother," I said.

"I'm selling myself at street prices," he said. "I can live with that. What's your price?"

I left without telling him I had no minimum. What I did have was a pocketful of Eleanor Roosevelt's cash. Seidman didn't see me leave. Across the room I saw his thin frame leaning over to finish filling his artichoke crate. Cawelti was out of sight, probably discussing current events or Goethe with the Mexican in one of the interrogation rooms down the hall. Slaughter and a uniformed kid were in earnest, head-to-head conversation with the Negro kid still handcuffed to the bench. He was nodding his head in full agreement to everything they whispered to him, probably confessing to crimes committed a century before he was born.

I almost collided with a well-dressed woman wearing a tiny black hat with a large black feather. She was about forty, maybe a little older, good-looking in a way that reminded me of my ex-wife, and perfumed heavily enough to break through the squadroom smell, at least at close range.

"Excuse me," she said, looking around the room with obvious distaste, "can you tell me where I might find the detective in charge of providing security for bridge parties?"

"Bridge parties?" I said.

"We are going to have a bridge party to raise funds for the USO and we would like a detective present to keep unwanted people out, if you understand," she said with a smile reserved for people like me, who could not possibly understand people like her.

"Sergeant Cawelti," I said. "That's his desk right there. You just have a seat. He'll be right back. Tell him Captain Peters said he should take care of you."

"Thank you," she said, taking off her glove and offering me her hand. I took it. It felt soft. "Thank you, Captain

Peters. It's difficult to know what the right thing to do is at times like this."

"You're doing the right thing," I assured her, taking her hand in both of mine. Behind us, Slaughter grumbled, "No, no, no," to the Negro kid, who had apparently given a wrong answer. The woman drew her hand away.

"My son's in the army," she said, trying to keep her eyes away from the scene on the bench. "It's hard to know what to do."

"Leave it to Sergeant Cawelti," I said, feeling guilty but not knowing how to get out of it. "Good luck."

"Thank you, Captain," she said as I walked out the door and left her perfumed presence to be engulfed by hell.

Veldu called, "Take care, Toby," as I walked past him and into the light of Wilshire Boulevard. A lone cloud crossed in front of the sun, and I looked down at the watch I had inherited from my father. It was his only legacy to me, besides a tendency to feel sorry for most of the people who staggered into my life. The watch could never be relied upon for the right time. Now it told me that it was six, but it couldn't have been later than two.

My car radio, after "Wendy Warren and the News," told me that it was two-fifteen. A stop at a drugstore got me a Pepsi and a phone book that let me know that I was a twenty-minute drive away from Dr. Olson's office in Sherman Oaks. I called the number in the phone book and a man answered, "Dr. Olson's office."

"I'd like to see the doctor," I said. "This afternoon. It's an emergency."

"What kind of pet do you have?" he said. "And what is the problem?"

"Little black Scotch terrier," I said, a sob in my voice. "He just seems different, like a different dog. You know what I mean?"

"I'll tell Doctor," he said with dull efficiency. "You can bring your dog in at four. The dog's name?"

"Fala," I said. "We named him after the president's dog. My wife thought it was kind of a cute idea. What do you think?"

"We see lots of Scotch terriers named Fala," he said. A phone was ringing behind him. "Sorry, Mr. . . . ?"

"Rosenfeldt," I said. "Myron Rosenfeldt. That's why my wife, Lottie, thought it would be cute to name the dog Fala."

The man grunted and the phone continued to ring behind him. "Four o'clock," he said and hung up.

Having given Dr. Olson something to think about in case he might be guilty of dognapping, I made another call to a second doctor, Doc Hodgdon, who agreed to cancel his two-thirty patient and meet me at the YMCA on Hope Street. Doc was thin, white-haired, and well over sixty. My hope was that he would slow down enough soon so that I could finally beat him at least once at handball. I sometimes wondered why he wanted to continue to play with me. "Sadist and masochist," Jeremy had suggested. "He likes beating you and you like being beaten. A symbiotic relationship."

I didn't like thinking about that so I turned on the radio when I got back in the car and headed for Hope. One hour later, after having lost three straight games to Hodgdon, I was showered, resuited, and heading for Sherman Oaks singing "I Came Here To Talk For Joe."

I was refreshed, unshaved, and unworried as the gas gauge in front of me bounced happily from full to empty. I was ready to do my part for victory by confronting what might be the most important dognapper in history.

4

A collie with a bad cough, a white Persian cat with a missing ear, a whimpering spaniel, and a white parrot in a cage with what looked like a bandage on his right leg, were ahead of me in Dr. Olson's waiting room. The people who had accompanied the patients were a silent lot: a thin, chain-smoking woman in a cloth coat had the collie, a teenage girl wearing a jacket with the letter L on it comforted the spaniel, an old couple holding hands guarded the Persian in the woman's lap, and a birdlike man with a straight back wearing glasses, a small smile, and a white suit rested his hand protectively on the cage of the white parrot at his side.

Dr. Olson's Sherman Oaks Hospital for Pets was on a cul-de-sac one block off Sherman Avenue. It was a new one-story brick building. The street itself had a number of driveways with houses set back beyond the trees. The only building near the street was Dr. Olson's place. There was no parking lot, but finding a place on the street had been no trouble.

My trouble came when a door opened off the waiting room and the sound of barking and whining accompanied the appearance of a white-coated giant who looked like a block of ice. His face was bland and dreamy under straight blond hair that tumbled across his eyes. The white coat was generously dappled with blood, some of it still moist.

"Mrs. Retsch," he announced in a surprisingly high voice. The woman with the collie stood up nervously, looked for someplace to put her cigarette, found an ashtray, and, head down, moved past the huge blond man and through the door, her collie coughing docilely at her side.

"You," the man said, looking at me. "You got no animal."

He was observant.

"That's what I want to see the doctor about," I said. "I'm looking for a pet. My name's Rosenfeldt. I made an appointment."

"But you got no pet," he repeated.

"Mr. . . . ?"

"I'm Bass," he said. "You've got an appointment and no pet."

"That's about it," I agreed.

Though I didn't see that anything had been settled, Bass nodded, wiped his hands on his coat, and looked at the others waiting.

"You're next," he said, pointing at the parrot man. He turned and disappeared through the door.

Amidst the smell of blood and animal I passed an hour with *Collier's*, enjoying particularly a story about Chiang Kai-shek's vow that China would never fall to the Japanese. He certainly looked determined in the pictures, and his wife at his side looked even better.

At five, one hour later, the door to the interior of the building opened and the teen with the spaniel emerged and sped past and out. Bass stood looking down at me, so I assumed since I was alone that it was my turn. I stood up and put *Collier's* and the Orient aside.

"Doctor's ready," he said.

"I'm ready," I said and followed Bass down a narrow corridor. The walls were white and the little surgery-examining rooms we passed were white and stainless steel and looked clean. The blood smell, however, was strong, as was the sound of whining animals.

Bass stopped and put out a hand. I almost ran into it.

"In there," he said. "Doctor will be with you."

I went into the room he was pointing to, and he closed the door behind me. It was like the others we had passed, one chair in a corner, a cabinet, a sink, a counter against the wall with bottles and instruments on it, and in the center of the room, firmly bolted to the floor, a stainless steel table with lipped sides. The table was big enough to hold a fair-sized dog or a very short man. I didn't think I could fit comfortably on it. I didn't think anyone, even my friend Gunther, who doesn't top four feet, could be comfortable on that table.

My thoughts were on the table when the door opened and a man who looked like Guy Kibbe came in, rosy-cheeked and rubbing his hands together rapidly. His freckled balding head was fringed with white hair that grew down over both ears. He wore an open white jacket over a very neat, three-piece suit with a matching blue striped tie.

Without looking at me, he moved to the counter, opened a cabinet, turned a knob, and music filled the room. It sounded like a tinny piano.

"Harpsichord," explained Dr. Olson, turning to me with a benevolent smile, rubbing his palms together. "Louis Couperin, Suite in D Major," he said. " 'Le Tombleau de M.

Blancrocher.' Seventeenth century. Louis Couperin lived from 1626 to 1661. Some people confuse him with his nephew, François Couperin, who was sometimes called Le Grand Couperin. This is Louis. Listen.''

We listened for a minute or two with Olson leaning back against the wall, arms folded.

"Animals like music," he said. "Most animals anyway. Not orchestras, not the big loud stuff like Beethoven. That scares them, but baroque they go for every time. Bach, Mozart, Haydn. Cats even like Vivaldi sometimes. Don't know what to make of that. What can I do for you Mr. Rosenfeldt? Bass says it's something about a dog?"

"I'm looking for a dog." I said.

"Wait, wait, listen to this part." Olson said, holding a finger up to his lips. His hands were clean and looked as if they had just been powdered. "That trill, holding back, the undulation. What can you compare it to, Mr. Rosenfeldt?"

"Sex?"

Olson looked at me seriously.

"Why not," he said. "Heightened emotion, combination of mind and body like good music. The animals have it. They are not inferior to us, not at all. We've just moved away from our origins, made things more artificial. That makes us think we're better. Is thinking better than feeling, Mr. Rosenfeldt?"

"I came about a dog," I said.

Olson scratched the inside of his ear with a clean pinky and with a sigh moved to the cabinet, reached in, and turned off the record.

"I'm attentive," he said, turning to me.

"My dog is sick," I said.

"So Bass told me, though it seemed a bit cryptically stated to him when you called."

"My dog is dying," I said without emotion. "I'd like another just like it, a small black Scotch terrier, just like the president's Fala. You familiar with the dog?"

"Alas," sighed Olson, "I'm not in the business of selling dogs, only in keeping them healthy. Perhaps if you bring your dog in there might be something we can do to help him or, if you are correct, make his final days less painful."

"Alas?" I said.

"I beg your pardon?" Olson said, beaming at me.

"I never met anyone before who used *alas* in normal conversation," I pushed. Olson was not unsettling as easily as I hoped he might, which suggested that he was one hell of a liar or had nothing to hide.

"Well, you have now and may your life be enriched for the experience, Mr. Rosenfeldt," Olson went on. "I'm afraid we have no business together unless you or your missus wishes to bring your pet into the clinic. Believe me, if anything can be done, I will do it."

He put out a friendly hand across the small room to guide me to the door. I pushed away from the wall and took a step toward it before turning.

"You sure you wouldn't know where I could pick up a dog to replace Fala," I said. "It would save me and other people a lot of trouble."

Olson shook his head sadly and, arm out, came to my side to guide me to the door. "I'm afraid I simply cannot give you solace or help," he said. "Many people want black or white Scotch terriers. Now, I've had a long day with my patients. Between us, Mr. Rosenfeldt, there is no essential difference between what I do and that which is done by an expensive Beverly Hills surgeon who makes incisions into movie stars. The anatomy of the mammal is essentially the same regardless of species. The knowledge needed to treat, to cure, is essentially the same. Ah, but the mystique is different. As a veterinary surgeon, I remove the mystique. For example, I see you have a slight limp. Sore back?"

He guided me with a surprisingly strong arm to the door of the room.

"Sore back," I agreed, "but it comes and goes."

"Yes." He chuckled. "If I were a big downtown surgeon, I could put you right up on that table and have you taken care of within an hour."

"Taken care of?" I said, pushing the door closed as he opened it.

"Yes." He smiled. "I could take care of all your problems."

"I'm determined to get that little black dog, Doc," I whispered.

"Who are you?" he whispered back, licking his lower lip.

"The name is Peters." I pushed, feeling that I was getting through to something. "I'm a private investigator looking for a missing dog."

"A missing dog?"

"You make a nice echo," I said. "Let's try for some original material."

"Leave," he said, his voice cracking, but the smile still frozen in place. "You've come to the wrong place."

"I don't think so, Doc," I said.

"Bass," Olson said. He hadn't raised his voice much, so the big blond must have been right outside the door waiting. He came in fast, the door catching me on the shoulder as he pushed through.

"Doc?" he said.

"This man's name is Peters," Olson said slowly. "Please look at him."

Bass looked at me obediently.

"He is not to be allowed in this clinic again," said Olson, shaking his head sadly. "He is not a lover of animals."

"He's not?" said Bass.

"I am too," I stuck in, but Bass wasn't listening to my voice. I wondered if he, too, was soothed by baroque music.

"So," Olson went on, putting an immaculate, paternal hand on Bass's substantial arm, "I'm afraid he will have to leave now. I would prefer that he not be hurt, but we cannot be responsible if he offers resistance, can we?"

"No, we cannot," said Bass, grabbing my shoulder as I tried to work my way behind him to the door.

"I'll leave quietly," I said, trying to remove my jacket from Bass's grasp.

"Let us hope so," sighed Olson. "Alas, Mr. Bass is a former professional wrestler. I would not like you to get hurt on the premises. It might result in some trauma for you, perhaps an emergency situation in which I would have to treat you as a patient."

"That's a threat," I said, unable to free myself from Bass.

"That is a statement of true concern," said Olson, nodding his head to Bass, who caught the signal, opened the door with his free hand, and pushed me into the narrow white corridor. I slammed against the wall and would have fallen if Bass hadn't pulled me up. Olson stood in the open door.

"It's not this easy, Olson," I said.

The smile on his face almost dropped as he quietly closed the door. Bass gave me a shove down the corridor and I banged off of another wall. The crash of my body sent a shiver through the walls, and animals all over the place picked it or something up and went jungle-wild. Down in the darkness behind us dogs barked, and a parrot voice screamed, "I'm Henry the Eighth I am."

I pulled myself up as bloody-coated Bass stalked forward, expressionless.

"Now hold it," I said, holding up a hand. "I'm going and I don't need any help."

He pushed me with an open palm and I staggered back as the sound of Louis Couperin, not to be confused with his nephew François Couperin, came from some speaker in the ceiling.

Bass reached out for another push, which would have sent me up against the door to the waiting room. As his hand came out, I pushed it out of the way with my shoulder as I stepped in and threw a solid right at his midsection. I wanted to knock the wind out of him. I never punched at the face. It usually led to a broken hand. The place to hit was the solar plexus. I hit. I know I hit, but Bass's reaction might have suggested something else to a passing Doberman. Bass looked displeased.

"I don't like fighting," he said.

"That's because you never have to do it," I said. "Now just let me—"

His left hand caught my neck, and his right arm went around my waist. I could feel his fingers digging in to a catchy passage from Couperin and the increasingly hysterical counterpoint of "I'm Henry the Eighth" and assorted dog howls. Up in the air I went, feeling light and dreamy. I floated through the door to the waiting room, which was now dark, and swooshed across the room to the door. The hand on my neck came loose, opened the door, and then returned to my neck. It was at this point that I had the sensation of defying gravity. The setting sun was above me when I landed against a bush. Something scraped against my arm, and I slid to a sitting position, facing the doorway in which Bass stood.

"Watch your hand," he said emotionlessly.

I looked down at my dangling left arm and saw that it hovered over a small natural mound probably left by an animal.

"Thanks," I said, moving away from it.

Bass didn't answer. He closed the door. I rolled over and stood up, looking down the street, but there was no one watching. My neck hurt, my stomach was sore, and my arm was scratched. That would all heal. The problem was my torn sleeve.

There is, I am sure, an easier way to get information than making people angry, but we each go with our own talents. Mine happens to be that of a class-A, number-one, pain-in-the-ass. I've got the wounds to prove it. I'm a walking, or crawling, museum of proof. I could give a tour of my body. Here's the hole made by a bullet when I got a movie star with a gun in her hand angry. (It was at that point that I should have learned not to go with my talent for provoking when the provokee has a gun in his or her hand.) Here's a bullet scar earned the following year from a crooked cop under similar circumstances, and my skull is a phrenologist's nightmare of scar tissue, lumps, and unnatural protuberances. Each success had brought with it a permanent memory for me to wear.

My limbs worked and I was pleased with the results of my sparring with Dr. Olson. Unless I had read him wrong, and I doubted that I had, he was my man. In case I was being watched from the clinic, I limped very slowly to my car, doing my best to look defeated and demolished. I climbed in with a grunt, started the engine, and pulled slowly away after making a U-turn. I went as far as Sherman, turned right, found a driveway where I almost collided with a garbage truck, and pulled back into going-home traffic. A left turn had me back on the cul-de-sac, where I pulled over to watch the clinic from a distance.

The sun was still up but about to drop behind the hills when Bass came out of the front door. He was out of his bloody coat and wearing a light jacket. He carried a little gym bag in one hand as he went massively up the sidewalk and headed for Sherman. I slouched down after a quick adjustment of the mirror, and watched him in its reflection as he came to the corner and turned out of sight.

When I sat up again, the clinic looked dark. My stomach growled and my body throbbed. It would have been nice to get something for my arm and take a hot bath but I couldn't afford to give Olson time to recover. Without Bass around, I was sure I could break him; well, I was sure I had a chance at it.

Darkness came in about an hour and I slipped out of the car and stood to keep my back from locking. I felt awful. I felt tired. I felt like great things were about to happen, but where the hell was Doc Olson? Was he working late doing a Bach-accompanied appendectomy on a dancing bear? Do animals have appendixes?

I gave it another ten minutes and then moved across the dark street toward the clinic. Lights shone through the trees from some of the houses set back from the street. Some of the lights came from a house directly behind the clinic and down a driveway. I circled the clinic, careful of where I was stepping, found no lights on and heard no sounds of music, only a crying dog and the parrot, who had stopped talking and was now croaking.

I moved back to the driveway and began to make my way down the gravel path to the house behind the clinic. There was still a final flare of light from the sun, which merged with the house lights to let me make my way to the front door of a two-story brick house of no great distinction.

No one answered my first knock or my second. The knocker was large, cast iron, and in the shape of a tiger's head. It was loud. I tried again and something stirred inside.

"Coming, coming, coming, for chrissake, coming," a woman's voice said from inside.

There was a fumbling and grumbling behind the door and it came open to reveal a very ample and not sober woman in her thirties in a red silk blouse and matching skirt.

"Mrs. Olson?" I said with a gentle smile, which, I guessed, would make my pushed-in face less jarring.

She was all right for quantity though I couldn't say much for quality at that point. She was dark, her hair black and straight, down to her shoulders. She was made up for a night out rather than a night in and she was coming out of the red thing she was wearing. She looked at me without answering, so I repeated, "Mrs. Olson?"

"Right," she said.

"Can I come in?"

She shrugged, opened the door wider, and gestured with a free hand with bright red nails that I should step through. I did and she closed the door behind me.

"I've got some business with your husband," I said.

She looked at me again and said, "Someone bit a hole in your arm."

Before I could make up a lie, she turned and moved into a room to the left of the little hallway we were standing in. I followed her and found myself in a living room with old-fashioned furniture and one table lamp that gave off enough light to see everything dimly. Mrs. Olson moved nicely to a small table, where she picked up a glass of something amber and took a sip.

"A drink?" she said, holding out the glass.

"I recognize it," I said.

"You want one?"

"Maybe after I talk to your husband," I said.

She moved out of the darkness and stood in front of me, her mouth open in a little smile. Her hand came out and touched my sleeve.

"Why don't you take that jacket off," she said with clear mischief playing around her mouth. "Roy is taking a bath. Roy takes long, long baths. You know why Roy takes long baths?"

"Because he gets dirty," I tried.

"Because he dreads smelling like the clinic. He is con-

stantly cleaning, scrubbing," she said. "He'll be in the tub
for an hour." Her eyebrows went up as if it was my turn and
I could see that she was swaying slightly, as if she heard
music too high-pitched for human ears.

"I'll wait," I said.

"Maybe we can do something while you wait," she said,
the smell of alcohol coming from her breath as she moved
close to me. "Roy's usual callers are not very interesting and
not very friendly. Are you interesting and friendly?"

"I am interesting and friendly," I said. "Let's talk."

"My name is Anne," she said.

"My wife's name was Anne too," I said.

"Was? Is she dead?"

"No, remarried."

"Poor man," she said, showing mock sympathy and taking
another sip. "Maybe we can help you to forget. What's your
name?"

"Toby," I said.

"Roy treated a schnauzer named Toby last year in Washington," she said. "He had cataracts."

"Terrific," I said as she reached up to touch my cheek.
"Tell me about Washington."

"People were too busy to pay attention to each other,"
she said. "Are you too busy to pay attention, Toby?"

What the hell. I kissed her while her husband was upstairs
washing away the day's blood. It felt good. It felt more than
good and it was going to get a lot more complicated if I didn't
do something, but I couldn't do anything except think that
she tasted great, that her name was Anne, and that the world
didn't make much sense.

While we were pressed together, I felt her right hand move
under my jacket and travel down my chest. My eyes were
closed and I didn't give a damn about the sound from far
away. I told it to go away, to wait, to turn into music.

"Water," I said, pulling my mouth from her, but not too
far.

"Huh," she said dreamily.

"Water," I repeated.

"We can't, honey," she said opening her eyes. "Roy's up there taking a bath."

"I hear water dripping from upstairs. Listen."

She gave me a look of impatience, blew out some air from puffed cheeks, and listened.

"You're right," she said without great interest. "Water dripping."

"It's dripping on my head," I added.

Anne Olson looked up at the low ceiling, a move that almost made her lose her already unstable balance. There was a distinct spot on the ceiling.

"Bathroom?" I said.

She tried to figure out the layout of the house and then, coming to a conclusion, said, "Bathroom."

"I'm going up," I said as she reached for me again, moving forward, her lips open in that smile. I jumped past her, went for the hall, took the stairs two at a time, turned the corner, and moved down a small hallway to the bathroom door.

"Olson," I called. "Are you all right?"

There was no answer but something moved behind the door.

"Olson?" I tried again, my hand on the knob. More silence. Water was coming through the opening under the door. I turned the handle and stepped in, trying not to slip on the wet tile.

Doc Olson was in the bathtub, pink and nude but not smiling. His neck was purple and the water flowed slowly and steadily over the rim of the tub. His eyes were open. His mouth was open. And I could see that he was dead.

A sloshy brown bath towel floated over my foot and I glanced down. Something moved behind me and I knew I had made a mistake. Doc Olson and I were not alone in the bathroom.

5

The order of events that followed is still a matter of speculation for those who delve into the blotters of the Los Angeles Police Department for tidbits, tales, and history. *I'm* not even sure of what happened. I know I turned. I know that when turning I stepped on the floating towel and slipped. What I don't know is whether the hand that pushed me struck before I slipped or was the cause of my slipping. A minor point, you might say, but if I could have managed to keep my balance while others were losing theirs, at least one more murder might have been prevented, not to mention what happened to me.

So I tripped backwards, seeing ceiling and the right arm of a murderer as it went through the bathroom door attached to the man himself. That told me one thing that should have been of comfort. He wasn't sticking around to do to me what he had done to Olson. But I wasn't thinking about that at the moment, or about the fact that for the second time in a few hours I was up in the air after being roughed up by someone associated with the late Doc Olson, upon whom I now found myself lying.

His body cushioned me neatly and kept me from a concussion or worse. There was no point in thanking him. My added bulk displaced a wave of water and my clothes took in moisture like a loan shark takes in IOUs. I reached back with a grunt to push myself up and found my hand in Olson's face. It was at this moment that the bathroom door pushed open and instead of letting go of Olson, I pushed harder to get myself up to face the killer, who had decided to come back and do me in. It was Anne Olson, however, who stood in the doorway to the bathroom, almost up to her ankles from a new wave of water I had displaced. She watched my hand pushing her husband's face under and she did a most reasonable thing; she screamed.

"No," I said, letting go of Olson and falling forward on him to take in a lungful of water. When I came up sputtering, she was still standing there, her hands to her mouth.

"Wrong," I gagged, coughing up water and managing to get one leg over the side of the tub. "I—" and a cough took me. She backed away into the hall and against the far wall. Her blouse was open. Drunkenness was gone. Seeing some-one sitting on your dead husband in the bathtub can have a sobering effect. I flopped onto the floor, dripping, and tried to hold a heavy arm up to her in explanation.

"Not . . . what you think," I gasped, down on my hands and knees. "That man, the one who ran past . . ."

"Man?" she whimpered, looking at me as if I were Harpo Marx. "What man?"

I tried to stand, slipped, and, with a magnificent effort, managed not to cry. There is no limit to man's heroic possibil-ities when the last nickel is on the numbers.

"I didn't do this," I said, managing to get back to my knees. "I didn't have time . . . just got up here."

"He's dead. Roy's dead," she cried.

I looked back at Roy because she was looking at him, though I didn't expect to see anything new. The naked corpse had turned sideways, away from us as if he were trying to sleep and our loud conversation had disturbed him.

"He's dead," I agreed, reaching for the toilet to help myself up. I managed and took a step forward. Anne Olson rushed forward. I thought she had experienced a change of heart and was going to help me. Instead, she closed the bathroom door. I lurched forward and tried the handle. My hands were too wet to turn it.

"Hold it," I yelled. "I didn't do this. The killer might still be around. I might be able to catch him."

I grabbed the knob with two hands and turned but nothing happened. What the hell kind of bathroom door locked from the outside? The answer was clear: a bathroom in the house of Anne and the late Dr. Roy Olson.

"Anne," I shouted, hearing her breathing on the other side. "For God's sake let me out. Listen to me."

Some water decided to come out of my lungs at that point and I was paralyzed with coughing. Over it I could hear Anne Olson's footsteps padding down the hall.

"Wait." I coughed again, but she was gone.

I tried the door again but it was solid and locked. The room was too small and too soggy for me to back up and throw my shoulder against it.

"Open the damn door or I'll use his corpse as a battering ram," I shouted stupidly.

There wasn't much I could do. Using the sink, I went back to the tub and turned off the running water. Then I sat on the closed toilet seat and looked at Olson's corpse. He had nothing to say so I tried the door again. Nothing. Taking off my shoes and socks, I climbed onto the rim of the tub, being careful not to put my footprints on the corpse, and opened the small pebble-glass window in the wall. It was too small to crawl through, and I couldn't see anything. There wasn't much point in shouting. The nearest house was a few hundred yards away through the trees and there was no way, without stepping on Olson, that I could even get my head out the window. The open window did let in some cool air.

It was time to think. Time to act. I took off all my clothes, dried off with a towel Olson probably had planned to use, checked my dad's watch, which was ticking merrily away and telling me it was three o'clock on some day in never-never land. With the spigot turned off, the water drained out, mostly under the door. I sopped up most of what remained on the tile floor with the towel I had used and a stack of other towels. I didn't let the water out of the tub. There had been enough tampering with evidence. Having done all that, I sat on the toilet and checked myself for wounds. The scratch on my arm from the bushes didn't look too bad. The bruises were minor on the rest of my body.

So, I sat naked with a naked corpse in a bathroom in Sherman Oaks and for a nutty moment considered posing as The Thinker. Maybe five minutes passed, during which I turned Olson over so I could see his face. I couldn't decide what was worse, not seeing him and wondering how he looked or seeing him. In another five minutes I was shivering and had made a decision. There were dry clothes in the room neatly hung on wooden hangers, the clothes Olson was going to put on after his bath. We were approximately the same size, so I put them on.

I had the underpants on, a few sizes too big, and one foot in the trousers when the door popped open and I turned off-balance to face a uniformed cop about sixty years old. He had probably seen it all, but he had never seen this.

"It's not what it looks like," I said, removing the pants carefully, to keep the gun in his hand from getting jumpy.

"Son," he said, looking from me to Olson, "I don't know what the hell this looks like and I'm gonna do my damned best not to think about it. Now you just step out here in the hall nice and slow like a good fellow, or I'll start pulling this trigger and not stop till I'm out of bullets."

"I'm moving," I said with as pleasant a grin as my battered face could muster.

My hands were out to show they were empty, and as I stepped into the hall he backed away, the gun level at my stomach.

"My clothes were wet," I explained.

"Don't talk," the cop said, still looking at me. "This is crazy enough without you giving me the fantods. We'll just call the station again."

"My name's Peters," I said. "I'm a private investigator. I didn't kill that man. The killer went out as I came in."

"Makes no never-you-mind to me," the cop said. "Just stand there quiet, or better yet, sit yourself down on the floor till I get some help here."

"My brother's Lieut—Captain Phil Pevsner of the L.A.P.D. He knows about this case," I said. "Call him."

It was the first thing I could think of and probably not a particularly good idea since it was a partial lie and Phil might be less willing to listen than some unknown sergeant working Sherman Oaks.

"All in good time," said the cop, reaching for a phone on a little white table in the hall. "You're just talking to a soldier of law here. Now sit."

I sat on the floor, resigned, while he made his call.

When he finished, the old cop took off his cap without taking his eyes from me. He was on the thin side except for his little basketball belly and he wore a dark toupee that didn't match his sideburns.

"You got your share of scars there," he said conversationally, trying to humor the madman.

"Right," I agreed. "You want to know what happened in there?"

"Nope," he said, showing a little smile. "I want to get home and finish reading the copy of *Dragon Seed* my wife bought me. I don't want to think about this at all. Who you got in the Kentucky Derby tomorrow? Picked up a bookie the other day who told me to back Shut Out."

The conversation for the next ten minutes was one-sided. The old cop, who said his name was Max Citron, talked and I tried not to listen as I sat in Olson's undershorts, shaken by an occasional chill. I don't know how long it was till the next two cops came. The first thing they decided after consulting with Citron was that I could put on an old suit of Roy Olson's. He wouldn't be needing it. Citron disappeared, came back with a gray suit, and I dressed while the new cops, both detectives, whose names were Downs and Hindryx, examined the bathroom, listened to my tale, wrote down what I said, and appeared to have no interest in the whole business.

"So the dead guy is a vet named Olson," Downs said, looking down at his notes as we stood in the hallway downstairs. He was dark-suited, thin, weary, and wore a toothpick in the corner of his mouth.

"Roy Olson," his partner, a squat redhead, filled in.

"Right," Downs said. "You had some beef with him or something sick going. You were in th tub together and things got out of hand. All a mistake, right?"

"That's not what happened," I said, shaking my head patiently. "Ask Mrs. Olson. Where is she?"

"No Mrs. Olson here. Nobody but you," Hindryx said, nodding back into the house.

For a second time, I explained what had happened. The two cops wrote it down dutifully so that my two tellings could be checked against each other and whatever additional tales I might tell. Hindryx wrote it, grunted occasionally, and put his notebook away.

"Where's your car?" said Downs.

I told him and he decided it would be fine right there until it could be checked out.

"Cop who found you said you're Phil Pevsner's brother, that right?" said Downs.

"It's right," I said.

"He's an asshole," said Downs, looking at me for contradiction.

"You want me to tell him you said that?" I answered.

Downs shrugged. "Suit yourself," he said, shifting his toothpick to the other side of his mouth.

The next hour was a trip down memory lane. Printed, booked, checked for priors, questioned again, and headed for the lockup. I had a single call I could make. I told the cop at the local that I wanted to make a few calls, that there was no law that said I could make only one, that the cops got that idea from William Powell movies, but he didn't budge. One call it would be.

I'd been through this before. I wouldn't get a bail hearing on a murder charge so there was no point in calling Gunther to get me out. They'd want to keep me for a psychiatrist to talk to after what had happened. So I called the Wilshire District station. Veldu was still on duty, a double shift he explained as the lockup cop checked his watch to be sure I didn't take too much time. Phil was home but Seidman was still there. I talked to him and gave him a quick explanation.

"Steve," I said when he didn't answer. "You there?"

"I'm here," he said wearily, "but I'm not sure you're all there. I'll tell Phil and see what he wants to do." He hung up and I gave the phone back to the lockup officer.

It was night and the cell I was taken to was small and

smelled of nightmares. There were two bunks in the cell and a weak light in the ceiling. On the wall between the bunks was a chalk drawing of Smokey Stover. Someone was lying on the bunk on the left. Doc Olson's clothes and I took the bunk on the right.

"I didn't do it," said the voice from the other bunk. The guy in it was lying on his back, his right arm across his eyes.

"I believe you," I said, checking the bunk for bugs.

The other guy began to snore and I lay back trying to think. Had I stumbled into some unrelated murder? Had some jealous hulk that Anne Olson picked up strangled her husband, and I just had the dumb luck to walk in at the wrong time? Where was Anne Olson? Had Olson been knocked off because of the kidnapping of the president's dog? Why? I knew I was too edgy to sleep, but knowing is not the same as feeling. I was asleep in minutes. My body had been through enough in forty-seven years to know when it needed a break, even if my mind didn't.

I dreamed that Guy Kibbe and I were sitting on Doc Olson's naked stomach. He was floating and we were out in the middle of the ocean. From a faraway island, a woman's voice called, "Out here damned spot." Using our hands, we paddled for it on the bouyant corpse. When we reached the island, my ex-wife Anne and Koko the clown were hand-in-hand, dancing on the beach. We got off of Olson, and the four of us watched him float out to sea. For some reason, it was a tender moment. Something was about to happen. Anne was about to speak and tell me something important, but she never did. Someone shook me awake and I was back in the cell.

"Come on," said Seidman.

"She was going to tell me the answer," I said, sitting up and looking over at my cellmate, whose arm was still covering his eyes.

"Sure," said Seidman. His jaw was slightly swollen.

"You snore," said the guy from the other bunk.

"You did it," I answered, following Seidman out of the cell.

Some bookwork, discussion, and dirty looks passed between Seidman and Downs, but in a few minutes the final
touches were made and I was on my way, seated next to
Seidman.

"I got the report from Hindryx," he said, heading into the
night. "That the way it was?"

"The way I said it."

That was all we said for the next half-hour till we got to
the Wilshire station. It was four in the morning according to
the clock downstairs and the night man had replaced Veldu.
I didn't know the night man so we exchanged nothing. We
bypassed the squadroom and went to an office in the hall with
CAPTAIN LOWELL B. PRONZINI stenciled on the door in black
letters that were peeling off from years of scratching and a
few dozen washings. Lowell B. had just retired. It was, I
found, the office of Captain Phil Pevsner. It was bigger than
his old one, had three chairs besides the one behind the desk,
and probably looked out on the parking lot. I couldn't tell. It
was too dark. The desk was just as old as the last one and
there were two battered file cabinets in the corner.

"Coming up in the world, ain't you Rico?" I said to Phil,
who sat rocking in his new swivel chair behind the desk.

"What's Eleanor Roosevelt got to do with this shit?" he
said, still rocking.

Seidman took one of the chairs, moved it to the corner,
and sat down to swallow a pill and massage his right cheek,
beneath which lurked the work that Shelly had done on him.

"Nothing," I said.

Phil stopped rocking for a second, looked forward at me,
a day's stubble of gray beard on his chin. He said nothing
and went from rocking to swiveling in his chair.

"Try again," sighed Seidman from the corner.

Phil paused, looking bored, and reached for the metal cup
of coffee on his desk. He discovered it was empty, got mad
at the cup, and threw it in the garbage can near the desk. The
garbage can was brown, metal, and not new.

"Ruth can make some curtains," I said, "turn this into—"

"Eleanor Roosevelt," Phil said, rubbing his temples.

"Eleanor Roosevelt," I agreed, and told him everything, her fears, the dog, everything. "You believe me?" I concluded.

Phil's hands went up in a resigned gesture of indecision. He looked at Seidman, whose tongue was in his cheek testing his inflamed gums. He had no opinion.

"Go home," Phil said, swiveling away from me to look out of the dark window.

"Aren't you going to tell me to stop looking for the dog?" I asked. "To keep out of it, to—"

"Would it do any good?" Phil said.

"No," I agreed, "but that's the routine. Aren't we partners anymore?"

"We never were," sighed Phil. "Downs and Hindryx gave me four days to come up with something or they're pulling you back in. I leaned on them a little. They're a pair of shits."

"They have great respect for you too," I added.

"And they've got a friend in the Wilshire who'll be watching things for them," Seidman added behind me.

"Let me guess," I said. "Cawelti? Hell, Phil, just pull in Anne Olson. She must have panicked. She'll back my story."

"Go home," said Phil. "Now." He spun around, stood up, and turned his red face to me. The tie was back on. Old habits.

"I'm going," I said, backing away. "My car is in Sherman Oaks. It's on your way back to North Hollywood. How about dropping me off?"

"Go," said Phil so softly that I could only tell what he was saying by watching his lips. I went.

I was almost to the front door of the station when Seidman caught up to me.

"I'll take you to your car," he said.

"You don't live in the valley."

"Can't sleep with this toothache," he said. "Besides, Phil doesn't want to take a chance on you going back to Olson's when you get the car."

Seidman led the way to his car and we drove without talking. The sun was just coming up on the far side of the valley when we made the turn onto the cul-de-sac. It was

Saturday morning. Seidman took my thanks without comment and waited to be sure I made a U-turn and drove away. He followed me and then veered off when he was sure I was on my way up Coldwater Canyon Drive. He had no worries. I was headed home wearing a dead man's suit. When I got over the hills, a stop light caught me and a guy on the radio said Robert S. James, the rattlesnake killer, had just been hanged at San Quentin. He was, said the announcer with a pregnant pause, "calm to the end."

I looked in the rearview mirror at my face. My chin was covered with stubble just like my brother's, the same gray field of hard times.

6

Mrs. Plaut was singing her Fanny Brice rendition of "I'm Cooking Breakfast for the One I Love," complete with Yiddish accent, when I pushed open the door of her boarding house on Heliotrope. My plan was simple, to get to my room and fall asleep, but to accomplish that I had to make it past Mrs. Plaut.

She didn't hear me come in. There wasn't much that Mrs. Plaut could hear, but she made up in determination what she lacked in hearing. She stood about four and a half feet high and was somewhere in the range of eighty years old. Her age, sex, and hearing impairment deprived the U.S. Army of the services of the most able assistant General Patton could have hoped for.

The door to her rooms on the main floor was open. I moved past slowly and quietly, noticing that she was back in the kitchen and the smell of something good was wafting into the hall. I got to the first step when her voice stopped me.

"Mr. Peelers," she shouted. "Mr. Peelers. You must wait for comments and messages."

I put one hand on the wall and turned to face the inevitable. Not only did Mrs. Plaut not know my name, but she had latched onto the delusion that I was a pest exterminator who was somehow involved in the publishing industry. My periodic efforts to explain something approaching the truth to her only managed to tire me out and thrust the woman deeper into delusion. The situation was complicated by the fact that Mrs. Plaut was, with great and typical determination, writing the definitive history of her family. She had completed over fifteen hundred pages, neatly printed. It was my task to edit and comment on the chapters as she finished them.

Why didn't I move? Answer: The rent was low. My best friend, Gunther Wherthman, a Swiss midget who made a living as a translator, was a tenant at Mrs. Plaut's, and, with the war, housing had almost disappeared in Los Angeles. Rents were flying as high as Doolittle, a sign of the times that, fortunately, had not entered Mrs. Plaut's interest or awareness.

She appeared through the door below me, wiping her bony hands on her apron, which was muslin and carried a stenciled message in black: PROPERTY OF THE U.S. ARMY AIR FORCE. She adjusted her glasses with a clean finger.

"I'm very tired, Mrs. Plaut," I said wearily.

"You look very tired," Mrs. Plaut said, looking me over, her head cocked to one side critically.

"What can I do for you, Mrs. Plaut?" I said with a smile.

"I have a list of items to relate," she said, fishing into a pocket in her apron and pulling out a small notebook, which she opened. "First, have you finished reading my chapter about Aunt Gumm and Mexico?"

She looked up at me patiently, waiting for an answer.

"I have finished," I said, speaking slowly, clearly, and loud enough to awaken whoever might still be sleeping in the boarding house. They would be sloshing down soon for Mrs. Plaut's breakfast, those who were willing to pay the price in conversation. "But I don't understand why your Aunt Gumm thought she owned Guadalajara. You never make it clear why—"

"You know Aunt Gumm owned Guadalajara," she beamed, interrupting me.

"I'd heard something about it," I said, leaning on the wall.

The chapter, which lay on my table upstairs, was even less coherent than most of the previous ones Mrs. Plaut had been giving me. I really didn't mind reading the manuscript. I just couldn't take discussing it with Mrs. Plaut.

"How did your Aunt Gumm meet the bandit," I tried.

"You are in need of a shave," she said critically. "Though your new suit is an improvement over what you have worn previously."

"I got it from a dead man," I said, grinning evilly.

"I see," she answered with a grin. "That is no concern of mine. I am quite aware of your line of business, as you know. Let us return to Aunt Gumm."

"Let us," I said, and then desperately, "Your buns are burning."

Mrs. Plaut gave me a tolerant look and clasped her hands together.

"Buns," I repeated.

"Uncle Parsner was the one for puns and such like," she said gently. "Aunt Gumm was devoid of a sense of humor. You must keep my relations in order if you are to help, Mr. Peelers."

"I'll try," I said in weary surrender. "Aunt Gumm is wonderful, a critical member of the family. The chapter should be longer, more about the bandit."

"The bandit," she said, glancing at the open door from which the smell of buns came, "was a distant friend of Joaquin Murietta, who kept his toenails in a jar. Aunt Gumm's bandit did no such of a silly thing though he was, I am told, given to telling dialect jokes, mostly at the expense of those less fortunate than himself, though who that might be remains a mystery not only to me but to Uncle Jerry and other branches of the family. My buns are done."

"Good," I said, turning to go up stairs. I had made it up four steps when she stopped me.

"There are other items to relate," she said. I turned and watched her tiny figure as she glanced at her notebook. "Calls galore. The policeman brother of yours called."

"He found me," I said.

"And," she concluded with a flourish by slamming closed the notebook, "you are now involved in the politics."

"I am?"

"One of the many Roosevelts who run this country called you," she said with disapproval. "I do not recall if it was Anna. I rather hope it was since I voted for her father. Teddy Roosevelt was the last good president we had. Before him all was abyss except for Jackson and Polk."

"Did you vote for them?" I said softly, my eyes closing as I rubbed the stubble on my chin.

"Rude disrespect will not get you into heaven," she said, pointing a flour-covered finger at me. I wasn't sure if she had miraculously heard what I had said or had come up with an even more unpleasant invention.

"I'm sorry, Mrs. Plaut. I really am. I'm tired and—"

"She should not have married him," she went on.

"Who?" I tried, feeling the tears of sleep.

"Franklin and Eleanor are cousins," she explained patiently as if I were a backward second-grader. "That is incest."

"Let's hope so," I said. "If I don't get upstairs and into bed, I'm going to tumble down these stairs and make it difficult for Mr. Hill and the others to climb over my body."

"We'll talk again when you are in a less jovial frame of mind," she said, disappearing into her rooms before I could find out when Eleanor Roosevelt had called. My goal was a few hours of sleep followed by a call to Eleanor Roosevelt and a search for Jeremy Butler, who might be able to tell me something about Bass, the former wrestler who seemed to be the only suspect I had in Olson's murder. That would be followed by a search for the missing Anne Olson.

I didn't have to fumble for the key to my room. The rooms in Mrs. Plaut's boarding house had no locks. Mrs. Plaut's philosophy was that adults should change clothes in the bath-room down the hall and decent people should have nothing to hide beyond their own crude nakedness. She respected closed doors only for the time it took her to knock once and enter. If one wanted privacy in this barracks of the outcast and elderly, one resorted to a chair under the doorknob. Even this had been known to do no more than slow down the determined landlady.

I liked my room. It was nothing like me. There was one old sofa with doilies on the arms which I was afraid to touch, a table with three wooden chairs, a hot plate in the corner, a sink, a small refrigerator, a few dishes, a bed with a purple blanket on which *God Bless Us Every One* had been stitched in pink by Mrs. Plaut, a painting of someone who looked like Abraham Lincoln, and a Beech-Nut gum clock on my wall, received in payment from a pawnshop owner for finding his runaway grandmother. Every night I took the mattress from the bed and put it on the floor. This morning I repeated the rite. I slept on the floor because of a delicate back crunched in 1938 by a massive Negro gentleman who took exception to my trying to keep him from asking Mickey Rooney a few questions at a premiere at Grauman's Chinese.

I removed Olson's suit, dropped it on the sofa, ran my tongue over my furry teeth, decided I was too tired to eat and too sensitive to examine my bruises, and fell like an uprooted radiator on the mattress. My Beech-Nut clock said it was 6:34. My father's watch said it was noon or midnight. I fell asleep clutching my second pillow to keep from rolling over on my stomach and ruining my back.

There were dreams, but I didn't remember them well. A city, probably Cincinnati, about which I dream frequently though I've never been there, a plump young woman with glasses saying something to me, a tree and a stag whose branches and antlers had grown together so that they couldn't be separated. I woke up to someone knocking at my door. The clock on the wall told me it was eleven.

"What, what, what?" I grouched.

"Toby?" came Gunther's high precise voice, complete with Swiss accent. "Are you well?"

"Come in, Gunther," I said, sitting up.

He pushed at the door and stepped in, all three feet nine of him in his usual sartorial splendor. He wore a light brown, three-piece suit with key chain, tie, and tie pin. Gunther was somewhere in his late thirties. We had met two years earlier, when he was my client, and had been friends since then. If given one wish, Gunther would have made me a reasonably clean human with minimal taste.

"You did not come home last night," he said evenly, indicating concern without interference.

Sitting up on the floor, I was almost at eye level with him.

"Case," I said, tasting my tongue. "Secret, big."

"Mrs. Roosevelt," he said.

"My secret mission seems to be this morning's news," I said, getting up and groping for my—Olson's—pants.

"Mrs. Plaut and I exchanged information while attempting to take a coherent message," he explained. "I assumed from your converse just now . . ."

"You assumed right," I said, unable to resist the urge to scratch my stomach. "Listen Gunther, I've got to shave my teeth and brush my beard. You want to put some coffee on? I'll be right back."

Gunther nodded politely and moved to the corner of my room, which served as my kitchen and which Gunther always approached as if on a mission to deal with an attacking horde of army ants.

No one was in the bathroom so I managed to finish my shaving and brushing with a new bottle of Teel in less than ten minutes. I put Olson's shirt and tie back on, slipped on my second pair of socks, the ones with only one hole, and went back to my room. The coffee was poured, and a bowl of Wheaties stood waiting for me with a nearly empty bottle of milk next to it. Gunther sat sipping his coffee with great gentility and dignity, his feet not quite touching the floor.

Gunther had a book in front of him and was deep in thought over something in it.

"What's the problem?" I said helpfully, now that I was awake and capable of thought and movement.

"Passage that requires a translation," he said, tapping the tome in front of him. "What does it mean, 'Take a deep breath, and call lung distance'? Should that not be 'long distance'? And even so, I believe there is intended some crude form of wit in this."

I was well into my second bowl of Wheaties and had used the last of the milk on it when I concluded my explanation. Gunther had sipped coffee silently, nodding occasionally to show that he followed my explanation.

"Would you say it is a good joke?" he asked seriously. "I mean in English."

"It sounds like Lum and Abner," I said, finishing my coffee.

"Then I'd best find some means of rendering it in French," he said seriously. Then he changed the subject, coming to something that I could see had been on his mind.

"What is it, Gunther?"

"If you are engaged in something that will even in a small way help in the war effort, I should like to offer my assistance, even in a small way."

With anyone else I would have been unable to resist the opening and get in three or four small jokes.

"I have great loyalty to this nation," he said, back erect, "as you know. Many of my people, most of my people, my own relations in Berne, assure me of their similar feelings though to be neutral is of a necessity."

"You don't have to explain to me, Gunther," I said, getting up and gathering the dishes. Gunther must, indeed, have been grappling with weighty thoughts because he didn't stop me. Usually, the thought of my cleaning anything up was repulsive enough for Gunther to not only volunteer, but to insist that he take over. He wiped the corners of his mouth neatly with a paper napkin and hopped with dignity from his chair.

"I have offered my services," he said. "They are sincere."

"Okay," I sighed, "I'll take you up on the offer. I'll give you the address of a veterinary clinic in Sherman Oaks. I want you to go there, wait for a blond hulk. His name is Bass. Follow him but don't let him see you. That shouldn't be too hard. There aren't too many smarts rattling inside him.''

Gunther nodded knowingly, and I explained the whole thing, including Olson's murder, the missing dog, everything.

"I'm relieved," he said with a small grin. "I was afraid you had chosen that suit. While properly conservative, it does not accommodate your personality."

"It'll have to do," I said, thinking that Gunther would also have to do. Normally, it is not a wise thing to send a midget out to tail a suspect. There is no such thing as an inconspicuous midget or little person, but then again there are few people as dense as Bass seemed to be.

Gunther hurried to his room to get on with his assignment, and I decided to do the dishes some other time. In the hallway I flexed my muscles, decided that they still functioned, and moved to the phone on the wall to make a few calls.

Eleanor Roosevelt did not answer at the number she gave me, but a woman with what sounded like an English accent did. I gave her my name and she told me to wait. Gunther passed me, still suited, nodded seriously, and went down the stairs. The phone rang.

"Mr. Peters?" came Eleanor Roosevelt's voice.

"Mrs. Roosevelt," I said. "Things are getting a bit complicated."

"I have been informed about Doctor Olson," she said. "Do you think it has something to do with Fala? I should hate to think that a man actually died because of some intrigue over a dog, but then regard for human life has not been this low since the reign of the Teutons."

"I guess," I said. "But this might be getting beyond the stage where I can handle it. You might want to call in the heavier guns, the FBI, whoever."

There was a pause while she considered what to say next.

"Mr. Peters, it is quite evident to both of us that you wish to continue this inquiry. You have my trust, and I feel confident that you will not betray it. Beyond loyalty, there is little else that can be asked or received."

"Intelligence would be nice," I said.

She laughed gently. "You do not strike me as an unintelligent man," she said. "There are those who pose as men in the heart of our own government, even those who have been elected, whose intellect does not surpass that of a small terrier and whose loyalty lags far behind. The canine reminder is, by the way, quite intentional."

"I'll get back to work and get to you as soon as I can," I said.

"Remember," she said, "I have only a few days. I must be back in Washington for the Peruvian dinner, and Mr. Molotov is coming."

"Sounds like a fun-packed few months," I sympathized.

"Mr. Molotov is, in fact, quite nice," she said. "His English is good, his sense of humor mischievous, and his manner poor. He actually brings his own food and carries a loaded gun in his suitcase."

There I stood chatting with the First Lady in the hallway of Mrs. Plaut's boarding house when Mrs. Plaut herself appeared at the bottom of the stairs, saw me, and began her resolute way up.

"I'll have to go now, Mrs. Roosevelt," I said. "Something important just came up. I'll report as soon as I can."

"Be careful Mr. Peters," she concluded. "The dog is important, but it is, after all, a dog."

"I'll remember that," I said, hanging up and wondering if I could make it back to my room before Mrs. Plaut caught up with me. But she was too fast.

"Mr. Peelers," she said, cutting off my retreat with her wiry body. "Now, I think, would be a good time to discuss Aunt Gumm."

"Mrs. Plaut," I began, "I've got . . . forget it. It's a fine time to discuss Aunt Gumm and Mexico."

"The Mexicans," she said knowingly, "pronounce it Me-he-co."

By noon I had developed a headache from shouting, but managed to break away from Mrs. Plaut. I didn't use the phone in the hallway for fear that she would want to talk further about her proposed next chapter dealing with her mother's encounter with the Mormons.

I darted down the stairs, out the door into the sunshine, and made it to my car in near record time. I found a Rexall drugstore and called Jeremy Butler's office/home number at the Farraday. He didn't answer but Alice Palice did. Alice and Jeremy had become "good friends." It was a union that did not bear too much fantasy. Alice more than occupied space on the third floor of the Farraday. She ran Artistic Books, Inc., an economical operation, consisting of one small printing press that weighed two hundred and fifty pounds. Alice, who looked something like a printing press herself, could easily hoist the press on her shoulder and move it to another office when the going got rough.

"Jeremy's in the park," she said. I thanked her and hung up.

It was one o'clock, so I switched on the radio. It was too early for the baseball game so I found KFI and listened to "Mary Noble, Backstage Wife." Soap operas always gave me a lift. It was nice to find people, even pretend ones, who were having a harder time than I was.

I drove past the office on Hoover and down Hill past Angel's Flight, the block-long railroad that carried passengers up the steep slope of Bunker Hill between Hill and Olive. When I was a kid, my old man once took me and my brother to the observation tower at the top of the hill that rises about a hundred feet over the mouth of the Third Street Tunnel. I remember seeing the San Gabriel Mountains and wanting to tell Phil that it was beautiful, but Phil had always been Phil. Back then it had been a tourist attraction with about twelve thousand passengers a day going up the railway and to the top of the tower.

I turned off of Hill at Fifth and found a parking spot near Philharmonic Auditorium. The sign outside the hall told me Volez and Yolanda were, indeed, playing there and I could get tickets for as little as fifty-five cents. I stopped at the box office and splurged on two one-buck tickets, then nodded to the statue of Beethoven on Fifth, and moved into Pershing Square. When I was a kid it had been Central Park, but had been renamed in 1918 in honor of old Black Jack. I passed by the banana trees and bamboo clumps that surrounded the square, and in the shade of the Biltmore Hotel I squinted around searching for Jeremy. I took a few steps down the broad brick walk that forms an X across the square and looked at the fountain in the center of the X. The place was full of men, almost no women, most of them wearing suits, most of them with ties. Arguments were going on all over the place. Near the fountain a guy with glasses was pointing off in the distance and showing a handful of papers to another guy without a hat who had his hands on his hips. Another group was gathered around a bench on which was standing an ancient man who looked a little like John Nance Garner. John Nance was shouting at a small Negro man wearing a fedora and a mustache. I weaved my way through the knots of men arguing. One guy conversing with some students from the Bible Institute down the street was going at it about where God was now that men were being killed by heathens. A pair of cops weaved in and out, keeping things from getting out of hand, which they often did. Then I spotted Jeremy. He was hard to miss since he stands about six two and weighs slightly over two-fifty. He was under the Spanish War Memorial in the northeast corner of the park. Under the shade of the twenty-foot statue of a Spanish War veteran, Jeremy had his right hand on the shoulder of a white-whiskered, barefoot messiah, and was gesturing with open palm at the bronze cannon a few feet away.

The war had brought out a battalion of prophets who wandered through downtown Los Angeles strongly suggesting that the end of the world was well under way. This did not strike most Los Angelenos as news.

I listened politely to Jeremy telling the bearded man that hope and not fear should be the basis of progress, but the bearded guy was not about to turn in his staff and head for the barber. He just stroked his beard and nodded sagely. Jeremy spotted me out of the corner of his eye and excused himself from the man.

"He doesn't lack intelligence," Jeremy said, "but there is nothing more difficult than to get a man to give up an obsession in which he has invested his faith, no matter how unreasoning that obsession may be."

"You've got that right," I agreed. I always agreed with Jeremy because he was wiser than I was and could break my neck by breathing on me if he felt the need, which he never did.

"What can I do for you, Toby?" he said seriously, stepping out of the way of a pair of old men, one with a newspaper under his arm, who barreled past us.

"I'm looking for information on a former wrestler. A guy named Bass. Big guy, bigger than you, maybe thirty-five or younger," I explained.

"He may look that young, but he is almost your age," Jeremy said, looking around for the messiah who had disappeared in the crowd. Jeremy rubbed his shaven head and returned his attention to me. "A close look will show that Elmo Bass's youthful face is that of a man who has not been furrowed by experience and life. It is an unformed face, not a young face. It is a face that has experienced no depth. It is a face unlike yours or mine."

"Got you," I said. "What about him?"

Jeremy shrugged and unzipped his gray windbreaker to give his massive chest some room to breathe.

"Very dense," said Jeremy sadly. "Very little sense of the moral. Never having truly suffered, he has no sense of what suffering means. A dangerous man, Toby. One to stay away from. I fought him three times. He beat me but one of them, the last one at the Stadium in, let me see, 1935 or '36. He was removed from the sport that same year. No control, no sense of the game, the art of enactment. He did not know how to act. He could only fight. Consequently, no one but me wanted to enter the ring with him, though he did end his career against the Strangler, and Pepe the Giant."

"So you think he could kill?" I said.

"With little excuse and no remorse," Jeremy said.

"Where does he hang out?"

Jeremy shrugged and said, "We have not kept in touch, though I have heard less than kind things said about him, particularly from Pepe with whom I still play chess from time to time. It would be best to stay away from Bass. You know what his nickname for himself was? *Le Mort*, Death. Pepe called him Badass Bass. If you must encounter him, I strongly suggest that I accompany you."

"I'll keep that in mind Jeremy, thanks."

"Alice and I," he said seriously, changing the subject, "have a new enterprise. She has agreed, at least for the time, to put aside the pornography, and publish a series of books of children's poetry that I am writing. While I have no great quarrel with pornography, I think it tends to simply reproduce itself and make the pornographer carry guilt instead of pride. Would you like to hear one of the poems I have written for our initial book?"

"Sure," I said, noticing that a scrawny man in a sweater and jacket was listening to our conversation. A cigarette dangled from his lips, and the skin on his neck hung down like that of a forgotten turkey.

"Ah," Jeremy said, suddenly remembering, "Academy Dolmitz. Academy hired Bass for debt collecting a few years ago. I thought I heard that he still did some part-time work for Academy."

"Thanks, Jeremy," I said. Academy Dolmitz had a used bookstore on Broadway. The bookstore was a front for a bookie operation.

"The poem," Jeremy reminded me, a gentle but massive hand on my arm. I stood politely with the turkey man and others as Jeremy recited his poem to a growing crowd, which numbered about ten by the time he finished.

> *"The wife of the king*
> *continued to sing*
> *though his majesty said*
> *he would render her dead*
> *if the queen did not cease*
> *and give him some peace.*
> *'If my song was too loud,'*
> *said the queen to the crowd*
> *which had gathered to see*
> *a monarch hang from a tree*
> *'then a strong admonition*
> *might have changed my position,*

but the king would not dream
of a choice less extreme
than to tie off, garrotte,
my tender white throat.
And so the next time
a tune leaps to your mind
  cut it off in mid-note
  and commit this to rote:
If the queen can hang
for a song she sang,
then might not the noose, come
for a tune that you hum?'
Brought on by hysteria,
the queen then sang an aria
but a black-hooded fella
cut short her a capella,
as a voice from the crowd
shouted angry and loud,
'Not a moment too soon,
she can't carry a tune.' ''

The turkey neck looked puzzled while another guy in the crowd applauded and a voice from the back said critically, ''It got no goddam onomatopoeia for chrissake. A poem gotta have onomatopoeia.''

I backed away from the coming debate, wondering what a kid would make of Jeremy's creation and if he and Alice were planning to illustrate their book. I also filed in the back of my mind the possibility of bringing Mrs. Plaut and publisher Alice Palice together. Object: publication, and my own curiosity.

On the way back to Burbank for another try at Jane Poslik, I turned on the news and found that it was Saturday, which I already knew. What I didn't know was that the sugar shortage had gotten worse. Hoarding syrup was now a crime and ice-cream manufacturers were being limited to twenty flavors of ice cream and two of sherbet. Beyond that, Laraine Day was engaged to army aviator Ray Hendricks, who used to sing with Ted Fio Rito. Shut Out had won the Kentucky Derby, and a Japanese transport and six fighter planes had been destroyed in an attack on enemy bases in New Guinea.

I had time for about ten minutes of Scattergood Baines before I pulled up in front of Jane Poslik's apartment in Burbank. My workday had begun in earnest.

Jane Poslik was home. She didn't want to open the door at first, but I dropped some names like Olson, Roosevelt, and Fala, and she let me in. Her apartment was small and neat and so was she. There were sketches on the wall in cheap, simple frames, more than a dozen sketches of women in a variety of costumes. My favorite was a pencil sketch of someone who looked like Lucille Ball in a fancy French dress all puffed out, white and soft.

"Looks like Lucille Ball," I said, nodding at the drawing.

"It is," she said, watching me carefully with puckered lips.

Jane Poslik was somewhere in her late thirties, hair cut short. She wore a brown dress with a faint pattern. She was not pretty and not ugly. If her nose had been less chiseled, her chin a little stronger, she might have come out all right, but if she was one of the Pekin, Illinois, beauty pageant runners-up or an actress who had played the second female lead in a Dayton theater company production of *Street Scene*, she wasn't going to be any competition for the hundreds who tripped over each other coming to Los Angeles every week.

"You an actress?" I said, taking the seat in the small kitchen she pointed to.

"Designer," she answered, filling a pot with water. "Coffee or tea?"

"Coffee," I said. "You work for a studio?"

"No," she said, hugging herself as if she were cold and turning to look at me. "Not yet. So far I've managed to design for a theater company in Santa Monica. I've had to take a variety of jobs."

"Like working for Dr. Olson," I said.

"Like working for Dr. Olson," she agreed, fishing a package of Nabisco graham crackers out of a cabinet and placing them on the small table in front of me. "Right now I'm doing part-time work for Gladding, McBean, and Company in

Glendale. I'm designing some mosaic tiles. If it goes well,
I'll be put on full time."

"Sounds good," I said.

"It's good," she agreed, standing near the coffee pot.
"But it's not designing."

"Olson," I said.

"Olson," she sighed. "You work for . . ."

"A private party close to someone quite high in the government," I said, nibbling a graham.

She looked at me for a long time trying to decide whether
to trust me or not.

"I know about the letters you wrote to the White House,"
I said. "I know that the FBI talked to you."

"All right, Mr. Peters," she said, deciding to take a
chance. "What do you want to know?"

"What made you think something was going on with Dr.
Olson and the president's dog?"

The coffee was perking now. She checked the pot, made
another decision, and said, "I'll answer your question when
you answer one for me."

"Go ahead."

"Why are you wearing Dr. Olson's suit?"

The explanation took about five minutes, with me leaving
out a few things and pausing for her to react when I told her
that Olson was dead. She reacted with a quick intake of air
and silence.

"Killing people over a dog," she said, pouring the coffee.
Her hand was shaking so I helped her.

"I don't know why they killed him. You have some
ideas?"

She sat sipping coffee and told her story, making sketches
on the table with her finger. Her mind was creating another
century, another life for Joan Crawford or Olivia DeHavil-
land, while she gave me her suspicions. Her memory was
good and she didn't waste time or words. According to Mrs.
Roosevelt, Jane Poslik was reported to be mentally unreliable.
She was, as far as I was concerned, the sanest person I had
met in weeks outside of Eleanor Roosevelt.

She had begun working for Olson soon after he moved to

Los Angeles. Back in Dayton, where she said she was from, her family had bred dogs, so she was familiar with them. Olson, apparently, had been easy to work with though he had made a few clumsy music-accompanied passes at her in the operating room. She had handled him with no great trouble. The revelation seemed a bit strange since Anne Olson was a Lana Turner to Jane Poslik's Ann Revere, but Olson was probably one of those guys with active glands from too much contact with goats. Olson had, from the start, been nervous, but Jane had chalked that up to normal behavior. He had brought several dogs with him from Washington, which he kept in a special section of the clinic and wouldn't allow anyone else to handle. One was, indeed, a small black Scottie. Once Jane had walked in on a telephone conversation between Olson and someone named Martin. The word "Roosevelt" had been part of the conversation, which ended abruptly when Olson spotted Jane in the room. For the next few weeks, other bits and pieces began adding up to the conclusion that Olson and someone named Martin were involved in some way with President Roosevelt and his dog. She also concluded that Olson had left Washington because of the dog business and that Martin had, somehow, found him. Then one morning Bass came to work. Jane had the distinct impression that Olson had not hired Bass, that he had been sent to watch Olson, possibly protect him from questions and doubts.

"I'm not sure," she concluded, pouring herself and me another coffee, "but I had the impression that Martin or someone would come to the clinic to give Dr. Olson instructions, pep talks, or a good scare."

"What makes you think that?"

"Well," she said, making circles on the table with her finger, "there were afternoons when after a normal series of examinations or procedures, and no phone calls, he would be pale and shaken. More than one poor animal suffered in surgery those evenings. In any case, I must have given some indication of my suspicions because Bass began to ask me questions. What do you know about the dogs Dr. Olson brought from Washington? What do you know about Dr. Olson's friends? That sort of thing. Bass is far from subtle.

I became more suspicious, obviously. Within a week I had sufficient evidence from phone calls, conversations overheard between Bass and Dr. Olson and Mrs. Olson, to lead me to the conclusion that Olson had taken the president's dog. I can't imagine why he would do it.''

The major emotional change in her telling had come when she mentioned Mrs. Olson, so I pushed that after getting down another graham cracker. I wanted to dip it in my coffee but kept myself from doing so.

"Anne Olson," I said.

"Mrs. Olson's name is Laura," Jane Poslik answered, looking up at me from her imaginary drawing.

Anne or Laura Olson had had a few belts when I met her so she might have been playing non-sober name games with me. I let the puzzle pass for the moment and went on.

"Was she, is she, part of the business with the dog?"

She shrugged. "It's possible, but I'm a prejudiced source. I didn't like Laura Olson. She was on a free ride. While Olson was not my favorite human, he was a troubled man who needed support. She gave him quite the reverse."

"Was she fooling around with Bass?" I tried.

"Possibly, but I doubt if you could call anything Bass does fooling. More coffee?"

"No thanks. Go on."

"I once walked in on her nose to nose with a man who had brought in a sick cat for treatment. She didn't take long."

That I could confirm from my own experience.

"That's it?" I said.

"That's it," she agreed, standing up. "That's what I wrote in my letters after the FBI came asking questions last month and I started to put things together as I told you. I know it isn't courtroom evidence, but it was enough to make me think it was worth reporting. I don't know how, but I thought it might have something to do with the war. Mr. Peters, my parents are both dead. There's just me and my brother. Charlie's in the navy somewhere in the Pacific. Am I making sense?"

"You're making a lot of sense," I said, heading for the front door. "And I like that dress on Lucille Ball."

"Thanks," she said, offering me her hand. "Let me know if—"

Whatever it was she wanted to know remained unsaid. There was an insistent knock at the door a few feet away from us.

"Yes," she said.

"Police," came a voice I recognized.

She looked at me, took a few steps, and opened the door to John Cawelti, who didn't look in the least surprised to see me. He gave both of us a knowing smirk and stepped in.

"Listening at the door, John?" I said with a smile.

"Call me John again and I ram you through the wall." He grinned back.

"John and I are old friends," I said to Jane Poslik, spreading my legs slightly in case he decided to pay off his threat. He took a mean step toward me and she stepped between us, facing him.

"This is my home," she said softly. "And you'll touch no one in it. What do you want?"

"I'm investigating the murder last night of a Dr. Roy Olson," Cawelti said, looking at me and not her. "You used to work for him, and I understand you didn't get along, that you quit a few weeks back. You want to tell me about it and let me know what you told my friend Peters?"

"Miss Poslik and I were just leaving," I said, showing my most false smile.

"No, Mr. Peters," she said, "you go ahead. I'll talk to Officer—"

"Sergeant Cawelti," he said.

"Suit yourself," I said, brushing by Cawelti. "I'll be seeing you, John. You won't be able to miss me. I'll be the guy a step ahead."

I stepped quickly past the door of the as yet unseen Molly Garnett and headed for my car parked across the street. It was early in the afternoon. The sun was shining, and a couple of small birds swooped by playing tag as the black Chevy that screeched away from the curb rushed out to kiss the side of my Ford. I would have been caught in the middle of the kiss if I had not heard an unexpected but familiar voice call out, "Toby."

I managed to sense the Chevy, rolled forward on the hood of my car with my feet in the air, and tumbled over on the sidewalk to the sound of metal scraping metal. When I looked up, the Chevy was weaving down the street wasting precious rubber.

"Toby," came Gunther's voice.

I looked back to see his small form hurrying toward me.

"I'm okay, Gunther," I said. "Was that . . . ?"

"Bass," he finished, coming to help me up. Gunther was strong for his size. He had done some circus work back when he had to, but he wasn't quite what I needed. It was extra work getting up and pretending that he was helping me, but I managed it.

"I followed him as you said," Gunther explained. "He came here, started to get out from the car, saw you, got back into the car, and then tried to compress you. Shall I pursue him?"

"Not now," I said. "You saved my life again, Gunther."

"I was fortunate to be in vicinity," he answered, embarrassed. "I'll continue my pursuit tomorrow then?"

"Tomorrow will be fine."

We shook hands after agreeing to meet back at the boarding house that night, and I inspected the side of my car. The paint was streaked with metal showing through as if some massive bird had scratched its claws along it. The door was dented slightly, but there seemed to be nothing else wrong other than that I couldn't open the passenger door. I'd worry about that later.

I got in and drove downtown.

Jeremy was seated in his room on the second floor of the Farraday when I got there. I had once referred to Jeremy's room as an office, but he had politely corrected me. "It is the room in which I often work, but I work in other rooms, other spaces, while I walk, sleep, dream," he had explained. There was no desk in the room and no name on the door. If you didn't know he was in 212, you'd never find him. The room itself contained an oversized leather chair near the window and a couch of matching black leather. A low table in the middle of the room was surrounded by four stools. On the table were neat stacks of lined paper, some with poems and notes written in Jeremy's even hand. Others were blank. The walls were lined with books from floor to ceiling. There wasn't a speck of bare wall in view. I knew that beyond another door in the corner was a room I had never seen, in which I guessed Jeremy slept.

When I entered the office, Jeremy was seated in the leather chair. The two reading lamps in the room were off and he was backlit at the window with a book in his lap.

"Jeremy," I said, "I'm sorry to bother you but I need some help."

He was looking at me without expression, the book held open in front of him. I went on. "A woman named Jane Poslik in Burbank may be getting a visit from Bass. I don't think he plans to be friendly when he visits. I'm going to try to put a penny in his fuse, but for a day or two someone should keep an eye on her. I know you have your book to—"

"The address, Toby," he said, finding a bookmark and placing it carefully in the page he was holding open with his huge thumb. "The day is clear. I can sit in my car and meditate. Look for the secret moment of the day.

"There is a Moment in each Day that Satan cannot find Nor can his Watch Fiends find it, but the Industrious find This Moment and it multiply and when it once is found It renovates every Moment of the Day if rightly placed."

"Byron," I guessed, going with one of Jeremy's favorites.

"Blake," he corrected, getting up. "The last victory went to Bass in the American Legion Stadium before four thousand. It would be interesting to meet him with only a passing bird, the bending grass, and the sun upon our heads."

"Sounds fine to me," I agreed.

"Do I have time to do a quick cleaning of the lobby?" he said, putting the book neatly back in a space on the shelf near him.

"I don't know, Jeremy."

Leaving Jeremy's office, I knew there had been another choice. I could have gone back to Jane Poslik, tried to talk her into moving out of her apartment till I got the whole thing settled, but that would have meant giving her a hell of a scare, which she didn't need. Besides, she might have turned me down. No, my best bet was to track down Bass, try to find the dog, locate the guy Jane had mentioned—the guy named Martin—and hope for the best.

Back on the fourth floor, I could hear Shelly humming over the sound of Emmett Quigley in the office next to ours. Emmett had been in the Farraday for two weeks. He was either giving voice lessons to the deaf, writing modern versions of Gregorian chants, or engaged in some elaborate self-torture. Why he needed an office was a question that merited about five minutes of discussion each morning between infrequent patients for Shelly and even less frequent clients for me.

"Any calls?" I asked as I stepped into the office to a startling sight.

"No calls, nothing," said Shelly, who was on his knees cleaning the floor. His glasses had slipped to the end of his nose and he was twitching madly to keep them up. His hands were covered with soapy suds. The dishes and instruments in the sink had been cleaned and the sink itself scoured. The coffee pot was gone and something about the wall was somewhat strange. Then I realized that the coffee stain near my door had been scrubbed away.

"What's going on Shel, Mildred moving in?"

He puffed to his knees, wiped his hands on his filthy white coat, and found his soapy cigar.

"Inspection," he explained. "County Dental Association inspections. They got complaints. Can you imagine? Complaints about me."

"I can't imagine that Shel," I said with sympathy.

"Of course you can't," he agreed. "It's unimaginable. There's nothing wrong with this office. I use the most modern techniques, equipment."

"Then why are you cleaning up?"

Shelly got up, removed the soapy cigar butt from his mouth, gave it an evil look, and threw it in the bucket of water near his feet. "So they won't have anything, not a thing to point to, to say Sheldon Minck is not sanitary, not ethical. I am both sanitary and ethical."

"While you're at it," I added, "you should lead a safari into the waiting room. I think some of the bugs out there have tusks worth showing to a dental inspector."

"I'm doing the waiting room next," Shelly sighed, pushing his glasses back on his nose and leaving a sudsy white mass over the left lens. "And you should clean up your office. In fact, you should clean it up and move out till the inspection is over. I don't know what the ethics are about having subtenants."

"Speaking of that, don't you think you'd better scratch out some of those degrees you have listed on the outer door?"

"Right," he said, trying to snap his wet fingers. "I'll get right to that. You wouldn't want to give me a hand here?"

I didn't answer.

"I didn't think so," he hissed. "Gratitude stops at the dental chair. I learned that in dental school. How can they do this to me? Why me? You know who taught me techniques of basic oral surgery? I never told you this. It was Maling, Maling, damn it. You think Dr. Arthur Maling has to be inspected? He'd turn over in his grave if he knew I was being inspected, me his star pupil."

"Hold it, Shel," I said. "I can't tell from what you just went through if Maling is alive or dead."

Shelly's eyes went to the ceiling at my stupidity. Suds trickled down his left lens and dropped like a snowy tear.

"Does it make a difference?" he asked. "Does it really make a difference?"

"Happy cleaning," I said, and went into my office where I discovered where Shelly had put the hot plate, coffee pot, and some of the more uncleanable and rust-infected instruments that had turned to antiques at the bottom of his sink.

"Shel," I screamed, stepping back into his office.

"Hold your fillings," he said, backing away. "I'll clean it out by tonight."

"I'm coming back in the morning," I said. "If it isn't all out of my office, I'm going to dump it on your nice clean floor."

"You are a tenant," he reminded me, stepping forward again and almost slipping on a moist spot.

"I'll be back in the morning," I whispered, looking at him and then stepping into the waiting room and out into the hall. Emmet Quigley was still gargling as I stomped past and went down the stairs. I was shaking my head on Hoover when a bum came up to me.

"You work in there?" he asked.

"Right."

"You ain't no cop?"

"I ain't no cop," I agreed.

"They're giving out sugar ration books come Monday," he said, breathing muscatel into my ear. "I got one coming. I'll sell it for a price. I can get plenty more from guys, you know?"

"Not interested," I said, walking down the street. He followed me.

"You know a guy who might?" he said. He was wearing a long coat under which I guessed there might be nothing.

"Dentist back in the Farraday," I said. "His name is Minck. You and your friends might go see him."

I moved faster and left the bum behind muttering his thanks.

My life is and was a series of lows, lows, lows, and highs. There weren't many highs, but those that came were right up there with going a full round with Henry Armstrong. The trouble was the lows. I legged it to Arnie's and ignored his warnings about the scratches on the side of my car.

"The whole damn chassis is going to rust out in maybe a month, two," he said, pronouncing chassis as chas-siss. "You better let me fix it up."

"We'll talk about it Arnie," I said, moving past him. "I turn most of the little I earn over to you as it is and what do I have to show for it?"

"Transportation," he said emotionlessly.

"A zombie line of wrecks without fenders, paint, working gas gauges," I went on.

"Having a bad day, huh?" he said, spitting into a corner.

"You could call it that," I agreed.

I had three boxes of cereal stashed back at Mrs. Plaut's but I wasn't about to go there. Instead, I stopped at a restaurant off of Melrose called Herrera's, ordered two tacos, a bowl of shredded wheat, and a Pepsi. Herrera didn't blink his lazy eyes. He brought the order and I downed it. Back when I was first married, Anne had spent two years coaxing, threatening, challenging, and tricking in the hope of getting me to change my diet. For the last two years of the marriage, she hadn't cared much, though she had occasionally brought it up in her quite reasonable catalogue of my faults.

"You eat like a nine year old whose parents don't give a damn," she had once said. Since she was probably right, I hadn't answered. I get along fine with nine year olds.

My stomach filled, I paid the buck I owed, including a dime tip, waved to Herrera and the belching guy who had taken up the stool next to mine, and set off to do what my brother had warned me not to do. My answers, if there were any, were back at Olson's clinic or house.

7

One slow drive down the cul-de-sac alongside Olson's animal clinic convinced me that no one was watching the place. There were no cars on the street and as far as I could see there were no cars down the narrow lane that ran back to Olson's house. However, as far as I could see was not very far. There were many ways to handle this. Most of them involved exercising some caution. Caution was a word that, in spite of many attempts to engrave it on my skull and spine, had never made its way into my brain.

I found a driveway across from Olson's, drove in far enough to be sure the car wouldn't be seen from the street, and found a space between a pair of trees. I took out my little notebook and pencil and left a message under my windshield wiper for whoever lived there that my car had broken down, that I had come to deliver something to them, and that I'd be right back. That should hold off a call to the police, at least long enough for me to do whatever I was going to do.

It must have been around four. My watch was no help. The sun was bright and I was in a hurry. I walked straight across the street and up to the front door of the clinic. The door was locked and there was a sign on it saying the clinic was temporarily closed due to Dr. Olson's death. It was spelled correctly and in an even hand.

In case anyone was watching from a nearby bush, I knocked at the door, tried to peer through the tiny window, and then started up the driveway. Out of sight of both the street and the house, I doubled back and circled the clinic from the rear, looking for a door or window.

There was a door, but it was locked. Behind it I could hear barking and some sounds I didn't recognize. The first two windows I tried were locked and unforgiving. The third window was locked too, but the lock didn't have its heart in the job. I managed to get my fingers under the bottom of the window, trying not to think of what would happen in the next second or two if Bass were behind the window and decided to lean his weight down on my fingers.

There was a guy named Stumpy Fredericks, California middleweight champ around 1924 or '25. He had no fingers on his hands. Stump's were like rocks, fingers never got sore, but his seconds had a hell of a time keeping his boxing gloves from flopping around. I tried not to think of Stumpy, who never told how he had lost his fingers. I failed. Maybe it was the thought of those fingerless boxing gloves flapping in the face of some confused kid out of Monterey that gave me the extra push that broke the lock. The window flew up and rattled a dozen dogs into something like song.

Instead of jumping through the window, I stood still for a second listening, trying to hear if someone were inside, or if someone outside might have heard the noise. I waited, waited, and waited, and then I crawled in, closing the window behind me.

The dogs had calmed down a bit but the parrot I had seen in the office the day before was somewhere croaking "I'm Henry the Eighth I am."

There was plenty of light from the window. I was in one of the surgery/treatment rooms. I moved around the metal table in the center and went to the door. The door wasn't quite closed so I pushed it open slowly, carefully, and stepped into the hallway looking both ways. "Monks, monks, monks," the parrot called and I followed his voice back into the building to a closed door. Even with the door closed I could tell from the smell that I had found what I was looking for. I opened the door and the barking and croaking started again.

"Shh," I whispered. "Everything's okeydokey. No one's going to be operated on. Everyone's going to be fed."

One massive German shepherd in the cage on my right didn't believe me. He rolled back his upper lip and showed some less-than-inviting teeth. The room was big, but the cages weren't full. It took no more than a few seconds to scan the cages and see there was no black Scottie.

My next step was going to be a look through Olson's papers. It would have been my next step if, when I turned, Anne Olson hadn't been standing there. Her hair was combed straight. Her slacks were dark and her sweater white. Her eyes were also clear and sober and the gun in her hand was blue. She was color-coordinated.

"What are you doing?" she asked. Her voice quavered and quivered a little but it was a reasonable question.

"I came to return the suit," I said. "Is mine dry?"

She shook her head no.

"Well," I sighed, "then I'll come back some other—"

"That's not why you came back. You're looking for something. You killed Roy for something and now you've come back for it."

"I didn't kill your husband," I said. "If the police haven't told you that by now, you should figure it out yourself. Remember, the water was dripping? I ran up the stairs. How the hell fast could I have drowned him? And by the way, what happened to you last night? And since I'm asking questions, is your name Laura or Anne?"

The gun stayed on my chest and the parrot behind me cackled more about Henry the Eighth and monks.

Mrs. Olson said nothing.

"I came here looking for a dog," I said, "a black Scottie. I think your husband took President Roosevelt's dog and brought him to California. I think that had something to do with his being killed. If I can figure it out, the police can figure it out and they will. I've got a deal to make with you. You put the gun away and tell me what you know about what your husband did, and I'll see that you get no trouble and a lot of credit for finding the dog."

The gun stayed up as I smiled and held out my right hand. The bullet, which would have made a hole in it had I not slipped on something wet, pinged off the bar of the cage behind me and took off the head of the parrot in mid-"monk."

"Cut it out," I shouted, backing away, trying to make myself heard over the animals, which had gone wild from the noise, my fear, and the feeling of sudden death.

The second shot took a piece of the ear of the German shepherd, who was nowhere near me. Anne or Laura Olson was now crying and shooting, her eyes full of tears and her finger not knowing what it was clicking off. I took the three or four steps toward her, grabbed her hand, and pulled the gun away. The one-eared shepherd managed to get its snout out and sink his teeth into Olson's pants. I pulled away hearing the tear and feeling the tug. The noise shivered through me as I reached behind the woman, opened the door, and pushed her through. I followed her and slammed the door closed behind us. It was better but not perfect.

"You're going to kill me now," she sobbed. "That's what I get. I've never hurt anyone or anything in my life and this is what I get."

I considered reminding her that she had just sent a bird to parrot heaven and created a funny-looking dog, but I let it pass. Instead I led her to the small operating room, where I found what looked like a clean cup and filled it with water for her.

She took the water in two hands and downed it in the same number of gulps.

"You're not going to kill me," she said, looking up at me from the one chair in the room. "If you were going to kill me, you wouldn't give me water, unless you're some kind of sadist or you plan to torture me for some sick reason, or you want to tell you something I don't know, or . . ."

"You want some more water?"

She shook her head no and went silent. Her right hand came up automatically to brush back her hair. I took the cup and touched her hand.

"I was drunk the other night," she said.

"I didn't notice," I answered. "You want your gun back, without bullets?"

"It was Roy's. I got it out of his office. I don't know much about guns," she said.

"I wouldn't know it by the way you were mowing down pets in . . . I'm sorry."

"I accept your apology," she said with dignity, finding a handkerchief in the pocket of her slacks. "I didn't love Roy Olson."

Since I hadn't asked, I nodded in sympathy.

"He was a friend of my father's back in Washington. It just happened. I'd been through a divorce and Roy was there and going to California and I wanted out. It was a mistake. Have you ever made a mistake?"

"Never," I said. "Did you make a mistake with Bass?"

The shudder was real. "He's a . . . a . . . one of those things with no sex."

"Politician," I helped.

"No . . . you're joking."

"I hope so," I agreed. "What do you know about the dog?"

"He had a black Scottie when we came here," she said, looking up at me and taking my hand. "But I never thought it was, what's his name, Fala. I still don't understand. Why?"

"That's what I want to find out. Do you know a friend of your husband's named Martin something?"

She stood up and seemed to be trembling a little more. "You think this Martin killed Roy."

"Or Bass, or both," I said.

"You didn't do it, then," she said, stepping toward me.

"That's how we started this conversation. I didn't do it. All I want to do is find the dog. To do that, I might have to find out who killed your husband."

"Could you come back to the house with me for a while," she said, holding my hand. "I . . . I don't want to be alone in there, where he was killed. Whoever did it might come back. I thought it was . . ."

She put her arms around me and laid her head on my shoulder.

"You have a bad habit of not finishing your sentences," I said, putting the gun on a nearby table so I could hold onto her and keep from toppling over.

"I wasn't completely drunk the other night," she said. Her hair was in my nose. It was dark, clean, and smelled like some flower I couldn't place. "I don't see people, go anywhere. My husband never even wanted to make love." Her head came back and her mouth was inches from mine.

"I've got to find a dog," I said.

"You can come up to the house for a little while," she said, touching my cheek.

"Well," I said, "maybe for a little while."

This time no dripping water fell on our heads. She pushed me back gently onto the operating table, where my head hit the gun. I moved the gun and made room for her. With a dead parrot in the next room, we did something like making love on an animal examining table.

When we were finished, which was not long after we

started, she put on her underpants, bra, slacks, sweater, and gun, and I put on her husband's suit.

"We'll get another one of Roy's suits for you at the house," she said, smiling and touching my nose.

"Is your name really Anne?" I said.

"Laura Anne," she answered.

"I've got a phone call to make," I said.

She kissed me and told me to go ahead and make the call from the clinic and then come up to the house, where she would have a surprise waiting for me.

"I'm not up to another surprise right now," I said with a stupid grin.

"We'll see," she said, backing out of the door.

I called Mrs. Plaut's, praying to the ghosts of dead parrots that she would not answer the phone. My prayers went unanswered.

"Yes?" she asked the phone in that voice that made it seem as if she couldn't understand how any human sound could come from a machine.

"It's me, Mrs. Plaut, Toby Peters."

"Yes," she said reasonably.

"Can you hear me?"

"Yes," she repeated.

"Good, please get Gunther on the phone," I said, dropping my voice only slightly from the level I used to threaten boxers who were safely busy in a ring a stadium away.

"Is anyone there?" Mrs. Plaut said, making it clear she had heard nothing of my end of the conversation.

"Gunther Wherthman," I screamed.

"Mr. Wortman," she said, "will you please answer this madman. I can make no sense of him."

"Can I help?" came Gunther's voice.

"Thank God," I sighed. "Gunther, I won't be able to make it back for dinner."

"That is most unfortunate, Toby. I am preparing a buttery quiche and have purchased several bottles of Lucky Lager beer which, as I recall, you are fond of."

"The fact is," I said, feeling guilty, "I may not make it back to the boarding house at all tonight."

"May I ask," he said, pausing to frame his question with dignity, "if it is a business situation or a young lady."

"It's business and the lady isn't exactly young, but neither am I."

"The quiche will hold till tomorrow," said Gunther. "In fact, my aunt who taught me the recipe believed that it tasted best on the second day. Take care of yourself, Toby."

The hole in my pants, or rather Olson's pants, was large enough to shove a dead parrot through, but the thought didn't appeal to me. I thought of getting a veterinarian for the shepherd with the missing ear, but the resident vet was dead. Laura Anne Olson might have a suggestion. The dog and I weren't exactly friends, but I'd been in his position enough times to know how it feels.

I trotted up the pathway to the house and stopped short. There was a car parked at the door, a car I had seen parked in front of Jane Poslik's apartment earlier that day. If it was Mrs. Olson's car, I had a few questions about her travels. If it wasn't, then she might be inside with a visitor she at least wanted to meet. I tried the front door. It opened and I stepped in.

"Anne," I shouted. "Laura?"

Something, someone moved in the living room. I stepped toward it carefully, considering a run to my glove compartment for my .38, but there might not be time.

"Anne," I repeated, staying out of the doorway that would set me up in backlight for whoever might be standing or sitting in the shadows beyond.

Someone was in the room, in the distant corner in a chair. The figure stood up and moved into the light.

"Anne, huh?" said Cawelti with a smirk. "Laura."

"Where is she?" I said, moving forward to meet him.

"Who, Mrs. Olson?"

"You know that's who I mean."

"She's dead," he said.

I looked up at the spot where water had leaked through the ceiling two nights before and took a step toward the hallway. If I hadn't stopped to call Gunther, I would have been with her, but it had only been a minute or two and Cawelti was here. Something was wrong.

"Is this a sick joke of yours, fireman?" I asked, turning to him again.

"No joke, little brother," he grinned. "She's dead. Died two days ago, on Tuesday, in the Victor Hotel just off Wilshire, private room and a bath. Just found the body today. Very messy."

"Cut the crap Cawelti, I saw her five minutes ago down in the clinic, and there was nothing wrong with her. She—"

"—wasn't Mrs. Olson," he finished. "That's why I'm here. Laura Olson, middle name Faye, was about fifty, short, fat, and no beauty. The woman who was here when you were parading in the negative was another broad, if there was really someone here."

"You're full of—" I began.

"She took you in." He chuckled, looking down at my pants. "The way Captain Pevsner figures it, if she exists someplace outside of your troubled mind, she and someone else did in Olson just as you came knocking at the door. She came downstairs to keep you busy while he finished the job and then they set you up. That's the way your brother figures it, but I'd like to keep you involved."

"Let's go find her," I said, turning to the door.

"Come on, Peters, as far as I figure, there is no 'her,' just you. You're a sorry sight."

We were a few feet apart by now and all it would take was the wrong word. He searched for it.

"The way I figure it, you were playing with yourself," he said, looking down at my pants leg.

"Let's go to the station and talk to the captain," I said.

"Day off," Cawelti said, enjoying the moment.

"Seidman," I tried.

"Home, sick, tooth problem. You wouldn't know anything about that, would you?"

"How badly do you want a nose like mine," I said, sweetly.

"I'm ten years younger and twenty pounds heavier than you are, Peters," he answered.

"And I've got a bad back and a weak skull, fireman, but I've got something you don't have. I'm the most stubborn terrier you ever ran into. I don't give up. I just keep coming. You knock me down and I get up again. I get up and up until you're too tired to move your arms and you ask for mercy and I stomp on your face.''

Something was in Cawelti's eyes now that told me he thought he was looking at a crazy man. That was just what I was shooting for. What I told him was the truth. I'd take twenty in the gut to give one good one back. I could live with the twenty, but I had found that the other guy would usually do whatever he could to keep from getting that one good one.

"You're nuts," Cawelti said.

"I do my best," I grinned. "Someone shot some animals in the clinic. You'd better call a vet."

"Get out of here," he said, not backing away but not pushing for the fight. If he was going to lay into me, it would be in front of an audience, someone who could pull us apart after I got hurt and before he did.

When I got back to my car, the note was still there. A man was standing in the doorway of the house nearby apparently waiting for me and the package the message on my car had promised. I waved to him, got in my car, and drove away.

I stopped at a pay phone and called a North Hollywood number. My sister-in-law Ruth answered.

"You're coming for dinner tomorrow, aren't you, Toby?" she said.

"I'm coming," I answered. "Listen, I've got two tickets for Volez and Yolanda tomorrow night. You and Phil can go. I'll sit with the kids."

"I don't know," she said, her voice making it obvious that the idea excited her. "Let me ask Phil."

She put down the phone and wandered away and then I heard light breathing on the other end.

"Smush," said a little voice.

"Lucy?" I said. "This is Uncle Toby."

"Lock," she said and clobbered the phone with her pet lock, a lock that had found my head more than once with velocity well beyond what you could expect from a two year old. She had her father's arm and probably his disposition.

"Terrific," I said. "Get Mommy."

"Toby?" came Ruth's voice. "He said okay. Can you come early for dinner then, about four?"

"I'll be there," I said.

When I hung up, I checked at a nearby restaurant and found out that it was almost five in the afternoon. I had expected a night with someone who called herself Anne Olson. A tailor on the corner was closing his door when I caught him and persuaded him with an ugly look and the promise of a good tip to let me in. It took him about five minutes to sew up the tear in Olson's pants.

"Good as new," he said, stepping back to admire his work after I had the pants back on and he had two bucks in his hands.

"You want to come around with me and tell that to everyone who thinks different?" I asked.

"It's what I tell them all," said the tailor, tucking the two bucks away. "And it is good as new, better, only it don't look so good. Looking and being good is different," he said with some slight European accent.

"You got a point," I agreed and went back to my car.

My session with the fake Mrs. Olson should have left me satisfied, but I couldn't hold back the urge to get over to Spring Street and Levy's Restaurant. My appetites were up and to avoid figuring out what was happening in the Fala case, I decided to make an assault on a Levy corned beef sandwich and on Carmen the cashier.

The corned beef proved easy, complete with pickle and a chocolate phosphate. Carmen proved to be, as always, Carmen. She sat dark, placid, a counter fighter with formidable front, and large brown eyes.

"You're voluptuous," I said, holding up the line of three people behind me wanting to pay their tabs.

"You're holding up the line," she said without a smile.

"Phil Harris is still at the Biltmore Bowl," I whispered. "Name a night."

"Come on, bud," a guy behind me whimpered.

Carmen gave me a look that could with imagination be read as a smile. She was a widow of great reserve and resistance and I was probably one of the more resistible elements in her life.

"No wrestling this week?" she asked softly.

"Thursday at the Eastside Avenue over on Pico," I said. "I'd like to get together before that."

"I am sure you would," came the voice of the guy behind me, "but I've got a show to get to."

"The wrestling match next Sunday," she said, ringing up my bill.

"I can't wait," I said.

"You'll wait," she said, promising nothing. So it would have to be five days before my next assault on the Mona Lisa of the restaurant world.

"Ain't love grand?" said the little guy who was late for his show as he plunked down a half a buck to pay for his sandwich.

"Ain't it," I agreed before stepping outside to see the sun coming down over Spring Street. I got back in my car, ignoring the bruised far side, and drove up to Eleventh and then across to Broadway, where I found a parking space right in front of the Peerless Book Shop. I'd been in the place a dozen times or so, twice to look for books and ten times to look for leads on missing people or people with not too savory reputations.

The Peerless Book Shop had a good collection of cheap used books. There were also some new ones that went for used prices because the owner, Morris "Academy" Dolmitz, would, from time to time, pick up four or five hundred copies of some title from a source he didn't want to know too much about. When I walked in this time, the place was piled with copies of John Steinbeck's *The Moon Is Down* and Robert Frost's *A Witness Tree*. There were other books all over the place, in boxes, on shelves. If Academy had to rely on book sales, he would have been a poor man. As it was, his main income came from bets he placed in the back room.

No one was in the shop but Academy, who sat behind the counter on his stool, his mop of white hair falling into his eyes, a white zippered sweater over a red flannel shirt covering a little pot belly. Academy was around sixty-five and had seen and heard it all.

"What can I do you for?" he said, looking up at me with tiny gray eyes and a smile of even false teeth.

"I'm looking for a fella," I said.

"I deal books," said Academy, holding out his hands, "not fellas. You know that, Peters. Ask me one. You know what I mean. Ask?"

He sat up, waiting.

"Best actor, 1934," I said.

"Victor McLaglen, *The Informer*," he said, in disgust. "Give me a hard one for chrissake. Whatdya think I am, a dumb putz here?"

"Best cartoon, 1935," I said.

"*Three Orphan Kittens*, Walt Disney, Silly Symphony. One more." He grinned, eyes open wide.

"Sound recording, 1929," I said.

Academy was bouncing in his chair like a kid.

"You're a good one, Peters, a good one. Douglas Shearer, MGM, for *The Big House*."

"I'm looking for a mountain named Bass," I threw in, and Academy stopped grinning. His mouth closed tight, and his false teeth went clickety-clack. "You can't miss him."

"Not a familiar name," he said through his teeth, trying to go back to his book.

"Your memory's suddenly failing you?"

"It happens like that," he said with a shrug. He opened the book and pretended to go back to his reading. I reached over the counter, closed the book, and looked at it.

"That's a dirty book," I said.

"It's a classic," he answered, reaching for the book. "What do you think you are doing here anyway?"

I held the book away from his hand and he sat back, shaking his head. "Peters," he clacked. "You know I got a button down here and you know I can push it and you know two guys'll come through that door and squash you like a rose between the pages of a Bible."

"Colorfully put, Academy, but I've got questions and a

big mouth," I answered, handing him the de Sade. "You know my brother's a captain now?"

"I know," he said. "Things like that I know. It's my business. What are you, threatening me or what?"

"Threatening you," I agreed.

"So that's the way it is," he said, feigning defeat. "Human nature. All these books, you know, they're about human nature. I know human nature."

"And who won the Academy Awards," I said impatiently. "Bass. He worked for you. I want to know why you hired him, where he is now, who his friends are, or who else he's been working for."

"Ten bucks," said Academy, folding his arms on his chest.

"Come on Academy," I said. "You don't need my ten bucks."

"Principle's involved here, Peters," he said. "I give you something for a threat and pretty soon every bit player on the avenue's in here paying in closed fists and loud voices instead of cash. I'm running a business here. Know what I mean?"

I fished out the ten and handed it across the counter.

"Bass is a putz," he said.

"Everybody's a putz to you. Give me something hard."

"Bass is special putz," he said. "Doesn't show a temper. Cold, a little dumb, one of those that likes hurting. You know the kind?"

"I'm waiting for news here, Academy," I said impatiently.

He clacked his teeth and went into the spiel.

"He did about four months in the back room. Customer named Martin, got an office around here someplace, sometimes a customer, recommended him. Bass was some ways okay. He collected for me when a guy came up slow with the gelt. Trouble was when Bass collected, the guy he collected from didn't show up here anymore. He was making guys pay but he was losing me repeat customers. You need a kind of festive atmosphere back there," he said, nodding over his shoulder at the solid wooden door. I'd been back there once.

"There is no way short of Cedric Gibbons and an MGM

crew of making that dirty brown betting room festive,'' I said.

"You know we got free coffee going in there all the time?'' he went on. "So, I told this Martin that it would be nice if Bass found another job. I didn't want, you might guess, to tell Bass myself. Anyway, this Martin guy says it's all right, he's got a good job for Bass working for some animal doctor.''

"Two questions," I said, holding up two fingers. "Where does Bass live and how do I find this Martin?''

Dolmitz puffed out some air, clacked his teeth and said, "Bass lives some place on Sixth near Westlake Park. I don't know the address. Martin's got an office around here is all I know. He's maybe fifty-five, young guy, thin, gray hair, not too big, wears those little glasses like Ben Franklin. I don't know what he does. That's the best you get from me, pally.''

"That wasn't ten bucks' worth," I said, holding out my hand for change. Dolmitz's hand went under the counter where I knew the button was.

"Take a book or two," he said. "We'll call it even."

I grabbed a copy of *The Moon Is Down* and the Frost poems and went for the door.

"You want to know who won best film editor in 1938?'' he called, as I went to the door, the books tucked under my arm.

"Ralph Dawson for *The Adventures of Robin Hood*," I said. He had come up with the wrong question. I had been on the security force at Warners when Dawson won. I'd seen him come back with the Oscar in his hand.

"Son of a . . . '' Dolmitz began, but I was on the street before he could finish.

Half an hour later I was back at Mrs. Plaut's knocking on Gunther's door.

"Come in," he called and turned around in the small chair at the small desk where he worked.

"Did you eat yet?" I said. "I had a change in plans.''

"No," he said with a small smile. "I wanted to finish this troublesome passage. The quiche is best at room temperature, in any case. I shall bring it right in with the beers.''

Back in my room I set the table, took off Olson's jacket and tie, and turned on the radio. The quiche was great. So was the beer. We ate and listened to "Truth or Consequences" and I gave Gunther the Steinbeck book, for which he thanked me.

"Gunther, if you've got time tomorrow, you could do me a favor and go down around Broadway and Eleventh and try to track down a guy involved in the case."

Gunther, after finishing the final small morsel of quiche on his lap, agreed with enthusiasm, and I told him what I knew about Martin.

"You've had a busy day, Toby," he said, sympathetically. "I'll go back to my work and leave you to your rest."

"A good dinner, Gunther, thanks."

Gunther gathered his plate and his book and had made it to the hallway when we heard the phone on the landing ring. I ran past him to beat Mrs. Plaut in case she might be hovering around. I caught it on the third ring.

"Hello," I said, "Mrs. Plaut's boarding house."

"Toby Peters, please," said a man's voice I had heard somewhere but couldn't place.

"You're talking to him," I said.

"You have been making some inquiries about me," he said. "I don't like that at all. I would prefer that you stop."

"I can't stop, Marty," I said. "I've got a client. Why don't we just get together and talk it over. I've got some questions about who scrubbed Doc Olson and his wife, who the lady pretending to be Mrs. Olson was, and what you have to do with a hulk named Bass."

"I was afraid you wouldn't listen," he said patiently. "But I wanted to give you the opportunity. What happens next will be your responsibility, not mine."

"Is that the way it works? You drop the bomb and if I don't get out of the way, it's my fault?"

"Something like that," he said.

"Give back the dog and I stop looking," I said. "Maybe I don't care who gave Olson and his wife a bath."

"You care," he said. "I know that sound in your voice. We have nothing further to discuss. You have my sincere warning and, if it will do any good, you have my assurance that what I have done has been for the security of our country."

"And which country is that?" I said.

"The United States of America," he answered and hung up.

8

No one tried to kill me on Sunday morning, but then again I didn't try to find Martin or the fake Mrs. Olson. I read the L.A. *Times* over a couple of bowls of Wheaties and a cup of coffee. I went right for the funnies after finding out that the Japanese were a few miles from the Chinese border. Dixie Dugan, Mickey Finn, Texas Slim, and Dirty Dalton kept me company through breakfast. I had to wait for the bathroom because Joe Hill the mailman was taking a bath, but some time after ten I got in, shaved, washed, and made ready.

I was dressing in my room when Mrs. Plaut burst in with a bundle in her arms. She paid no attention to my near nudity and plopped the bundle on the sofa.

"Found this on the doorstep this a.m.," she said.

"Thanks," I said, getting into my pants. She just stood there in her blue paisley dress and waited. There would be no getting rid of her till her curiosity was satisfied. I started to put on my shirt.

"I'm late for church," she said.

"I'm sorry," I said, getting my second arm in and moving to the bundle without buttoning up. TOBY PETERS was printed on the outside of the brown paper wrapper in neat letters. I pulled off the string and found my neatly pressed suit, the one I had traded with Doc Olson. The torn sleeve had been neatly repaired. Lying on top of the suit was a card on which was written in what looked like a feminine hand: *Sorry, really.*

"It's your suit," said Mrs. Plaut, disappointed.

"I'm sorry it's nothing more exciting," I apologized, and Mrs. Plaut left in disgust.

For about an hour I sat making notes and trying to sort the case out. Nothing came so I finished dressing, hung my suit in the closet, and went out into the late morning with a book under my arm. The sun was bright and the two little girls who lived next door to Mrs. Plaut were throwing a ball against Mrs. Plaut's steps.

"My mother says you're a criminal," said the younger girl. She was about eight and wore pigtails. There were blue ribbons in her pigtails.

The older girl, about ten, looked embarrassed, and whispered, "Gussie, no."

"I'm a private detective," I said.

"My mother said you kill people," the girl went on, looking up at me.

"Only them what needs killing, little lady," I said in my best Harry Carey. "Now if you'll excuse me, I've got my work to do."

My work consisted of a run up to Burbank with some worry about how much gas might be left in my gaugeless tank. Rationing was soon going to officially cut me to five or six gallons a week. I knew I could get more through Arnie, but I wasn't sure I could pay the price.

Jeremy was parked halfway down the block where he could keep his eye on the stairs leading up to Jane Poslik's apartment. I parked behind him and walked over to lean through the window and hand him the Robert Frost poems and the paper bag I had stopped for on the way.

"Tea, hard rolls, and some poetry," I said, handing him the bag. "Your favorite."

"You are very thoughtful, Toby," he said, laying aside the pad of paper he had been writing on and taking the book and the package.

"Right, very thoughtful. I send you out on a Sunday morning to wait for the Frankenstein monster and I go off for dinner with the family," I said.

"Sunday is like any other day to me, Toby. It holds no special significance. The sun is warm. I am relaxed and this is a good place to work and to read. Forget your guilt. Would you like a roll?"

I declined and he told me that Jane Poslik had gone out an hour earlier to pick up a newspaper but was now safely back in her apartment. No one had come or gone.

"I'll relieve you this evening," I said.

"I would prefer," Jeremy put in, examining the first roll, "that you devote your time to finding the person who threatens this woman. That would be more effective than protecting her at the point of her greatest vulnerability. It's a simple principle of wrestling."

"Okay," I said. "I'll keep at it."

When I arrived at my brother's small house on Bluebelle in North Hollywood, it was about three. Lucy greeted me at the door, her hands behind her back probably concealing her padlock. Nate and Dave, my nephews, were seated in the small dining room playing with toy soldiers. Nate was almost fourteen and Dave about eleven. I picked Lucy up carefully to avoid hidden locks and said hi to the boys.

"Uncle Tobe," Nate called. He touched something in front of him and a toothpick flew across the table mowing down a lead soldier. Dave groaned.

"How's it going, Huey and Dewey?" I said, pinching Lucy's nose gently.

"Okay," said Nate. "I'm smashing him. He's the Nazis."

"No I'm not, Nate. You're the Nazis."

Ruth came in, skinny, tired, with tinted blond hair that wouldn't stay up and a gentle smile.

"Toby, you're early," she said.

"I'll go away and come back," I said, starting to put Lucy down.

"No, Uncle Toby," Dave said.

Phil came through the front door, a package in his arms, and grunted at me.

"Take this and put it on the kitchen table. Make yourself useful."

I put Lucy down, took the package, and went into the kitchen.

"How's Seidman?" I said over my shoulder.

"Minck almost killed him," Phil said, following me in after picking up his daughter, who stuck her finger in his hairy ear. "He has a hell of an infection. An oral surgeon at the university is taking care of him. Steve may kill that dirty dentist when he gets out of the hospital."

The rest of the afternoon went fine. Lucy clipped me once on the shoulder with a wooden toy. We listened to a baseball game on Nate's short wave. The Red Sox snapped a thirteen-game Cleveland winning streak, 8–4, in Boston. Charlie Wagner was the winning pitcher. Bobby Doerr had three hits. Pesky picked up a couple and Ted Williams had one. Foxx and DiMaggio were blanked. Nate, a Red Sox fan, was happy.

Ruth had made turkey, salad, iced tea, and a Jell-o mold with little pieces of pineapple in it.

"Remember when I used to think you killed people every day," Dave said after dinner. "That was dumb. No one kills people every day except maybe in the war. My dad doesn't even kill people every day."

"Dumb, dumb, dumb," Nate said, looking at the ceiling.

"Dumb, dumb," Lucy repeated, giggling.

"It's not funny, you little twerp," Dave said to his sister, which made her giggle even more.

Ruth and Phil took the tickets I gave them and went off to Volez and Yolanda after dinner. As soon as they were gone, Nate said, "Okay Uncle Toby, tell us about someone you beat up or shot this week or something."

With Lucy on my lap, I made up a tale of scarred Nazi villains and assorted gore, none of it mine. By the time I was finished Lucy was asleep in my lap sucking her thumb.

"Is that a true story?" Dave asked when I was finished.

"Would I lie to you guys?" I said.

By ten the boys were asleep and Lucy was up crying for Ruth. I played with her, let her pull my hair, gave her rides on my back, and blessed the moment Ruth and Phil came through the door to take over.

"Thanks, Toby," Ruth said, giving me a kiss on the cheek at the door after she took Lucy.

"My pleasure," I said.

Phil's hands were plunged deeply in his pockets. He bit his lower lip, ran his right hand across his bristly hair, and put out his hand. I took it.

"Business as usual tomorrow," he said, pointing a thick finger in my face.

"I wouldn't have it any other way," I said, meaning it, and went out into the night.

When I was a kid back in Glendale, Sunday nights were for reading, talking, and playing board games. Sometimes we would go to a movie. My father liked comedies. Harold Lloyd was his favorite. I liked anything just so it moved. A late movie would have been nice, but I couldn't leave Jeremy on that dark street all night.

I pulled up behind him and walked to the car. His eyes were closed and he was snoring gently. I hadn't thought about it before, but now it hit me that Jeremy Butler was not a young man in his prime. He was at least five years older than I was. Even a bull deserves some time in the pasture.

"Jeremy," I said softly through the open window.

His eyes came open instantly and he looked at me.

"Relief is here," I went on. "I can't sleep and it's too late to do anything else. Go on home. You can take over tomorrow. If I don't turn anything up by afternoon, we'll talk to Miss Poslik about moving."

"I was asleep," Jeremy said softly.

"It was a reasonable thing to do," I said. "It's almost midnight and you've been sitting here all day and night."

"I had a responsibility," he said. "The meaning of one's life is measured by the responsibilities he accepts and lives up to."

"We agree pretty much on that, but you haven't let me down."

"We must check on Miss Poslik," he grunted, getting out of the car and motioning me aside. He closed the door and moved down the street, a huge dark cutout moving lightly. I caught up with him.

"I don't think the sight of you at her door at midnight would reassure her," I said. "I'll check. She knows me."

That seemed reasonable to Jeremy, who zipped up his windbreaker and went with me to the apartment. There were no lights on as I started up the steps, but my footsteps must have sent a shock inside. The living room lights came on as I reached the top and brought my hand back to knock.

"Who's out there?" Jane Poslik's voice came through the door.

"Me, Peters," I said. "I've got to tell you something."

The door came open and she stood there wearing a man's blue bathrobe with white dragons clutched over her chest. She kept the screen door locked.

"I think it best that you not come in," she said.

"Good idea. I don't want to frighten you, but I think Bass might pay you a visit."

She shuddered and clutched the dragon robe around her neck.

"Why?"

"Because I came here yesterday or because that Martin guy you heard Doc Olson talking to found out that you have been talking about Fala," I said. "He was parked outside your apartment when I was here. I think you should move out of here for a day or two. It shouldn't take more than that to clear all this up."

She stood thinking about it for a while, undecided, and I tipped the scale by repeating "Bass." It was enough. It was either scaring her or being responsible for another possible corpse.

"I haven't got anyplace to go," she said.

"I'll find some place; just throw some things together. I'll wait out here. Take your time."

She unlocked the door and told me to come in and wait. I looked at Lucille Ball dressed as Madame Du Barry for about five minutes while Jane packed. She came in wearing a brown cloth coat and carrying a brown, very worn leather suitcase.

"Ready," she said, and I led her out.

At the top of the stairs I told her that a rather large, very gentle friend was on the street waiting for us and assured her that he was more than a match for Bass, something that I was beginning to doubt but didn't want to share with anyone, not even me.

We closed the scene with Jeremy saying that he was sure she could stay with Alice Palice for a day or two. That sounded like a good idea to me since Alice was nearly as formidable as Jeremy himself. I wished them a good night and waited in the street to be sure no car was hidden in a driveway ready to follow. Satisfied, I got back into my Ford and drove home.

I made it to my room in the darkened boarding house without waking anyone, and removed my clothes. My original plan was to change my underwear, but I altered my plan. Never let the enemy anticipate what you might do. In this case the enemy was my own desire to keep reasonably respectable.

In my Sunday night dreams, Johnny Pesky threw me out in a close play at second, Lucy chased me through Pershing Square with a giant lock, and Koko the Clown kept saying "Monks, monks, monks." And then it all came together. Lucy threw her lock to Pesky who heaved it at Koko, taking off his clown's hat.

I woke up thinking it had been one hell of a throw and was disappointed to find that it had all been a dream.

"Are you stirring?" came Gunther's voice through the door just as I was sitting up.

"I'm astir," I said, and he came in.

He was wearing a lighter suit today, but it was still three pieces, including tie. My wall clock said it was almost eight. Gunther held a stack of cards in his hand and a very tiny satisfied smile on his lips.

"I have information," he announced, tapping the cards with his finger. "I could not work last evening so I made a sojourn to Broadway. It being Sunday there were not many people traversing the streets, but there were restaurants. And," he said triumphantly, "it was in one of these establishments that I encountered success."

"You found Martin?" I asked, sitting up further.

Gunther had not only found Martin Lyle, but had tapped some resources, mostly writers he knew, who gave him a profile of the man and his business. Lyle's office was in the 900s on Broadway right near Little Joe's Italian Restaurant. Lyle ran an office, the New Whigs, a political group of reactionary Republicans who had left the party deciding that even the most conservative branches were too soft. The New Whigs were, according to Gunther, believed to have plenty of money and no more than a few dozen members, six of whom lived in or around Los Angeles and the rest in Washington, D.C.

"And this I discovered this morning," Gunther concluded. "I made a most early call to an acquaintance who has actually written a piece on the group for the *New Politics Review*. He is, like me, a Swiss. He told me that a principal aim of the group is to discredit President Roosevelt and the Republicans so they can propose their own presidential candidate. Apparently, they have been in touch with both Generals Patton and MacArthur about running as New Whig candidates. My friend does not know how either of these army officers may have answered. And, finally . . ."

The pause was for effect and I didn't want to deprive Gunther of it since he had done such a first-rate job.

"Finally," he repeated, "your Doctor Olson was a founding member of the New Whigs. Is that not an interesting piece of datum?"

"An interesting piece of datum," I agreed, getting up and putting on my neatly pressed suit. The suit from Doc Olson was heaped in a corner. I'd worry about that, and about making the bed and changing my underwear, some other time.

"What is it that we now do, Toby?" Gunther said seriously.

"You stay here in case I get a call," I said. "Jeremy's guarding an important witness and Eleanor Roosevelt may be in touch."

"I will listen attentively and keep Mrs. Plaut from chaotic intervention," he said.

"Perfect," I said, putting my shoes on. "I've got time for coffee and some cereal. Join me."

"I have eaten," he said, "but I will have some coffee if you permit me to rewash the cups."

I permitted him and he drank while I downed two bowls of Little Kernels and we worked on a plan. It wasn't much of a plan but it might do. I read the side of the cereal box to Gunther using my best Georgia accent.

"To me it sounds correct," Gunther shrugged, "but having my own difficulty with exact pronunciation I am not able to know the subtleties of accent. I am sorry."

It would have to do. In the hall, I looked up the number of the New Whigs, dropped in my nickel, gave the operator the number, and waited. It was a few minutes after nine. Lyle himself answered on the fourth ring. I recognized his voice from the warning call on Saturday. I felt like shouting "Bingo."

"The New Whig Party," he said. "Can I help you?"

Dropping my voice and plunging in, I croaked, "Mah name is O'Hara. Ah've heard good things, good things about you from a friend in Washington, a big fellah, good smile."

"Allen Hall," he supplied.

"Sounds about right," I said. "Suggested I should get in touch with you should I get to this part of the country on business. That's just what I'm doing."

For some reason the image of Thomas Mitchell as O'Hara in *Gone With the Wind* had popped into my mind and now I was tangled in my awful Southern accent overlaid with an even worse Irish brogue.

"Well, Mr. O'Hara," Lyle oozed, "would your schedule permit a visit to our modest but adequate West Coast offices some time in the next few days?"

"Got a big meeting this afternoon with some folks at Pacific Electric Railway. Let's see heh. Could make it this mornin' if that's okay on your side of the border?"

Lyle agreed and we set the time for ten, one hour away. I hung up and tried to recite some Mother Goose with a Southern accent.

I was well into "Taffy was a Welshman," and almost to the bottom of the stairs, when Mrs. Plaut appeared, large wrench in hand.

"You are saying it all wrong, Mr. Peelers," she corrected. "There is an impediment."

"Thank you," I shouted and then had an inspiration that would better have been forgotten. "You have an old Western hat in the garage. White hat, in the back seat of the car in the garage."

Mrs. Plaut had a 1927 Ford in her garage. It had been there since 1928 when Mr. Plaut died. She had worked on it when the mood struck her but had never driven it. I had borrowed her tools a few times for minor surgery on the piles of scrap Arnie had sold me, and I remembered the hat.

"I'm sorry Mr. Peelers," she said, holding the wrench in two hands. "I thought you said you wanted Myron's hat from the car."

"That's just what I do want." I nodded furiously. "I just want to borrow it."

She stood blinking at me for a full ten seconds.

"Myron's hat?"

"Myron's hat," I agreed.

She shrugged, turned, and led the way through the house, out the back door and down to the garage, where sat the old Ford with Myron's hat in the backseat. I reached back, dusted off the hat, and tried it on. It was a bit small, but it would do. I looked at myself in the windshield, which Mrs. Plaut kept spotlessly clean. The effect was less than perfect.

"You look like Tom Mix," said Mrs. Plaut, eyeing me critically. "Though Mix had a very large shnoz and you've got practically none. Though you are a match in the homely department."

"Thanks for your honest appraisal, Mrs. P.," I said.

The hood of the Ford was up and she inserted the wrench, turning her back on me.

"That hat," her voice echoed from under the hood, "originally belonged to Uncle Cruikshank, the one in chapter four of the family book you will recall."

"I recall," I said, stepping toward the garage door.

"That's Uncle Ned Cruikshank, the assistant sheriff in Alemeda, Kansas, before the gout epidemic of 1867."

"I'm going now Mrs. Plaut," I shouted.

"Uncle Cruikshank died in that hat," she said. "A bully named Sousa or something like that blew him out from under it in the environs of Alemeda."

"A comforting thought," I said. "I must—"

"Myron was fond of that hat, Mr. Peelers. Try not to get it soiled or yourself blown out from under it."

I pledged not to, to her deaf ears. In the sunlight, committed to the hat, I began to have second thoughts, but a man's gotta do what a man's gotto do. I strode off toward my faithless Ford, climbed into the saddle, and barely made it to Arnie's garage as the gas tank went bone dry.

Arnie filled it up and gave me an estimate on fixing the door. The estimate from No-Neck was twenty bucks.

"I'll make it fifteen if you throw in that hat," he said as he pumped gas into the tank. "It'd be some good laughs around here."

"I didn't know you had a sense of humor, Arnie," I said, adjusting the hat on my own head.

"I'm as sensitive as the next guy," he said, pulling the gas nozzle out. "That's two bucks for the gas and another fifteen cents for oil."

I paid, took off my hat so I could get into the car without knocking it off, and drove away. A pair of boots would've helped, but I didn't have the time. My disguise would have to do.

Parking on Broadway was tough. I pulled around a corner and drove into a parking lot. I got out, put on my hat, and gave the guy in overalls a broad grin and told him I expected to be back in an hour.

"You got it, Tex," he said.

"How'd you all know I was from Texas?" I said.

He was climbing into my Ford and shaking his head. I figured him at about eighteen years old, maybe nineteen.

"It's the hat, Tex," he said with a wink. "Real authentic. You guys all have them authentic hats just like in the movies. You want a tip?"

"Sure enough, son," I said.

"You're layin' it on too thick," he whispered confidentially. "I'm from Lubbock. Anyone talk like that back home, we'd know he was a Yankee pissing around and we'd hog tie him and ship him north on a cattle car."

He screeched rubber and headed toward the corner of the lot. What did he know? I left the lot and headed down Broadway past Little Joe's to the building where Martin Lyle and his New Whigs had their office. It was a respectable building, if not in a high prestige neighborhood. It even had an elevator that worked at reasonable speed and carried me up to the eighth floor with no stops.

"Good weather you folks up heah are having," I told the bespectacled, pudgy woman who operated the elevator. She turned, looked me up and down, shook her head, and went back to work. I was beginning to seriously doubt the credibility of my disguise, but it was too late. I got off the elevator, touched the brim of my hat to her and went down the hall to room 803, which had stenciled in gold on its door THE NEW WHIG PARTY HEADQUARTERS, and below that in smaller letters, MARTIN LYLE, EXECUTIVE DIRECTOR. Below that there remained the outline of additional lettering that had been scratched away. I bent to look and was fairly sure that the removed letters read DR. ROY OLSON, PRESIDENT.

I was squinting at the door when it opened and a pale woman looked down at me. She was wearing a dark blue suit, her black hair back in a bun, and a serious look on her face.

"Can I help you?" she said.

"Name's O'Hara," I said, standing as high as five nine would take me. "I've got an appointment with your Mr. Lyle."

Damn, the Irish accent had taken over. I touched the brim of my hat to remind me of who I was supposed to be and cursed my stupid disguise silently.

"Come in, Mr. O'Hara," she said, and I did.

The outer office was small. Secretary's desk, some files, photographs, paintings of stern-looking old men in ancient suits. "Who are those fellas?" I said, pointing at the wall paintings.

"Henry Clay, Daniel Webster, William Henry Harrison, and Winfield Scott," she said, going back to her desk efficiently.

The photographs on the wall flanking the portraits were, according to the woman, of various congressmen, none of whom I recognized.

"Most impressive," I said, getting back my Southern exposure.

"We think so," she said efficiently. "I'll show you right in."

She got up from behind the desk again, knocked at the door behind her, and, hearing a "Come in," opened it and mentioned me to follow her.

I wasn't sure of what I expected Martin Lyle to look like. I was counting on his never having seen me before and of my accent being just good enough to disguise my voice. Lyle was standing behind his desk, which featured a tabletop American flag. Both hands were on the desk and he had a small smile on his face, the same small smile I had seen on his birdlike face in Doc Olson's waiting room when he had been sitting there with his parrot.

"You may leave us, Miss Frederickson," Lyle said. "In fact, you may simply close the office and take that package to Mr. Sikes in Santa Monica."

Without a word, Miss Frederickson closed the door and left.

"Now," Lyle said, apparently not recognizing me in the hat or never having paid attention to me in Olson's office, "let's talk about our old friends in Washington."

I had the big hat in my hands as I sat in the chair across from Lyle, who remained standing, a small smile on his face.

"Allen Hall," he said evenly.

"Big fellah." I grinned.

"And am I to understand that you would like to consider joining our organization?" Lyle said, still standing.

"Maybe so," I chuckled. "Maybe so. I'm ready to do

whatever it takes to save this great country of ours from going down with the likes of Franklin De-lay-no Rosey-velt.''

"And so are we," he said as the door to his right opened and Bass stepped into the room. "So are we, Mr. Peters."

Bass looked as close to respectable as it was possible for a moving truck to look. He wore a suit, white shirt, and tie, though the short end of the tie was too short and the long, too long. His washed-out blond hair was combed back carefully.

"Accent gave me away?" I said, trying to be calm.

"I knew who you were when you called," said Lyle, motioning to Bass with a nod of his head. Bass clearly did not understand the nod so Lyle had to sound it out for him. "Go stand at the door to insure that Mr. Peters does not leave before we've had a nice chat. You like chatting, don't you Mr. Peters?"

"I like chatting," I said, bouncing my cowboy hat on my knee.

"Good," said Lyle, still standing as he adjusted his rimless glasses. "I'm going to try to reason with you."

"At the moment I'm very much interested in listening to reason," I said amiably.

Lyle touched the tip of the gold-painted flag pole on his desk and looked at the flag as he went on.

"Your interference, your insistence on pursuing me and Mr. Bass, could result in publicity so devastating that it could reach the Whig Party. Did you know that we elected two presidents of the United States, two, both of whom were secretly assassinated to keep the Whig Party from flourishing?"

"Two?" I prompted like the congregation in a Southern Baptist Church.

"William Henry Harrison and Zachary Taylor," Lyle said. "General Harrison was poisoned by Martin Van Buren less than a month after he took office, and General Taylor was stabbed by minions of Polk after they first corrupted Taylor and forced Henry Clay to expell him from the Party."

"I never heard any of that," I said, pretending great interest.

"You mock me, Peters, but the proof is in our book, the manuscript of which will soon be going to the printer to coincide with our national campaign for the presidency. This war we are in would never have come to pass if Henry Clay or Daniel Webster, our founders, had been elected to the presidency."

"They were against the war with Japan?" I asked.

"Bass," Lyle said over his shoulder to the unseen Bass behind him. This time Bass understood. He stepped forward and hit the top of my head with an open palm. It felt like a steel beam falling from the top of a tall building.

"Clay and Webster were against our entry into the Mexican Wars," Lyle explained, though I had trouble hearing him over the vibrating in my ears. "Clay made the mistake of issuing the Raleigh papers early in his own campaign. He opposed the Mexican War. But . . ."

And with this Lyle raised a fist.

"But . . ." I agreed, solemnly glancing over to be sure Bass wasn't going to prompt me.

"But once we were in a war, the Whigs went to military leadership to lead the country as we always did. Tippecanoe, Taylor, and Winfield Scott. And that is what we want, Mr. Peters. A strong military leader to take America back where it belongs, behind its own strong borders, defended with a big stick."

"And with you behind the scenes as Henry Clay?" I added. "And Bass here will be Daniel Webster?"

"Doctor Olson was to have served that function," said Lyle. "Behind your sarcasm is accidental truth, Mr. Peters."

"So?" I said, twirling the cowboy hat in my hand until Lyle nodded and Bass stepped forward to take the hat from me.

"So, if you involve us in some tale of murder, threats, and this dog obsession, it will be very difficult to get a military figure of the stature of Patton, MacArthur, or Eisenhower to join us. We need credibility. Our ranks are small but our resources boundless and our determination unswerving. New members join us every day."

"Like Mr. Academy," said Bass, from behind me. I turned to face him, but he had sunk back into attention for his leader, who fixed him with a less than paternal look.

"We did not kill Doctor Olson," Lyle went on, returning his gaze to the flag. "Roy Olson was a man of great vision, though he had little fortitude for the essential actions of political realism."

"Like dognapping," I said.

This time I moved my head as Bass's palm descended. It was a good and bad idea. It kept my brain from turning to Kosto pudding, but it resulted in his hand hitting my left shoulder. My left arm, hand, and fingers went numb.

"The dog was . . . There are more important things than the dog," Lyle sighed.

"Mrs. Olson," I said, trying to get some life into my tingling fingers.

"Between us," said Lyle, "and no one will ever believe you outside this room—that was an accident. She found out about certain . . . things."

Like the dog, I thought, but I didn't say anything this time. I wanted two good legs if the chance came to get out of the room. I'd also need at least one good hand to open the door.

"Mr. Bass attempted to reason with her, but things got out of hand."

With this, Lyle's hands went up as if to show that the matter was out of his hands, a question of fate or bad timing.

"It was," he went on, "an accident."

"And the woman who pretended to be Mrs. Olson," I said. "The one who kept me from maybe saving Olson the night he was killed, the one who took off my pants in the clinic yesterday?"

Lyle looked at me with genuine curiosity.

"I may have misjudged you, Peters," he said. "You may simply be mad. Bass, do you know of any such woman?"

We both turned to face, Bass, who looked bewildered. The conversation had passed him by.

"Woman," I said. "You know what that is? Mrs. Olson, not the one you killed, but the other one."

"No," said Bass, but it sounded less like the answer to a

question than an attempt to ward off the one weapon with which he couldn't cope, words.

"Mr. Peters," Lyle returned to me. "This is getting us nowhere. Certain things have to be done if political viability is to be maintained, if this country is, literally, going to be saved. Your petty investigations of an inconsequential murder and a less consequential missing dog might well jeopardize the fragile but vital web we are constructing. It is, indeed, like the first, strong strand of the spider. It is the strand on which the entire structure is based, a structure that will grow and encompass our enemies, but that first strand must be protected until it is strengthened. Do you understand?"

"You're no Daniel Webster," I said. "Or Henry Clay. Spiders and webs. Come on, Lyle. People are getting killed out there. China's going to fall. The RAF is getting shot down over Germany and you're back in the nineteenth century."

"Bass," Lyle cried, and before I could move from the chair, Bass had his arms around me and had lifted me up. I lost my wind and gasped for air, but my voice came out in a little puff.

"Wait," I tried to say, but Lyle had opened the window behind him and nodded to Bass, who carried me easily around the desk.

"Wait," I tried again, but Bass didn't wait. He stuck my head and shoulders out the window, eight floors above Broadway. Traffic was heavy below me. I spotted my own car in the parking lot and even spotted the parking lot attendant from Lubbock.

"Since there is no reasoning with you, Mr. Peters," Lyle said within the room, "then you will simply have an accident or commit suicide."

"Others," I gasped as I felt Bass's arms loosen and tried not to imagine myself bouncing off the building.

"Others?" said Lyle. "Others what? What others?"

Bass's grip had loosened enough for me to cough out the words, "Butler. Bass knows him."

"I beat him," Bass said, proudly shaking me.

"One out of three," I said.

"Pull him in," Lyle's voice called out, and in I came. Bass threw me into the corner of the room, where I bounced off the wall and sat catching my breath.

"I think you're lying about your friends waiting for you," said Lyle, closing the window and advancing toward me with Bass right behind.

"Send Kong down to look," I said as I got up.

Bass looked puzzled and then something clicked.

"He called me a monkey," he said, pushing past Lyle and reaching down for me.

"Bass," Lyle shouted, stopping the hands inches from my throat. I could smell Bass's breath. It should have smelled of garlic, but it was more like mint, which was even more unpleasant than garlic would have been.

"I haven't time for games like this, Peters," Lyle shouted. "Let us call this little visit a warning, a friendly warning. If you persist, the warning will have been made. Now get your silly hat and take your silly ideas out of here. Out of here."

I picked up my hat, and using the wall, got up with Bass glaring at me.

"Monks, monks, monks," I said, limping to the door and brushing off my hat.

"What? What did you say?" Lyle croaked.

"Your parrot, that's what he said the last time I saw him. He said he was Henry the Eighth and then the bit about the monks."

"Those were Henry the Eighth's last words," Lyle said.

"Those were the parrot's last words too before that second Mrs. Olson you know nothing about blew his head off." My hand was on the door and I looked back at Lyle. His upper lip was trembling.

"Henry is dead?" he said.

"Unless a parrot can live without a head." I sighed. "Just thought I'd give you a little good news to start the day off right."

Before he could recover and consider having Bass remove my head, I went out the door, hobbled through the outer office, went into the hall, and headed for the stairs, the location of which I had noted before I had entered the office.

I wasn't sure what I had discovered beyond the fact that Bass had killed Mrs. Olson, but that was a start and a few things were fitting into place.

Jeremy was working on the mirror in the Farraday elevator when I arrived. He sprayed, scrubbed, looked at his own image. Since my ribs were bruised, I rode up with him.

"I should replace this mirror," he said, "but I like to maintain the original. Replacement is necessary in all things but there comes a point at which so much has been replaced that what you have is but the replica of what once stood. When that process begins, we are too often unaware of the transition. However, my fear, Toby, is that when singular replacements become necessary, I will lose my interest in maintaining the building."

"That will never happen," I assured him as we groaned up past the first floor, which reminded me. "How are Alice and Jane getting along?"

"Remarkably," he said, working away at the mirror. "Miss Poslik is very much interested in our children's book and has already begun illustrations. Of course, we could offer her no money at this point, perhaps at no point, but there is a communal feeling about this project. . . . What is wrong with you, Toby?" he asked, suddenly looking at me in his mirror as we squeaked past the second floor.

"I ran into your old friend Bass," I said, gently touching my rib cage to reassure myself again that nothing was broken. "He sends you his best."

"I doubt that," he said, turning to examine me. "You are fortunate that he simply toyed with you."

"He dangled me out of an eighth-floor window," I said as we approached the third-floor landing. The elevator came to a stop and Jeremy, tiny bucket in huge hand, stepped out after sliding open the metal door. He lips were tight in anger.

"He should have been dealt with long ago, before he had the opportunity to seriously hurt anyone," he said.

"He killed a woman last week," I said, as the elevator door closed.

"And he is on the streets?" asked Jeremy, looking up at the slowly rising cage.

"No proof," I said, sagging back against the mesh.

"Justice does not always require evidence of the senses," his voice came up. "It can even go beyond intuition."

Our voices were echoing down the halls now, vibrating off metal and marble and over the whine of machines and distant humming voices.

"I thought you were coming to the idea that there was no good and evil," I shouted. "What about your poem in the park?"

"I have no obligation to be consistent," he shouted back. "My thoughts and feelings are one. When enlightenment comes, it will come not because I will it but because I am ready for it."

"Whatever you say, Jeremy," I said, as the elevator came to a stop on four. I said it quietly to myself. It was hard to think about enlightenment with a ringing skull and bruised ribs.

When I reached the outer door, I knew that things had changed, that I would enter a cleaner but even less savory realm because it would be a false one. The still moist sign on the pebbled glass read SHELDON MINCK, D.D.S. There was no reference, even in small letters, to the existence of Toby Peters, Private Investigator. Inside the door, the waiting room had been scrubbed and a new, metal-legged trio of chairs sat waiting emptily. The small table was clean, the ashtray scrubbed and empty, and two editions of the dental journal, both recent, rested waiting for an eager patient to explore their visual wonders. The ancient poster of gum disorders was gone. In its place was a framed, glass-covered sign urging waiting victims to buy war bonds and stamps.

Beyond the next door, the wonders continued. The sink was still clean, the instruments lined up neatly on a white towel, and Shelly was wearing a freshly scrubbed white jacket buttoned to the neck. He was sitting in the dental chair puffing on the remains of a cigar when I came in. Before he peered up from his magazine through his thick lenses he heard me and cupped the cigar in his palm.

Coughing and choking, he bolted out of the chair.

"It's . . . you . . . for God's sake . . . for chrissake Toby.

I thought it was the inspectors. You could give a man . . ."
He returned his cigar to his mouth, still coughing and pushing
his glasses back on his nose.

"I thought they were coming tomorrow," I said, heading
for my office.

"They like to fool you," he said with a wry smile. "You
know, come in a day early or a day late. But I'll be ready.
How do you like the place?"

"Depressing," I said. "I liked it better the old way."

"Mildred likes it better this way," Shelly said defiantly.

"Then Mildred can come down and work in it. I think I'll
move out." The words came out before I had a sense that
they were coming.

"Out?" Shelly choked. "You wouldn't. We're friends.
Who would I get to rent that closet?"

"Why is my name off the door?" I said through my teeth.

"I'll put it back on as soon as the inspection is over," he
said, looking to heaven for help with my unbending position.

"You've got three days," I said. "Three days. It goes
back on or I move out. And if this hands-off-the-walls stuff
continues, out I go."

"You're threatening an old friend," Shelly said sadly,
flipping the pages of his magazine.

"I'm threatening *you*," I said. "That's not quite the same
thing."

"I was going to ask you a favor," Shelley said. "But with
your present attitude . . ."
He paused, waiting for me to ask him what the favor was.
I didn't ask.

"I was thinking that when the inspector came you could
pretend to be a patient. You know, sit in the chair, let me
clean your teeth, take an X ray."
I laughed. The laugh hurt my ribs.

"Anyone who lets you x-ray his mouth with that left-over
prop from *Metropolis* deserves the fate that awaits him."

"Never mind," he said, shoving his face into the magazine. "Just forget it. You'll get your name back on the door.
And in case you're interested, you've got a visitor."

The visitor was Cawelti, who was looking at the photograph of me, my dad, Phil, and the dog. Cawelti's hands were behind his back.

"Nice family portrait," he said.

"I don't want to talk to you, fireman," I said, getting behind my desk and biting my lower lip to keep from showing the pain in my aching ribs. My feet kicked something under my desk. Shelly had put the coffee pot, cups, and various pieces of junk and magazines in a box and shoved them there. I kicked them and the rattling turned Cawelti's head toward me.

"Seidman's doing better," he said, pulling out the visitor's chair and sitting on it after turning it around. I hated people who did that. It would be nice if the damned chair collapsed, but it didn't. "No thanks to your friend out there."

"Shelly would be happy to work on you for nothing," I said. "You got business with me, fireman, or is this social chitchat? Should I send out for coffee and cookies?"

"Jane Poslik is missing," he said. "You wouldn't know anything about it, would you?"

He leaned forward, his arms on the top of the chair, his head resting on his hands. I could see where he had cut his face shaving that morning.

"You cut yourself shaving," I said.

His hand inadvertently shot up to touch his chin and then backed down. His face went bright red.

"Jane Poslik, prick," he said, clenching his teeth.

"I don't think she's got one," I said back through my clenched teeth.

"You think you're funny," said Cawelti, standing and pushing the chair into the corner.

Shelly's voice came through the door in a petulant whine.

"Hold it down in there, will you? There's a doctor at work out here. Inspectors could be coming in any time now."

"Shut up, you hack," Cawelti shouted back.

"That's quack," Shelly shot back. "I'm a quack, not a hack. Get your insults straight at least in there."

"He's right," I agreed. "He is a quack." Then I whispered to Cawelti, "I'd say you get half credit for your answer. Any more questions?"

Cawelti's hand came across the desk toward my neck, but I was ready for him. I came up with the coffee pot in my hand and swiped at his advancing arm. I caught him at the elbow.

"You son of a bitch," he yelped, jumping back holding his arm.

"I'll be sure to tell my brother what you called our mother the next time I see him," I said, still holding the coffee pot like a hammer.

He turned and left, slamming the door behind him. In the outer office I could hear Shelly say, "Hey, try to stay away from here a few days, will you? I've got some classy people coming through. Hey, hey, what are you—" The door slammed and Cawelti was gone.

"Some caliber of people you've got coming to see you, Toby," he shouted at me. "Spitting on the floor. My patients don't even do that."

I put the coffee pot back in the cardboard box under my desk, pulled the box out, and carried it into Shelly's office. He was settled in his chair, the L.A. *Times* covering his face.

"Where the hell is Madagascar?" he said from behind the open paper. A puff of smoke popped over the back page.

"A French island, I think. Somewhere near Africa," I said, walking toward him slowly.

"British occupied it over the weekend," he said. "About time our side occupied something instead of moving out of somewhere."

Shelly was still behind his newspaper as he flipped the pages.

"Mildred and I didn't get away over the weekend," he said. "We were in here cleaning up, but I think we'll take in *The Man Who Came to Dinner* over at the Bliss-Hayden Theater. You know, a reward for passing the inspection. Right here Katherine Van Blau says Doris Day as Maggie the secretary 'proved herself to be an actress of scope and fine sincerity.' You think that's the same Doris Day who stole Cal Applebaum's mother's candleholders? Couldn't be. She wouldn't come back here with the same—"

I dropped the carton on the floor and cut off Shelly's

babbling. The newspaper came down and Shelly's eyes focused on the floor as an ash fell on his recently washed white jacket.

"What the hell?" he said. "Toby. I can't have that stuff in here with the inspection."

"Find another place for it. Take it home. Put it in the trunk of your car. Put it out in the hall. Someone will steal it within five minutes. I don't care where you put it, but not in my office."

"You don't plan on cooperating with me on this crisis, do you?" he said, nodding his head knowingly, a man who finally recognizes betrayal.

"You're beginning to understand that, are you?"

"All right. All right. Just leave it there. I'll take care of it," he said, looking down at the carton. "Just go on with whatever you were doing. It doesn't matter that I might lose my license, that I might not be able to help all those people out there who rely on me."

"Like Steve Seidman," I said. "You could at least go see him in the hospital or call."

"Me?" Shelly said, putting his newspaper aside and pointing to his chest. "I didn't do anything to him. If he has an infection or something, it's because . . ."

"Good-bye Shel," I said sweetly and left the office.

I had a hard time finding Jeremy. He wasn't in his office. He wasn't in the elevator recleaning the mirror. He wasn't Lysoling the stairs or polishing the name plates in the lobby. I went back up to Alice Palice's "suite" and found him there. Alice's suite consisted of much the same space Shelly occupied two floors above. In the center of the main room was a large oak dining room table. On the table was Alice's printing press. Surrounding the printing press were cans of ink, towels, and stacks of paper. In fact the room was a mess filled with paper and books. It looked like moving day on the Island of Yap just before the invasion. The smell of ink hit hard and not unpleasantly. Jeremy was standing and shaking his head over something he was reading, which had probably been printed on the press.

"Toby," he said, "one should be careful about one's

promises. I told Alice I would keep an eye on things for her, she is expecting a delivery. She and Miss Poslik have gone downtown to a sale at Bullocks. They are getting along very well.'' He put the printed material down and looked around the room. "I would be very willing to put all this in order, but Alice and I have an agreement.''

"Think you could close up shop and keep me company while I keep an eye on the guy who I think has the dog?'' I said.

"You need company?''

"I may run into Bass,'' I explained.

"Then it will be my pleasure to join you.''

We took my car, which proved to be a mistake. Since the passenger door wouldn't open, Jeremy had to slide in on the driver's side. It was a tight fit past the steering wheel and we almost had to give up. We didn't think of what might happen getting out. Fifteen minutes later we were parked in front of Lyle's building on Broadway. I left Jeremy and found by listening at the door that Lyle was still in his office. Then it was back downstairs and more waiting while Jeremy tried to educate me with poetry and a lecture on modern literature. At one point a guy who looked like an old George Brent came out of the shoe store we were parked in front of. He looked like he was going to tell us to move. Then he got close enough to see my face and Jeremy's body and decided instead to pretend he was looking for stray customers.

Around noon, just when I was going to suggest that I pick up some sandwiches, Lyle came out of the front door of the building followed by Bass. I could feel Jeremy sitting up next to me. Lyle wore a thin coat, which he pulled around his neck. He looked up at the sky and saw a wave of clouds coming that I hadn't paid attention to. Rain was on the way.

Lyle and Bass went down the street and I started the engine. They didn't go far. They got in a big Chrysler parked near the corner. Lyle got in back. Bass drove. The New Whigs didn't fool around with any of this equality stuff.

Following them was no problem. I was good at it and they didn't know enough to even suspect that I might be there.

It was a long ride. We followed the Chrysler west to

Sepulveda and then stayed safely behind as we took Sepulveda up through the hills into the valley past Tarzana. A turn on Reseda and in two more blocks, Bass and Lyle pulled into the small parking lot next to the Midlothian Theater, a small neighborhood cigar box.

I kept driving, made a turn in a driveway where a man in a baseball cap was watering his lawn, an effort that struck me as particularly dumb since Helen Keller could have told him that the rain would be coming down dark and heavy and not in minutes or hours. But the man didn't seem to care. He nodded at us as I pulled out of his driveway, somewhat relieved, I think, that we weren't coming to visit him, and went on with his watering.

We parked across from the Midlothian in front of a candy shop and watched Lyle and Bass as they were let into the theater. We already knew why we were there. The marquee read WHIG PARTY RALLY TODAY AT ONE. Then, below this sign in those little black letters was CELEBRITIES-CELEBRITIES-CELEBRITIES. The *t*s in the last two celebrities were red instead of black. Jeremy thought that was an interesting, eye-catching design concept that he might suggest to Alice for their book. I thought the kid who had put up the announcement had just run out of small black *t*s.

From where we sat we could see both the front entrance to the theater and Lyle's car. For the next hour we talked about design graphics, oriental healing (which Jeremy was learning), and the people who straggled into the theater. We didn't keep count but Jeremy, who was accustomed to gauging wrestling crowds, put the final total at forty-seven, mostly women. We also guessed that most of the crowd had been drawn by the promise of celebrities, none of whom I could identify going in. The most interesting attendee, as far as I was concerned, was Academy Dolmitz, who drove up a few minutes before one, parked in the gravel lot, and got into the theater as fast as he could, apparently hoping that no one would see him. Academy's pride in his political party was touching. Then Jeremy thought he recognized Hugh Herbert. I said the guy didn't look much like Herbert to me but maybe he was right.

At a minute or two after one, Lyle stuck his head out the door and looked both ways, either for the celebrities who hadn't arrived or in the hope of grabbing unwary housewives from the street to fill a few seats. His scanning of the street brought him quickly to me. With Jeremy at my side there wasn't any room to hide, so I threw a cool smile on my lips and looked straight back at the gleaming lenses of Lyle's glasses. Lyle's face went through a mess of emotions that would have been the envy of a starlet on her first screen test: surprise, curiosity, anger, mock confidence, smirk, shaken, superiority, and controlled but quivering anger. Then he pulled his head back in. It was replaced about a minute later by the bulk of Bass, who found us and began to cross the street, ignoring an Olds driven by a guy in overalls who almost ran him down.

"Out, quickly," said Jeremy, touching my arm.

I opened the door and got out, almost falling into the path of another car. Had my passenger door been working, which it was not thanks to Bass, Jeremy could have gotten out with dignity untested, but he did a fairly good job of it in any case and managed to be at my side just as Bass reached out a hand in the general direction of my throat.

I didn't back away. I couldn't back away without hitting my car or stepping into traffic, but backing away wasn't necessary. Jeremy's hand shot out and pushed Bass's down.

Bass looked at Jeremy, whom he seemed to be seeing for the first time, and said, "Butler. You're through. You quit."

"We both did," Jeremy said evenly, understanding what made little sense to me.

A woman of about fifty, dead black mink around her neck and a hat with a long black feather, had stopped on the sidewalk as she came out of the candy store. The sight of two giants in the street was enough to get her attention. I looked at her and shrugged as if I had been recruited as a reluctant referee.

"What are you looking at?" Bass said to the woman.

I gave her credit. She managed to keep from dropping her purse and candy as her heels clacked down the street.

"Go back across the street, Bass," Jeremy said calmly.

"I've got to do him," Bass said, nodding at me as if I were a package he had been assigned to gift-wrap.

"No," said Jeremy gently, as a guy in a black Buick stopped his car to complain about our standing in the street and then changed his mind and sped away.

"I'll do him and I'll do you again," Bass said, his eyes wide and his lips dry.

"You didn't beat me," Jeremy said.

"Two out of three," Bass hissed.

"I won the two," Jeremy said, his huge hands slightly away from his body, ready.

"Bass, I think you better go back and ask Lyle about this," I said. "He didn't count on Jeremy being here and I don't think he wants the two of you messing up Reseda. It wouldn't do the party any good."

"He's right," said Jeremy. "We're already attracting attention."

We gave Bass time to react to the argument. He didn't seem capable of fixing his attention on more than one major problem at a time, but the blast of a horn from a skidding car and the blue speck of a policeman about a block away got through to him. He clenched his fists, looked at me and Jeremy, and then pounded a dent into the top of a passing car. The driver just kept on driving and pretended he hadn't been attacked by the Minotaur of Crete.

We followed Bass across the street, let him go through the door ahead of us, and entered the Midlothian Theater. The small lobby behind the ticket booth smelled like stale popcorn. Posters hung on the wall inside framed glass scratched by the nails of maybe a million Saturday matinee kids. One poster promised a future with Olivia de Havilland, who wore an off-the-shoulder gown and looked toward the candy stand as if she was waiting for a seltzer delivery that was very late. Behind her, Dennis Morgan smelled her hair for remnants of eau de Milk Duds.

My foot caught in a strand of frayed, once-red lobby carpet, but I pulled it out before I fell, and followed Jeremy into the theater. There were about fifty people in a place that could have easily held three hundred or more, and they were scattered all over, only a few in front. Lyle was on the stage and the house lights were up. He had no microphone, but he did have a portable metal podium, the kind violinists use for solos. If he had leaned on the damned thing, his political career would have ended.

Jeremy and I found seats on the right about ten rows from the back. I moved inside. Jeremy took the aisle, which allowed him to put his feet out. Across from us a gray-faced man was eating a sandwich he had taken out of a brown paper bag. Something yellow dribbled out of the sandwich. I turned my attention to Lyle, who was getting the whispered message from Bass that I still existed. Lyle looked around, found me, eyed Jeremy, and nodded to Bass.

"Get started," shouted the sandwich man across the aisle.

"We will begin," Lyle said softly and cleared his throat. Behind him, pinned to the curtain, were big posters of MacArthur, Patton, and Eisenhower, all in full uniform. The right top corner of the Ike poster had come loose but Lyle had his back to it and never noticed.

"We will begin," Lyle said louder this time.

I found Academy Dolmitz about fifteen rows in front of us, hunched down. My eyes must have burned through his collar because he let out a big sigh, turned, looked at me and gave a massive "What am I gonna do?" shrug.

"Will you all move up," Lyle said. "It will be easier to talk and will leave space for those who come in late."

No one except the man with the sandwich across the aisle from us moved. He stuck his brown bag under his arm and, still holding his sandwich—from which an unidentified vegetable now dropped—tromped forward to answer Lyle's call.

"See the celebrities better," the sandwich-eater explained to those in his vicinity as he moved down to sit in front of Lyle, who did not have the talent to hide his distaste. Two well-dressed women seemed to have had enough even before the festivities started. They were in the far aisle from us and headed for the door. Bass hurried to head them off. They saw him coming and scurried back to their seats.

"The enemies of the Whig Party," Lyle began, looking

down at his notes on the unsteady music stand, "have for more than a hundred years done their best to silence our voice of reason. They murdered us when we earned the highest office in the land."

"Murdered?" came a woman's voice from the back.

Bass, who now stood, arms folded, in front of the stage, shot a glare of cold fury toward the voice.

"Yes," said Lyle looking up. "Murdered. They murdered Harrison. They murdered Taylor and they would have murdered Winfield Scott if he had been elected. And, most recently, just a day ago right in this city, they murdered the Dr. Roy Olson who, with me, had devoted his life to the revitalization of the Whig Party. And knowing them"—and with this he looked at Jeremy and me—"I am not at all surprised that they have sent the very murderers to our meeting today. Well, I tell them and I tell you they will not silence us."

He clearly wanted to thunder his first down for emphasis but there was nothing to thunder on but the wire music stand, or Bass's head. Lyle settled for shaking his fist and waiting for applause. There was none. Someone did cough up front.

"Who's this 'they' he's going on about?" said another woman, not aware that her voice would carry in the little, nearly empty theater.

"I'm glad you asked that, madam," Lyle said, aiming his words in the general direction of the comment. "*They* are the government, the Roosevelts, the Democrats, the Republicans. They are the ones who want to take away your right to be you, to be Americans, to take what you can take within the rightful limits of the law, to expand your horizons, to use the full power of God you were born with. They want to make you all alike, all weak, all dependent, all little wind-up dolls operated by them. They pretend to be against each other, but they hold each others' hands. And the others, the Socialists, the Communists, they're just waiting till the Megalops kill each other off so they can put you and your children and me in their prisons and make peace with the Nazis and the Japanese. We don't need crippled socialists standing in front of us as if we were children. We need strong leaders who stand up to enemies but maintain our borders. Don't tread on me. Leave me alone and I'll leave you alone. Responsible for my debts only. We need a Patton, a MacArthur, an Eisenhower.''

"A General Marshall," came a voice that might have been touched as much with Petri wine as enthusiasm.

"Not a Marshall," said Lyle, shaking his head sadly but glad to have some response. "I'm afraid he is one of them. We must choose carefully, find the powerful and the incorruptible to lead us. We must make our platform clear, begin with the dedicated few, and become the powerful many. At this point, are there any questions?"

The sandwich man now sitting directly in front of Lyle shot up a hand, and since there were no other questions, Lyle had to acknowledge him. The man got up brushing crumbs from his coat and said, "Where are the celebrities?"

The man solemnly sat down and Lyle said, "I'm glad you asked that. Our ranks right now are, admittedly, small, but among our numbers are the famous and the influential. Some of our strongest supporters are names you would recognize instantly but, because of the pressure of the great *them* who have opposed and suppressed us, unfortunately many of these famous people in entertainment, sports, and even politics and the military service must remain unknown till they need no longer fear for their lives."

"You said there would be celebrities," came a woman's cracking voice.

"We have celebrities," Lyle said, with a deep sigh; he didn't give in to despair. "I'll ask them to stand up and, perhaps, say a few words. Mr. Don Solval, famous radio personality."

A man, white-haired, lots of pretend teeth, stood up, turned around, and waved at the crowd. The wino in the back applauded alone.

"Who is that?" Jeremy asked me.

"Never heard of him," I whispered.

"Martin Lyle is a man of honor and integrity," Solval said in a deep bass voice that reeked of radio. I didn't recognize the voice. "In the years I have worked for him and his family in Maine, I have come to not only accept his political beliefs but to become a strong advocate of them."

He showed his teeth, waved again, and sat down. This time only Lyle applauded.

"Thank you, Don."

"That was no goddamn celebrity," said the sandwich man in the front row. Bass took two steps toward the man, leaned over, whispered something, and the man went white and silent. Bass returned to his position below Lyle and looked around the audience for more trouble, his eyes stopping significantly at Jeremy and me.

"We have other celebrities," Lyle said, placating the now restless little crowd with his upturned hands. "Mr. Robert Benchley."

"I heard of him," said the wino in back, clapping. There was a round of polite clapping as Lyle smiled and everyone looked around to find Benchley. Eventually a man who had been slouched over a few rows in front of Academy Dolmitz stood up and turned to the audience with a small, embarrassed grin. His face was round and his little mustache gave a twitch.

"Um," Benchley began, rubbing his hands together. "Um," he repeated and then let out a small laugh as if he had been caught eating the last cookie in the jar. "There seems to be some slight mistake here. I wasn't aware that this was a political rally." He laughed again. "I was told by my agent, or maybe I should say former agent or soon-to-be former agent, that this was a war-bond promotion. I'm not even a registered voter in this state. Thank you."

Benchley gathered up his coat and ambled down the aisle past us with a small, constipated grin as Lyle applauded furiously and a few others joined him.

"Thank you, Robert Benchley," Lyle said, applauding.

"Wait a minute," came the wino's voice. "He ain't even on your side."

"We promised celebrities," Lyle said patiently. "We never said they would support us. We begin by having them present and then the truth of our cause convinces them and you. Now that we have heard from our celebrities—"

"Hold it," called the wino, standing. "You mean that's it? No more celebrities? No free coffee, nothing?"

"Just truth," said Lyle, almost giving in to exasperation.

Bass was moving up the aisle now in search of the troublesome wino. While his back was turned, four women, probably a bridge club, escaped out of a side emergency exit. Bass found the wino and carried him at arm's length out of the theater.

"I want a refund," screamed the wino.

"You paid nothing and got much," shouted Lyle. "You got the truth and the truth will work on your conscience." The crowd was mumbling and considering following the valiant bridge club. One woman actually stood, but she had waited too long to make up her mind, and Bass, now returning, fixed his eyes on her coldly, and she sat.

"We have one more speaker," Lyle said clearly, sensing that he could hold the group no longer without a real celebrity or refreshments or, possibly, a good idea or two. "With the assassination of Dr. Olson I have had to go through the difficult task of assessing the qualities of the many qualified members of our party to select a successor as party organizer. I've agonized over this decision, consulted our leadership in Washington, New York, and Dallas, and come up with the name of a member of your own community, Mr. Morris Dolmitz."

Five rows ahead of us, Academy Dolmitz sank deeper in his seat and failed to hold back a gurgled "Shit."

Lyle applauded, and the crowd paused with minimal curiosity, looking for the one in their midst who had been selected by Lyle to make a fool of himself.

"Mr. Dolmitz is a prominent businessman in Los Angeles," Lyle said. "A man of great political knowledge who has much to say. Mr. Dolmitz, a few words please."

Bass applauded and grinned like a kid and Lyle beamed, waving for Academy to get up and speak.

"Go on, Academy," I called. "Your new career awaits."

"Blow it out the wrong way," Academy spat out through his clenched teeth loud enough for everyone to hear, but he was trapped. He shuffled into the aisle cursing that he was ever born, brushed his mane of white hair back, and went to the steps leading up to the low, small stage. Bass, clearly protective, hovered behind him to help in case his former boss and inspiration fell. Clearly uncomfortable, Dolmitz stood next to Lyle, who held out his hand. Dolmitz shook the offered hand and looked over at Jeremy and me apologetically as if to say, "See the things you have to go through to turn a dishonest buck?"

Academy stepped in front of the music stand, glared out at the uneasy audience, and said, "I've got nothing to say."

He turned and Lyle whispered to him urgently while someone in the audience started coughing and a voice, female, said, "Dorothy, are you all right? You want a glass of water or something?" But Dorothy stopped and Academy bit his lower lip, trying to think of something to say.

"I didn't expect this . . . honor," he finally said. "Did you know Robert Benchley won an Oscar in 1935, best short subject?"

"*How to Sleep*," I said. "MGM."

Academy nodded his head, one-upped by me again.

"I've met Oscar winners before," Academy went on, warming to his favorite subject outside of making money. "Lyle Wheeler, the art director who won the award for *Gone With the Wind*," Academy said quickly so I wouldn't get a chance to identify Wheeler from the audience, though I wouldn't have been able to do it. "Wheeler came into my bookshop one day and bought a couple of books by French writers, Flaubert, Zola, Balzac, that crowd. Wheeler was a nice guy. I tried to get him to put down a few bucks on a sure thing I had going out of Santa Anita, a two-year-old named Sidewalk, but Wheeler didn't go for it. That's all I've got to say."

Bass applauded furiously again as Academy climbed down from the stage and Lyle stepped forward as his political world seemed to be crumbling around him, but he had been through it before.

"Mr. Dolmitz has assured me that he fully supports the aims of the Whig Party," Lyle said as feet shuffled and Dorothy attempted to control her returning cough.

"No more states in the Union. . . . God meant us to have forty-eight adjacent states that we can protect and can protect each other. Peace with our enemies in Europe, peace with honor or we crush them. No quarter for the Japanese. The elimination of sales taxes. Establishment of a new cabinet position. Secretary of Women's Affairs."

"Right, right," said Academy, sinking back into his chair and trying to hide.

"My secretary will be in the lobby as you leave with written information on the New Whig Party, membership applications, and answers to questions you may have. Now, if you will put your heads down, we will have a full minute of silent non-denominational prayer."

Lyle looked at everyone in the auditorium as he clapped his hands and heads went down, even mine, Jeremy's, Dolmitz's, and the cowered sandwich man's in the first row a few feet from Bass.

Head down, eyes closed, I whispered to Jeremy, "You going to join the Whigs?"

"The line between dedication and madness is as thin as the space between two thoughts," said Jeremy. "The madman who bears away our faith is labeled a saint and the saint who fails to gather our faith is labeled mad."

"And?" I said, eyes still down, listening beyond Jeremy's voice to shuffling feet and clearing thoughts.

"And," he said, "you had best open your eyes and see where your moment of feigned faith has brought you."

I opened my eyes and looked up at nothing. The stage was empty. Lyle and Bass were gone. Jeremy was already in the aisle. I joined him noisily and eyes opened around us. When others saw that Lyle and Bass were gone they headed for the exit. I almost collided with the sandwich man, since I was going in the opposite direction.

Jeremy leaped on the stage. I was a beat behind him. He went for the curtain, pulled it open and disappeared behind it. I followed, finding myself in the darkness feeling my way across the movie screen on which Olivia de Havilland would soon be pining away. I followed the sound of Jeremy's feet

You want a tip?"

going to the right and, at the right side of the screen, found a small door and stepped through.

Jeremy was ahead of me, standing on the cement floor in a room behind the screen. Light was coming in through a dirty window. The room was a storage area: tables, old theater seats, boxes of light bulbs and electrical equipment, sacks of popping corn, a pile of movie posters, and a box of lobby cards. A few of the cards in sickly colors, with Lash Larue and Fuzzy St. John looking up at me, were on the floor. All very interesting, but not nearly as interesting as the wire cage in the corner, the door of which stood open. There was a small bowl of water in the cage and a general faint smell of dog.

I found the door to the outside before Jeremy. It was behind a painted Chinese screen with a gold dragon. It was a double door and I pushed it open with Jeremy at my side. We were in the back of the theater. The gravel parking lot was to our right. We ran the few steps and turned the corner in time to see Lyle's Chrysler shooting little rocks from its rear tires as it hit the driveway, almost hit a woman and a small boy, and barely make it into traffic in front of a delivery truck.

Jeremy and I ran for my car and lost additional time as Jeremy slid across the driver's seat and I followed him. By the time we pulled into traffic on Reseda a few seconds later, Lyle and Bass were out of sight.

"You got a suggestion?" I asked Jeremy, who sat placidly, eyes forward, thinking about a poem or another world, or a rematch with Bass.

"Intuition," he said. "Let your hands tell you. Let your mind go."

"Thanks," I said.

"You have a better plan?" He smiled.

I smiled back. "I'm taking a chance that he likes the same big streets and doesn't know we followed him to the theater," I said. "I'll cut ahead of him on Sepulveda."

Five minutes later I was cruising south on Sepulveda when Jeremy said softly, "Ahead, about two blocks."

I didn't see anything, but I trusted his eyes and kept going. Before we hit the hills, I spotted the Chrysler, slowed down, and kept my distance, trying not to think about how much gas I had left. Fifteen minutes later, we hit downtown Los Angeles. I reached over to turn on the radio but I changed my mind. Jeremy was not a radio fan.

Lyle and Bass drove down Broadway to Central, took Ninth across to Long Beach Road, and then went down Long Beach to Slauson Avenue. They pulled into a dirt driveway next to something that looked like an old warehouse just off Holmes Avenue across from the Santa Fe Railroad tracks. I parked half a block ahead and looked back to see them getting out of the Chrysler. The clouds had rolled in and were rumbling as Bass and Lyle moved to the trunk of their car, opened it, and removed a wooden crate that Bass hoisted to his shoulder.

They took the crate into the warehouse and just as I was deciding to follow them, they reappeared without it and got back into the car.

"Jeremy," I said, getting out of the car. "Stay with them. I'm going to find out if they just delivered what I think they delivered."

Jeremy nodded and, with great difficulty, squeezed himself behind the wheel.

"I'll make my own way back to the office," I shouted as he made a U-turn and darted off after the Chrysler, which was now a good block away.

The sky broke and the rain began to come down. I ran across Slauson ahead of a truck and found the door Bass and Lyle had gone through. Behind and above me, a tidal wave fell, sending up a wet dusty smell that lasted only a second or two.

The building was a gigantic warehouse. Beyond a pile of ceiling-high shelves filled with wooden crates I could hear voices. People were arguing. Murder seemed to be in progress. I moved slowly along the shelves toward the sound and turned a corner.

A pretty young woman with too much make-up and a ribbon in her hair and a man with a thin mustache and sagging jaw each had an end of rope that was tied around the neck of a man who looked slightly bewildered. They pulled and shouted and the man in the middle gulped, the center knot of a strange, deadly tug of war.

Then a voice called out, "Cut, cut, cut, cut, cut. Damn it, cut."

That was when I saw, beyond the bright lights blasting down on the trio of actors, a camera and a small group of people.

The man who had shouted "Cut" had a light mustache, a receding hairline, and wore no shirt. A towel was draped around his neck.

"What's wrong, Jules?" asked the man who had been holding one end of the rope.

"The noise," said Jules, pointing over his shoulder to the ceiling. "It's raining. We can't do sound in here with that." Jules put his hands on his hips and shook his head.

"Let's shoot the scene silent," said the man who was being strangled, the rope still around his neck. "Cut to a close-up of me and we can add rattling sounds later. You know, like my brains are getting scrambled. Then we do a point of view shot and I can see them moving their mouths, but the rope is so tight around my neck that it's cutting off my hearing."

Jules turned, thought about it, shrugged and said, "It'll do, Buster."

Buster Keaton, who had made the suggestion, put the rope ends back in the hands of the two actors and began supervising his own mock strangulation. He put his tiny hat on the side of his head and said, "Let's move the camera in and get going."

The camera operators said something I couldn't make out, and Jules called to the actors. "Don's having some problem with the camera. Let's take a lunch break."

Keaton took off his hat, removed the rope, shook himself off, and started to walk toward a door in the corner. A lighting man turned off the lights and I moved across the set, apparently a living room, and followed Keaton.

"Mr. Keaton," I called, catching up to him as he turned. There was no expression on his face as I stepped up. There wasn't any through our whole conversation. I was a few inches taller than he was and he was a few years older than I had fixed him in my mind. The dead-pan look I remembered from his silent movies was there, but the smooth face had turned to leather, covered by unconvincing light makeup.

"It's lunch," he said.

"I heard," I said. "Can I talk to you for a second or two? Won't take long."

"Can't take long," he said, waving at me to follow him. "We'll go to my dressing room."

I followed him to his makeshift dressing room, which was normally an office complete with desk, file cabinets, In and Out boxes with dusty paper. He opened the file cabinet, pulled out a bottle and a sandwich. The bottle was bourbon.

"Drink?" he said, turning to me.

"No thanks," I said.

"Good." He tossed me the sandwich. "You take the liverwurst. I'll take the bourbon, and I'll be in Forest Lawn before you."

I caught the sandwich as he opened the bottle, poured himself an unhealthy glassful, and sat in the wooden, creaking swivel chair, his little hat still on his head. He took a drink and looked at me.

"Let me guess," he said. "I owe somebody money and you've been sent to collect it?"

"No," I said, opening the wrapping of the sandwich, leaning against the wall and taking a bite.

"If you're looking for a job," he went on, "you've come to the wrong studio." He looked around the dusty office. "This production is so cheap we have to finish shooting a two-reeler by four o'clock so we don't have to buy coffee and sinkers for the six-man cast and crew."

"I'm not looking for a job," I said. "This sandwich is pretty good."

"I'll tell the chef," Keaton said, toasting me and taking another drink. "I'm out of guesses."

"What did those two men bring in here? The ones who just left?"

Keaton rubbed his nose and considered another drink. The question the bottle had asked him was more important than mine.

"You want to hear a confession and a declaration?" he said. "This"—his eyes went around the room and looked beyond the door toward the set—"is the bottom. From this, it can only get better. You're not a reporter, are you? No, you're not a reporter. You are . . ."

"A man who wants to know what two men just brought in here in a wooden crate," I said, my mouth full of liverwurst.

"You're a cop," Keaton said, his eyelids drooping slightly.

"Private investigator," I said. "Name is Peters."

"And they're dognappers," he said. "I've played a detective once or twice, done a lot of crime movies, mostly two-reelers for Educational."

"I've seen some of them," I said. "Why did you say they were dognappers?"

Keaton took off his hat and balanced it on end on the tip of his finger.

"Some of those shorts weren't half bad," he said. His lower lip came up over his upper as he concentrated on balancing the hat.

"Dogs," I reminded him.

"Not all of them," he whispered.

"I didn't mean the movies," I said.

"I know it," he answered. "A joke. Those two guys sold me a dog. Now I suppose I'll have to give it back. My own money too. There's not enough in the budget to hire a dog, and I've got a humdinger of a gag.

"Little dog comes running in, in the last scene, little black Scottie, and the camera moves over to show me, with little glasses and a cigarette holder, a Roosevelt gag. I play Roosevelt and Elmer, my character. We're in the same shot. Most expensive thing in the movie. Can't carry it off without special effects and a dog, and you want the dog back."

"I think he might be the real thing," I said.

"I wouldn't buy a fake dog," said Keaton, flipping the

hat in the air. It turned over three times and landed neatly on his head.

"I mean it might really be Roosevelt's dog," I explained, pushing away from the wall. "I've got reason to believe the guys who sold it to you took the dog. Now things are getting hot and they have to get rid of him."

Keaton didn't say anything, just looked at me blankly, but even in that whithered blankness I could see that he was considering whether I was a special movie nut or a general all-around nut who happened to be sleeping one off in the corner of the warehouse when the movie woke me up.

"That's Fala?" he said.

"I think it could be," I replied.

"I was going to call him Fella," said Keaton. "Why would someone take the president's dog and then sell it?"

"That's what I'm working on," I said. "Can I see the dog?"

From beyond the door a woman's voice called out, "We've got it working, Buster. Ready to go again."

"Coming," said Keaton, getting out of the swivel chair. He stepped over to me, almost nose to nose, and looked into my eyes. Then he shrugged and waved for me to follow him again. We moved back out the door and to the right, away from the set, down a dark row of shelves to a caged room that looked like a tool storage space. The dog was sitting in the middle of the room, looking up at us and wagging his tail.

"I'll have to take him," I said.

"That's fifty bucks and a good gag ruined," he said. "And how do I know you're who you say you are?"

"I've got a number you can call. Ask for Eleanor Roosevelt. Tell her who you are and ask her if she knows who I am," I said, reaching for the cage.

"I'll trust you," sighed Keaton.

"Buster," came the woman's voice from across the warehouse.

"Coming," said Keaton, opening the cage door.

The dog came running to us wagging his tail and leaped

up in Keaton's arms. The dog stuck his tongue out and licked the actor's face.

"Likes the taste of makeup," Keaton said.

"Looks that way," I said, holding out my arms.

He shrugged and handed me the dog, which was heavier than I thought—which surprised me—but smelled like a dog, which didn't surprise me. The dog didn't like me as much as he did Buster and let out a whining sound.

"I'll walk you to the door," Keaton said, petting the dog. "Think you can get my fifty back from those two guys?"

"I'll see what I can do," I said.

We had reached the front door through which I had come. The rain was still coming down hard and Keaton reached over to pet the dog once more. "I'll need a cab," I said, remembering that Jeremy had taken the car.

"Wait here," Keaton said, "I'll have April call one for you."

Before he could turn, I glanced out the window in the door and got what was probably the shock of my not-young life. The rain-soaked hulk of Bass shot up from below the window, blotting out the outside light and glaring at me. I almost dropped the dog, which let out a yelp, and Keaton turned to see Bass stepping through the door.

Bass, a dripping monster, hulked into the warehouse accompanied by thunder and the sound of dark pouring rain. I backed away clutching the whimpering dog and bumped into Keaton.

"The dog," Bass said. His hands were out reaching for the dog.

"You owe me fifty bucks," Keaton said solemnly.

"Let's let that drop for now," I said, backing away as Bass, his yellow hair dripping down in front of his eyes, reached out an arm to swat Keaton away.

Keaton dropped to a squat so quickly that Bass's swinging arm cracked into a metal shelf. Bass's face showed no sign of pain or feeling.

"The dog," he repeated.

"Why does Lyle want the dog back?" I asked reasonably. "He just sold it, got rid of it."

"The dog," Bass repeated as I backed into a stack of crates and felt the rough wood against my back.

"Excuse me," Keaton interrupted, tapping Bass on the shoulder. "I paid fifty bucks for the dog. I say Peters takes it and you give back my fifty."

Bass turned his head to the little actor, who barely came up to his chest. Keaton's jaw jutted out the way it did in *Spite Marriage* and almost collided with Bass's chest.

"He's a killer," I warned.

"Don't worry," said Keaton. "I won't hurt him."

Bass was surprisingly fast for a big man, but Jeremy had told me he was. But that was fast for a wrestler. He had never met a Keaton. Bass reached for Keaton's scrawny throat, but the actor dropped to the floor, rolled over once and came up on Bass's rear. The dripping killer had a moment of confusion and then turned suddenly as Keaton ducked under his arm. Bass's hand took the little hat, crushed it, and threw it at the actor, who caught it expertly.

Bass was now clearly distracted and challenged by this elusive gnat who he obviously didn't recognize. My impulse was to try to help, but to do that I'd have to put the dog down, which might lead to losing him. Besides, Keaton was doing fine without my help. There wasn't much room in the small lobby area, but it was too much for Bass to get his hands on Keaton. It was no match. Bass kept trying to cut off the space like a good clobbering puncher in the ring, but Keaton kept ducking right, left, or under his arms.

After two or three minutes, Bass was panting and damned mad and a voice behind me said, with exasperation, "Come on Buster, you can play with your friends later. We've got a crew waiting."

The man called Jules stepped into the space, towel around his neck, and watched for a few seconds before turning to me to whisper, "Big guy's not bad. Kind of scary. We could use him in the picture."

"I don't think he's got the calling," I said as Bass bellowed and took a massive plunge at Keaton, who seemed about to run into the front door, but made a sudden, impossible stop, pushed off the wall with his right foot and barely cleared

Bass's outstretched arm. Bass crashed heavily, headfirst into the wall, sagging apparently unconscious to the floor.

"Christ, Buster," Jules grunted. "If you've hurt that guy, we can't even pay the doctor bills."

"Don't worry about it," I said. "Just lock him in the cage back there and feed him once a week."

Keaton brushed himself off and moved to my side to pat the panting dog once more. He wasn't even breathing heavily.

"I'll have April get the cab for you, and we'll call the cops to take our friend away," said Keaton.

Our backs were to Bass and Jules had shouted, "Let's get back to work."

Something hit me hard and low and Keaton bounced away from a whirring arm. I spun into a corner and found my hands reaching for something to keep me from falling, which was why I knew I was no longer holding the dog.

When I did hit the wall and slumped down, I could see Bass in the doorway holding the barking dog. Keaton took a step toward him, but Bass had had enough. He opened the door and disappeared into the rain.

"I'll get him," Keaton said.

"No," I groaned. "He's my responsibility."

I did a poor imitation of a man running and followed Bass into the rain, but he was out of sight by the time I hit the street. A car, big and dark but not Lyle's Chrysler, was kicking up mud from the parking lot. I ran toward it but it made a right and shot off along the railroad tracks.

Keaton was still in the warehouse lobby when I sogged back in.

"No luck," he said.

"I'll get your fifty," I promised.

"I'd rather have the dog," he said.

Keaton went back to the set and I waited, watching the rain and trying to reach back to rub the spot over my kidney where Bass had heaved me into the cartons. The rain was doing my back no good either, but I ignored it reasonably well by wondering what Bass had been doing there, where Lyle was, and where Jeremy was.

A Red Top cab pulled up in about ten minutes—which,

considering the rain, was pretty good service. The woman driver reached back to open the back door and I made a dash for it. The rain was letting up a little as I filled the cab with water.

The cabbie wasn't a talker, which suited me just fine. I watched the rain while she drove me back to Hollywood. By the time we got to Mrs. Plaut's boarding house, the rain had stopped and I owed the cabbie a buck twenty.

"Pretty soon, there maybe ain't gonna be no cabs," she said, accepting a quarter tip. "No gas. No rubber. No parts. No cabs."

"You have a good day," I said, getting out and walking slowly to the porch.

I had been walking with my head down. My back hurt less that way, so I didn't see Jeremy sitting in the swing till I actually took the first of three wooden steps.

"I lost them," he said.

"That's all right, Jeremy," I said, making it up the last step.

"I managed to get close enough once to see that Bass wasn't in the car," he went on. "I don't know where he went. I think they spotted me following them."

"They did," I said, reaching for the front door. "Bass came back for the dog. Lyle probably figured it would be safe to hide the dog by selling it to Keaton."

"Keaton."

"Buster Keaton," I explained. "They could always steal it again when they needed it. They spotted you and decided the plan wouldn't work."

"I'm sorry, Toby," he said, getting off the porch swing.

"For what? I'll invite you to the next party I throw for Bass."

> "A shriek ran thro Eternity:
> And a paralytic stroke;
> At the birth of the human shadow.

"I think William Blake knew our friend Bass."
With that Jeremy declined my offer of a ride and I declined

his offer to help me upstairs. With hands plunged into over-sized windbreaker pockets, he went down the stairs, and I watched the muscle folds on the rear of his neck as he moved down the walk.

I was an easy target for Mrs. Plaut, a slow-moving target, but she wasn't in the house. It took me a long time to get up the stairs, but I wasn't in a hurry. It took me even longer to get into my room and get my clothes off, but I had stopped to turn on the hot water in the bathtub and I knew there was no hurry.

I soaked in the warm tub for half an hour after taking one of the pills Shelly had given me for pain resulting from a series of encounters over the years. The pills were designed for sore teeth but they did a hell of a temporary job on an aching back.

A new tenant in the boarding house, a Mr. Waltrup, knocked at the door in the middle of my bath to announce the urgent need for a toilet. I bid him enter, which he did with apologies, and we carried on a brief discussion about Mr. Waltrup's profession, tree trimming.

I learned all I wanted to know about tree trimming in the next five or six minutes.

"There really isn't much privacy here is there?" Waltrup said, buttoning himself. He was a solid young man with a nice blue eye and a false brown one that didn't match.

"Not much," I agreed, sinking back into the water and turning the hot tap on with my toes.

Shriveled and soaked, I felt much better and made my way back to my room with a towel around my waist. Mrs. Plaut's head was peeking up at the top of the stairs.

"This isn't a good time, is it Mr. Peelers?" she said.

"Not a good time at all," I said.

She turned and went back down the stairs and I entered my room, groaned my way into a pair of undershorts, managed to down a partly used bottle of Pepsi in the refrigerator, and then eased myself onto the mattress on the floor. I clutched the extra pillow and found it impossible to imagine getting up and making another run at finding the dog and Doc Olson's killer.

I didn't sleep. I just lay there for an hour watching the Beech-Nut clock and trying to put something together to tell Eleanor Roosevelt. Nothing came by three in the afternoon but a knock at the door.

I sat up in my shorts and watched Eleanor Roosevelt enter my room. She stopped for a beat, looked down at me without embarrassment, and said, "I'll give you a few moments to dress."

"I'm sorry," I said.

"I have sons and have seen a male body before," she said, with a little smile and a lot of teeth. "I'll wait in the hallway."

Struggling to my feet wasn't half as bad as knowing that I really didn't have much to get dressed in. I put on some wrinkled trousers and a pull-over shirt and looked at my room through different eyes. It wasn't much. I pushed the mattress back on the bed, threw the handmade spread over it, gathered my sopping suit, threw it in the closet, and went to the door to let her in.

"Sorry about the place," I said, stepping back. "But this is how the other two-thirds live."

She was wearing a thin, black coat and carrying a black oversized purse.

"Mr. Peters," she said. "I have seen squalor in New York that you can imagine only faintly. You live on a safe street, in a clean home. There is nothing to be ashamed of in that."

I offered her a cup of coffee, which she accepted. She sat at my little table. Me and the wife of the president of the United States. I should have had Mrs. Plaut come upstairs with her little camera and take my picture to prove it was true.

"I had the dog," I said, looking down at my coffee cup. "And I lost him."

"I'm aware of that," she said, sipping her coffee. "I had a message by phone less than an hour ago. I have been informed that I can have Franklin's dog back for fifty thousand dollars."

A knock at the door gave me a second to take in the new information. I wasn't sure what it meant.

"Come in," I said, knowing from the light rapping that it was Gunther.

Gunther, his suit gray and well pressed, entered clutching a sheet of paper, glanced at my visitor, and went pale. He said something to himself in German and Mrs. Roosevelt answered him, also in German. They went on, with Gunther regaining some of his usual composure, until I said, "Let's try it in English."

"I'm so sorry, Toby," Gunther said, without removing his eyes from Eleanor Roosevelt, who smiled and drank some more coffee. "I did not mean to interrupt."

"I'm pleased that you did drop in, Mr. . . . ?"

"Wherthman," Gunther said with a slight bow. "Gunther Wherthman. I'm—"

"Swiss," Mrs. Roosevelt finished for him. Gunther was beaming.

"Most people make the mistake of thinking me German," Gunther said. "That inaccuracy can, in these times, be an unnecessary embarrassment."

"I do not see how anyone with more than a superficial knowledge of language and culture could make such an error," she said, looking at both of us.

I nodded in complete agreement, trying to forget that I had been sure Gunther was German when I first met him.

Gunther began to say something, but it quickly turned to German and Mrs. Roosevelt answered him in his own language while I put cups away, avoided scratching my stomach, and gave Mrs. Roosevelt some more coffee. After about three or four minutes of this, Gunther was lost in conversation, but he must have caught something in my overly patient attitude and said, in English, "I'm sorry. I'll leave you to your business. It has been a great, great honor."

"The honor has been mine," said Eleanor Roosevelt.

Gunther backed out beaming, having forgotten what his original mission had been, and closed the door.

"That," she said to me, "is a gentleman."

9

"By tomorrow evening, as I told you, I must be back in Washington for a state dinner in honor of the president of Peru," Mrs. Roosevelt explained after offering to clean her own cup—an offer I declined. "It will be the first state dinner since Pearl Harbor, and it is essential that I be there. I must leave by tonight."

I accompanied her down the stairs and to the front porch, where Mrs. Plaut was standing with her 1918 Kodak Brownie box camera.

"When these first came out," she said pleasantly to Mrs. Roosevelt, "we used to send the whole box in and they'd make the picture and send the box back loaded."

"I remember," said Mrs. Roosevelt politely. "It was much easier then. I sometimes think that everything was easier then."

Mrs. Plaut smiled and took our picture, and Mrs. Roosevelt walked down the path to the dark-windowed automobile that was waiting for her at the curb.

"I shall tell my niece Chloe," Mrs. Plaut said, beaming. "Just think, Marie Dressler was in my home and I've got a picture of her. You do your best for her, Mr. Peelers. What is her problem, termites?"

"Roaches," I said, returning to my room.

Mrs. Roosevelt's message had been clear. The caller, a man, had said that she was to give me the fifty thousand dollars and I was to deliver it to the place where Henry the Eighth died precisely at eleven that night. I was to come alone or else. The problem was, simply, that Mrs. Roosevelt had no intention of paying fifty thousand dollars for the dog.

"This has gone much further than I ever anticipated," she had said during her second cup of coffee. "The political implications of this intrigue are, while not endless, certainly myriad. To pay ransom for Fala, regardless of Franklin's affection for the animal, might be ruinous. Imagine the consequences and the questions if the tale were made public. Are the interests of the United States in wartime not sufficient to occupy the time and attention of the president's wife? Is a pet more important than the tragedies taking place in the world? No, Mr. Peters, though I do not like the idea of deceiving Franklin, even if he has on occasion felt no comparable sentiment, I am quite willing to continue the charade that the dog in the White House is, indeed, his Fala."

So, my mission was clear. I was to try for another few hours to find the dog. Failing that, I was to do whatever I thought necessary to catch the dognappers. If Fala could be saved while doing it, she would be most grateful.

"The important thing," she had said, "is that they be caught. If, at this point, you wish to call in the FBI, I shall, but I must, in all honesty, tell you that once that is done, even if there is no leak of information to the press, there will be memos, comments, notes, and at some date in the future this incident will all come out. Franklin and I might be long gone, but there will be others and the Democratic Party to consider."

"There's not much chance of my getting the dog back in the next few hours," I had said. "Los Angeles is a big, dark closet with no clear walls. It's like searching for a lost cuff link in the Hollywood Bowl at midnight with a candle."

"A candle in the dark," she had said with a smile. "An appropriate metaphor, but if that is all we can do then it is better than not lighting the candle."

All right, Toby, I told myself. Think it through. I sat in my room adjusting my dad's old watch and nibbling Quaker Puffed Wheat right from the box. Who knew where the parrot had been killed? The fake Mrs. Olson who had killed him, Martin Lyle and Bass, who I had told, and anyone they had told, or anyone who had been in Olson's clinic since yesterday. But anyone who had been in the clinic wouldn't know that I had been there when the King Henry parrot lost its head.

Logic was simple. Lyle had the dog, or Bass was trying to be independent with someone's help. Lyle didn't need the money. If he was in on this, it was for some other reason.

I took a quick look at the newspaper and discovered that:

German Propaganda Minister Joseph Goebbels had begun a politeness campaign. Berliners were being asked to submit the names of the forty most polite people in Berlin. The first-prize winner would get a radio. Second prize would be theater tickets.

Another 2,370 Japanese in the Los Angeles area were being sent to the Los Angeles County Fair Grounds in Pomona for internment.

The R.A.F. had bombed Stuttgart and Le Havre.

But it was an item on the sports page that sent me running to the telephone in the hall. Carmen wasn't at Levy's Grill this early, I discovered, so I left a message with Sol, the waiter. Henry Armstrong was making a comeback, the only fighter in history to hold three crowns at the same time. Armstrong was going to do a four-round exhibition against two opponents at the Ocean Park Arena. It was a Red Cross benefit. Would Carmen be willing to go to that instead of the wrestling matches?

"You got that, Sol?"

"I got it," he said. "Listen, she don't wanna go, I will."

"I'll keep it in mind," I said and hung up.

Lyle's name wasn't listed in the phone book, but I knew the New Whig Party office on Broadway was. I called and the secretary answered.

"Mr. Lyle, please," I said, deepening my voice. "This is Colonel Strayer, Arnold Strayer. I'm General Patton's aide-de-camp. The general would like to speak to Mr. Lyle immediately."

"Colonel," she said, hyperventilating, "Mr. Lyle isn't in right now, but—"

"The general will not be reachable for some time," I said. "I'd explain why, but it does have military consequences. I'm afraid—"

"Wait," she said. "I'll give you his home phone number."

"And his address," I said quickly, "in case the general wants to contact him confidentially."

The request made little sense, but the woman was carried away with historical momentum. She gave me an address on Walden Drive in Beverly Hills just south of Sunset Boulevard, and a phone number.

"You have the general's thanks," I said and hung up.

I was headed for the address in five minutes wearing my semi-wrinkled trousers, the dark blue pull-over shirt, and a brown windbreaker with a small oil stain under the right armpit.

Beverly Hills was occupied more than a century ago by the giant Rancho Rodeo de las Aguas. In the mid-1800s the ranch was sold to two Americans named Wilson and Hancock, who already owned the adjacent Rancho La Brea. They tried to found a settlement in the late 1860s and again in the late 1880s, but it was no dice till 1906 when the Rodeo Land and Water Company laid out a subdivision between Wilshire and Santa Monica Boulevard and called it Beverly. The idea caught on and the next year Beverly Hills was laid out just northwest of it. The Beverly Hills Hotel went up in a bean field in 1912. By 1920 there were still only 674 people living in Beverly Hills, but Douglas Fairbanks, Sr., and Mary Pickford changed all that when they built Pickfair on top of one of the hills in the early 1920s. Celebrities began to pour in, trying and failing to outdo Pickfair.

John Barrymore built a mansion that he called the Chinese Tenement. When he tried to auction it off for half a million dollars, he had no takers and said, "Frankly, it was a kind of nightmare, but it might appeal to somebody, maybe some actor. Three pools. Incredible. In one of them I used to keep rainbow trout."

Before he died in 1935, Will Rogers was Beverly Hills's honorary mayor.

When the boom started in Beverly Hills in the 1920s, Rogers wrote in his column, "Lots are sold so quickly and often here that they are put through escrow made out to the twelfth owner. They couldn't possibly make a separate deed for each purchaser; besides he wouldn't have time to read it in the ten minutes' time he owned the lot. Your having no money don't worry the agents, if they can just get a couple of dollars down, or an old overcoat or shotgun, or anything to act as down payment. Second-hand Fords are considered A-1 collateral.''

I knew the town, knew the houses where Freeman Gosdon, Grantland Rice, Elsie Janis, Sigmund Romberg, and the automobile wizards E.L. Cord and C.W. Nash lived, but I didn't know Lyle's house until I pulled up to the driveway. The place was typical of the area: elaborate metal gate, eight-foot-high stone walls. Down a driveway lined with whitewashed bricks stood a sprawling adobe hacienda.

I had some choices. I could press the button next to the gate and try to talk my way in. I could climb the fence and brass it out. Each option had a drawback. Lyle would probably recognize my voice, even if his secretary hadn't. He had penetrated my Texas drawl with no problem. Climbing the fence might be possible, but my back told me it would be one hell of an effort and leave me in no shape for whatever I might find on the other side. Besides, that would be trespassing and Bass might well be in there. On the other hand, the dog might well be in there.

The hell with it. I took my .38 from the glove compartment along with the clip-on holster that went over my belt. I put them on and got out of the car to ring the bell and work my magic. If Lyle answered, I would improvise.

"Yes," came a distorted woman's voice from the speaker imbedded in the brick column to which the gate was anchored.

"Bullock's. Delivery," I croaked.

"Bullock's?" returned the woman.

"Gift," I said, straining my voice to its gravelly limits.

Something clicked in the gate and it popped open slightly.

I pushed it the rest of the way, got back in my Ford, and drove up the path, leaving the gate open in case I wanted to leave in a hurry. I drove up the driveway, turned the car around so it would be heading the right way, checked my gun, and got out. A curtain rustled in the room off the doorway, and I hurried to the door. It opened before I got there.

"Thanks," I said to the woman in the doorway.

"Thanks?" she said.

"For returning my suit," I told the woman I had known as Anne Olson. "It's drying out now. Got caught in the rain yesterday."

I wasn't sure she looked better, but she certainly looked classier in the doorway. Part of it was what she was wearing, a blue skirt and matching jacket with the high Joan Crawford shoulders. Her blouse was white and fluffy and her dark hair was pulled back.

"Can I come in?" I said.

She stepped back, holding the door open, and I entered, smelling some flowery perfume as I passed her.

The house was decorated in early Zorro, serapes on the wall, paintings of Mexican peasants. Even the furniture was rustic and covered in handmade blankets.

"How did you find me?" she said, walking ahead of me and into the open room on our right, the living room.

"Deduction, logic," I said. "Is Lyle a friend of yours, too?"

"He is my husband," she said, turning to look at me, her chin up as if to say, go ahead and hit.

"Your . . ."

"My name is Anne Lyle," she said. "The night you found me at Roy Olson's I was visiting as . . . as . . ."

"As . . ." I finished. "You and Olson were very good friends?"

She nodded in agreement, her mouth closed tightly without speaking.

"You have a lot of good friends," I said, sitting on the solid wooden arm of a sofa.

"Not too many, but a few," she said. "Roy Olson was a decent, sensitive man, not an obsessed . . . Would you like a drink?"

"A Pepsi, no ice, if you've got it," I said charmingly. "Is this story true? I mean, everytime I see you you have a new story and they're all good and all sincere. Is your husband here? I mean I'd like a little verification this time. Don't tell me. All I have to do is run up the stairs and find him. He wouldn't be in the bathtub, would he? No, you wouldn't hide him in the same place twice.''

"Pepsi," she said. "I'll see what we have. The maid is off and Martin isn't home."

"Don't surprise me," I said, following her out of the room and over the wooden floors covered with colorful throw rugs.

The kitchen was big, bright, and had a giant, heavy table of dark wood in the middle. She went to the refrigerator, found a Pepsi, and removed the cap with an opener attached to the nearby counter.

"No glass," I said, taking the bottle from her and gulping. "Won't you join me?"

"I didn't kill Roy Olson," she said. "I don't know who did. Roy was upstairs when you came. He was a decent man. His wife was the one who pushed him into meeting with Martin. When you came to the door, and assumed I was Mrs. Olson, I thought Martin had sent you, and I was admittedly a little drunk. I didn't know there was going to be a murder, that I . . .''

"And your husband killed Olson," I said, shaking the Pepsi bottle with my thumb on top.

"I don't know," she said. "Someone must have been waiting for him upstairs. Must you do that?"

I sprayed the Pepsi into my mouth.

"Sorry," I said. "I'm overdoing the you-can't-hurt-my-feelings crude act."

"I didn't trick you," she said sincerely. "Not to hurt you."

"But you tried to shoot me back in the clinic," I said, finishing the Pepsi and putting the bottle down.

"No," she sighed, her breasts rising softly. "I came to the clinic to do just what I did, to shoot that damn bird of Martin's. He loved that bird. I thought he killed Roy Olson because he was jealous, but I couldn't bring myself to shoot Martin, as much as I would have liked. Shooting Henry helped."

"The dog?" I said.

She shrugged. "That was for show. I didn't want you to think I knew what I was doing. It was just his ear. My father is an army general. I can shoot as well as you can with that gun you're hiding behind your back."

"If you can only shoot as well as I can," I said, "I was lucky to get out of that clinic with my ears. Who did you tell about shooting the bird?"

"No one, but Martin knew. He was almost in tears. Only that bird and the mention of Daniel Webster or Henry Clay can do that."

"Or General Patton," I added. "I told Martin about the bird."

"Thanks," she said with a small, pained smile. "I wasn't pretending with you in Roy's office."

"You didn't seem to be," I agreed. "But I've been fooled before. Hell, I've been fooled almost every time before."

"I'd like to prove it," she said, taking a step toward me, her hand out.

I didn't step back, and I didn't pull away. She took my left hand and kissed the palm.

"Where is Lyle?" I said.

It was a difficult moment. Her face was moving close to mine. I could smell her and I knew a Pepsi burp was on the way to spoil the mood. I beat the bad joke by pulling away and walking across the room.

"Not now," I said. "Maybe not ever, but not now. I've got to find your husband and I've got to find the dog. Is there a dog here?"

"Martin doesn't like dogs," she said, opening a cabinet and finding a bottle that looked like bourbon. "Dogs eat birds."

"So do people," I added.

She poured herself an unhealthy drink and shrugged.

"Martin isn't overly fond of people either."

"Where might he keep a dog?" I tried again.

She downed the glass of amber liquid, rubbed the glass against her cheek, and said, "Who knows? If he's in this with Bass, Bass probably has it."

"Then," I said, "I better have a talk with Bass."

"He's a scintillating conversationalist," she said, refilling her glass. "Another Pepsi for the road?"

I said no thanks and headed for the front door. She followed, drink in hand, opened the door for me and, holding my arm, rubbed her cheek against mine.

"You could use a shave," she said. "Martin has a collection of razors."

"Another time," I said, almost giving in.

"Another time," she repeated in a way that made it clear that she didn't expect there to be another time.

"I'll be seeing you, Anne," I said, going to my car. I seemed to spend a lot of time saying good-bye to people named Anne.

I didn't look back. The sky was cloudy but I didn't think it would rain. I stopped at the front gate, pulled out my notebook, and checked the address that Academy Dolmitz had given me for Bass. When I got there, however, Bass wasn't around. In fact, unless Bass lived in Manuel Ortiz's Shoes-Repaired-While-U-Wait shop, Bass wouldn't be around.

Dolmitz was in when I got to the shop. There were a few book-buying customers out front.

"Peters," he greeted me sourly. "No threats this a.m., okay? I talked to my lawyer. So, you turn around and march out." He demonstrated "march out" with two fingers of his right hand on top of the counter.

One of the customers, a young shy guy with glasses, tried not to look at us over the old book in his hand.

"Bass wasn't at the address you gave me," I said. "No one but a shoe repair guy was there."

"It's the address I got for him," Dolmitz said. "What can I tell you? You think Bass is such a brain he can't get his own address screwed up? Who knows where he is?"

"You couldn't give me another address," I said, smiling and walking over to the counter.

"I could give you a lot of them," he said. "2225 West Washington. That is the Arlington Bowling Center. Or—"

I eased my .38 out from behind my back and placed it on

the counter as gently and discreetly as possible. The young guy with glasses saw the gun, put his book down, and tried to walk to the door as if he were in no hurry.

"Threats?" said Dolmitz. "I get threats from you? You know what I can have done to you, to what remains of a face on you? Threats? I've got in the back room a zlob who'll tear your heart out for a sawski."

"This is big," I whispered to Dolmitz, leaning over the counter.

"Touch me and you are carry-out chop suey," he said, backing away against the wall behind the counter.

"I'm feeling crazy, Academy," I said. "I'll even take on a big political influence like you."

"Try the Gaucho Arms on Delospre," he said, "you crazy bastard you."

I put the gun away and smiled.

"Thanks," I said. "The best song, 1936?"

"The hell with you," Dolmitz said, resuming his seat but still sulking. But I could see it was too much for him to resist. "You mean original song written for the movie?"

"What else is there?"

"Nothing," he agreed. "In 1936 we're talking 'The Way You Look Tonight' from *Swing Time*. Kern and Fields. I got one for you. The last assistant director to win."

"I don't give a shit, Dolmitz," I said, sweetly turning to the door. "And if you've given me more crap about Bass, I'll come back and beat you to death with an Oscar."

"Ha," he shouted, "shows what you know. Robert Webb was best assistant director in '37 before they ended the category. Shows what you know."

Dolmitz hadn't lied about Bass's address. According to the man with the flannel shirt and suspenders who served as manager of the Gaucho Arms, Bass did have an apartment there.

"We ain't what you'd call amigos," said the manager, a tub-gutted type in his sixties with a pipe clenched in his teeth. "Less I see of him, the better."

"You wouldn't know if he has a dog in his apartment or

had had one there recently?'' I said, showing a five-dollar bill.

"You're overpaying, son," he said, taking the five and putting it in the shirt pocket next to his suspender strap. "I'd know. Walls are thin here and I keep an eye out. No dog in his place. Not much of anything. Truth to tell, I'd send him packing if I had an excuse and the nerve. 'Fraid I'm just a dandelion."

He chuckled, the pipe still clenched in his yellow teeth. "Got that from the cowardly lion in the Wizard of Oz," he explained. "Bert Lahr fella is a laugh."

"Bass have visitors?" I said.

"Okay, you paid for a lot of answers," he said, still chuckling. We were standing on the narrow lawn in front of the Gaucho Arms and he was holding a hose in his hand. He had been about to turn it on when I had come up to him. "Not a social type," the manager said.

"Mind if I look around his room?" I said, showing another five-dollar bill.

The manager rubbed his right palm against his faded pants, looked at the five, sucked in some air between his stained teeth, and said, "No, couldn't do it. Cash would be nice. Got a granddaughter visiting and I'd like to take her down to Pebble Beach for the glass-bottom-boat trip. Heard lots about it, but much as I got bad feelings about Mr. Bass, I don't violate his home."

"Take the five anyway," I said, holding it out. "I'm on an expense account."

"That don't give you the right to throw someone else's money away or me the right to take it," he said. "I'm not trying to offend you none, son, but that's the way it is."

I pocketed the added five and shook the manager's hand.

"I'll find another way," I said. "Thanks for the information."

He went back to watering the Gaucho Arms lawn and I found a place on Santa Monica Boulevard for a couple of grilled cheese sandwiches and an order of fries. It made my back feel better and I was starting to prepare myself for the showdown with Bass or whoever was going to show up at Olson's clinic with Fala.

Carmen was just coming on at Levy's when I called. She had the message from Sol.

"You said wrestling," she said blandly.

"We can wrestle after the fight," I answered. "Henry Armstrong, we can see Henry Armstrong, right there in the ring."

"The Mad Russian of Minsk is wrestling," she countered.

"The Mad Russian of Minsk is an ex-pug named Madigan," I explained. "He takes off the beard and he's Irish Joe Flannagan. He puts on a wig and he's The Wild Kentucky Hillbilly."

"All right," she said, not fully convinced. "Sol says Armstrong's fighting two guys."

"Two guys. One at a time," I said. "I'll pick you up at seven."

"Regular food this time," she said before I could hang up.

"All food is regular," I reasoned.

"Manny's tacos is not date food," she said.

"Regular food," I agreed.

I hung up and drove back to the Farraday.

I was halfway up to the first floor when Jeremy appeared from two floors above and called to me. His voice echoed, and I looked up to see him.

"Toby," he said evenly. "She is gone."

"Gone? Who?" I answered, but I knew it wasn't Alice.

"Jane," he answered. "Alice left her to go out for groceries at the apartment and when she came back, Jane was gone."

"Bass," I said.

"We must find him," Jeremy said softly, but the Farraday echo picked it up and sent his determined words echoing out of dark corners.

"Not so easy," I called back. "I just tried, but I think I know where he'll be tonight."

"And where will that be?" a voice said behind me.

I almost slipped on the marble steps as I turned to face Cawelti.

"What?" I asked.

"Jane Poslik," he spat. "You've had her someplace and now you've lost her. You think you've got troubles, dirty pants. Let's tag on obstructing justice, suspicion of kidnapping."

"John," I said, almost putting a hand on his shoulder. "Save that for the next Laurel and Hardy short you're in or for old ladies who heist shopping bags from Ralph's."

"Toby," Jeremy called down, seeing the exchange, but not hearing it. "Do you need some help?"

Cawelti looked up at Jeremy and something like worry touched his mouth. He had survived one run-in with Jeremy a few months earlier, and didn't want another, but I had to give him credit, he covered his fear and looked back at me.

"Let's talk down at the station," he said.

"I'll meet you there," I said, taking another step up.

"You'll come down and get in your car and drive and I'll be right up your ass all the way," he said.

"Well," I said, turning with a big fake smile, "if you put it like that, you old smoothie, how can a guy resist."

On the eastern end of Hancock Park, which we drove past on the way to the Wilshire Station, are the La Brea tar pits, ugly black bogs where oil and tar bubble up from underground pools. When it rains, a thin layer of water covers the gunk, setting up a trap for the dolts who climb the stone wall out of curiosity. At least the dinosaurs who got oozed in were looking for something to drink, not a cheap thrill. Usually, the screaming tourist is saved by a nearby cop, but once in a while a hotshot meets the same fate as the saber-toothed tigers and ground sloths. When I was a kid I was told that the bones of flesh-eaters were sometimes found nearly touching those of the smaller victims they had leaped into the pits to eat, only to find themselves as trapped as their prey. Los Angeles hadn't changed much in a few million years.

Cawelti gave me an impatient horn blast when I drove slowly past the station entrance. He wanted me to park on the curb, but I had picked up enough parking tickets in front of the station to know his game. If he wanted me that badly, he'd have to jump into the pit. I parked around the corner, and he pulled in behind me. I slowly locked my car, turned to look at him, stretched, and held out my right hand to indicate that he should lead the way. He decided to let me go a step ahead.

"Fireman," I said, holding the front door open for him to step in and for an overweight cop in uniform to step out, "did you ever take an hour off and look at the tar pits?"

His pock-marked face reddened and his eyes went narrow. He wasn't about to set himself up for an insult.

"Shut your mouth and get up the stairs," he said.

I obeyed, giving a nod to the old cop at the desk, who recognized me and nodded back without taking his attention from the pretty young Mexican woman holding the hand of a boy of about two and going nonstop in Spanish.

"When you maracas dry out," the desk sergeant shouted over her attack, "we'll try it in something like English, *comprende?*"

On the second floor, I automatically turned right to the squadroom door, but Cawelti's hand came down hard on my shoulder.

"Captain's office," he said, helping me in the right direction with more enthusiasm than was needed.

There was no name written on Phil's door now, which was a step in the right direction. Cawelti knocked, his eyes fixed on my face.

"Come in," Phil shouted, and in we came.

Phil was on the phone at his desk. He glanced up at us, gave a sour look to the desk, ran his free hand through his steely short hair, and went on with his conversation. Standing in the corner looking even more cadaverous than usual was Sergeant or Lieutenant Steve Seidman.

"How's the mouth?" I asked Seidman.

"You think I'm a violent cop, Toby?" he mumbled, the right side of his mouth rigid. I could barely understand him.

"No, Steve," I said. It was the truth.

"Then," said Seidman, saying the words carefully and not hiding a wince of pain, "you can believe me if I tell you that if I ever run into that mouth butcher again, I'm going to pull out two of his teeth with rusty pliers, the same ones he used on me if I can find them."

Cawelti bounced slightly, a near grin on his face. Seidman looked at him evenly.

"Something funny, John?" he said.

"Nothing," said Cawelti, still smiling. "I was just thinking about something a guy said on the radio."

"Get out of here," Seidman mumbled.

"Sorry, Lieutenant," Cawelti taunted. "I didn't understand you."

"Get . . . out . . . of . . . here," Seidman said slowly.

"I got you that time, Lieutenant," Cawelti said. He turned and left, closing the door behind him.

"He's got a great future," I said.

"Cawelti doesn't want a future," Seidman said, touching his cheek gingerly and gritting his teeth to keep from whimpering. "He just wants to make other people's presents miserable."

Behind me, Phil's voice droned on and Steve motioned to me to take the seat across from my brother. I took it and Seidman leaned back in the corner, his dark jacket open.

"Yes, Mr. Maltin," Phil said, still looking down at the desk. "We will. I'll see to it. You're right. It shouldn't have happened and it won't again. You have my word. I'll have a patrol there every night till we catch whoever's doing it. Pevsner. My name's Pevsner, not Posner. That's quite all right. Good-bye, Mr. Maltin."

He hung up the black phone and looked up in a black mood.

"Responsibilities of a promotion," I said solemnly. "Keep the public happy."

"We got a rape-murder," he said, folding his hands on the desk, "a strong-arm pair breaking into homes, missing kids, assaults, and I've got to talk to a shoe-store owner on Figueroa who complains about kids running off with his sale signs. While I have a patrolman checking out the local seven year olds, someone could be at the storekeeper's house eating his wife for lunch.''

"Well put," I said. Hell, he could have suggested that we surrender to the Japanese and I would have told him it was a good idea. He had just been handed a glob of frustration and he needed someone to throw it on. Having been the garbage can for Phil in the past, I wanted to keep it from coming, but I had a lot to hold out against: Phil's temper and my own tongue.

"Where is she?" Phil said, looking at me calmly.

"Phil," I said, "no wisecrack intended, but who are we talking about?"

"Jane Poslik," he said, quite calmly, unclasping his hands.

"How should I know?" I said, with an innocent smile, looking over my shoulder to Seidman for sympathy, which Steve was not ready to deliver.

Phil found a pencil, considered breaking it in half, decided not to, put it down, and then stood up slowly. I wished he had broken the pencil.

"You were in the house when Olson was sponged," he said. "And you say some woman who called herself Mrs. Olson was there with you. Now she's missing. You wouldn't know where she is, would you?"

"No, Phil," I said. "I swear to you . . ."

"And then you go to see this Jane Poslik who used to work for Olson," he went on. "A few hours later she disappears. Cawelti tells me you have her hidden some place."

"And Cawelti is an honorable man," I said.

"I want to know where people are and who killed the Olsons," Phil said, coming around the desk. His tie was open and he gave it an extra tug to get it all the way off. "And who shot the head off a goddamn parrot and did a goddamn Van Gogh on a German shepherd."

I looked up at him and shook my head.

"If I knew, I'd tell you. I would. But I'm pledged to secrecy. You'll just have to go to Eleanor Roosevelt."

"And you," he said, reaching down to put a hand on my jacket, "will be on a tour of hell by the time I'm through with you."

Something possessed me. It had been in me for a lifetime. Maybe a lot of things brought it out. Phil's promotion, his fiftieth birthday, my realization that I had finally lost the real Anne, the one I'd been married to and always expected to get back, my chronically sore back that would some day give up, the memory of Lucy on Sunday crawling into my lap. I pushed Phil's hand away and stood up fast, kicking the chair back.

"Enough," I said. "I've had a lifetime of you mashing my face and using me for a whoopie cushion. You hit me and so help me the second you turn your back I'll bring the closest chair down on your head so hard you'll wind up downstairs picking splinters out of your desk sergeant."

"You don't talk to me like that, you, you wasted, useless—" he started.

Seidman finally came out of the corner and mumbled, "Okay, Phil. Enough."

We both pushed Seidman our of the way and stood eye to eye.

"You know why you do that, huh? You know why you've been beating on me for forty years?" I said.

"Because you're a wise-ass, worthless bum," he shouted. "A bum who wasted his damned life, lost his wife, never had any kids, doesn't have a dime, and acts like a dumb kid even though he's pushing fifty. You know what it looks like, for—"

"Face it, Phil," I shouted back. "I'm going to say the dirty word. You love me, but you dumb lard-fist, the only way you can show it is by trying to kill me because you don't like what you feel for me. But I know it's there because I feel the same thing. You use your fists and feet and I use words. Which hurts worse, brother? So for a change why don't you just put your fists down and talk to me like people? When did you ever get anything out of me by kicking my ass? Don't you know by now I come back like a well-watered victory garden when I get corked? It runs in the damn family."

I'm a very persuasive person when I put my mind to it. Someone once told me that, but I don't remember who. Unfortunately, Phil had never heard it.

My brother's right hand grabbed my jacket and tugged me forward, tearing my zipper. His left hand shot forward, a short jab, his specialty, that caught me in the ribs. My lungs answered with a taco air. I slumped back trying to tighten up for the next shot, but it didn't come. Seidman was between us, whispering, "Phil. Phil, come on."

It was, apparently, a persuasive argument. Phil let go of my jacket and the metal end of the zipper tinkled across the floor. I sat back in the chair and Phil went back to his own chair. Seidman stood guarding the space between us.

We sat like that for about a minute or two with me panting softly and wondering if my rib was broken. Phil's chest rose and fell more than usual. His brows were down and he found the pencil to play with again. He turned it over and over again.

"Feel better?" I finally said.

"Yeah," said Phil.

"Good," I said, touching the tender flesh over the raw rib. "Shall we go on?"

Phil smiled. It was a genuine smile. He tried to hide it behind an open palm over his mouth, but he couldn't. His hand came down and he shook his head, smiling.

"I knew I could cheer you up," I said seriously. "What's a brother for?"

Seidman kicked the desk, which apparently sent a shiver of pain into his jaw. He let out a little grunt and walked back to the corner saying, "You're both nuts, crazy nuts. I'm not getting between you again. You both remember that. I wash my hands of you."

"Olson," Phil said, small smile still on his lips.

"I've got a real lead," I said. "Sure thing, tonight. You said I had till tomorrow night. Let's stay with that. I'll give you Olson's killer, tell you where Jane Poslik is, and maybe where to find the fake Mrs. Olson."

"Get out," Phil said, waving his hand. "I've got shoe stores to protect. Are you hurt?"

"Hell yes," I said.

"Good," he answered, still smiling. "I wouldn't want you to think I'm getting old and soft."

Cawelti was in the hall, arms folded, leaning against the dirty wall. He shook his head and said quietly with false sympathy, "Can you use some help getting down the stairs?"

"Only if we can go piggy-back and I can put the spurs to you if you go too slow," I said, walking away from him as normally as I could. It took me about a week to get out of the station, a week during which my entire life crawled before my eyes like a too-long French novel. The Mexican woman and her kid were gone and the old desk cop was on the phone, looking over his glasses at an advancing couple in their sixties. The man was cradling a big brown paper bag in his arms. I didn't want to know what was in that bag so I hurried out into the late afternoon, but before the door closed I heard the old woman's voice say, "I insist that we see Captain Pevsner immediately."

Getting into my Ford was lots of fun. It kept me from thinking. Driving to Doc Hodgdon's house was even more fun. Even Harriet Hilliard singing "This Love of Mine" on the radio didn't diminish the joy I was feeling. By the time I pulled in front of the frame house where Hodgdon lived, I was so tickled that I could barely move, but I managed to get out, groan my way up the walk and stairs and into the house, the first floor of which had been converted by Doc Hodgdon to offices for his orthopedic practice back in 1919 before anyone used the word orthopedic.

Hodgdon's secretary-receptionist, Myra, who had miraculously escaped the tar pits in the Pleistocene Period, gave me a sour look. No one was in the waiting room and she looked like she was packing her broomstick to go home.

"Doctor's office hours are over at four on Monday," she said.

"I'm dying," I said. "He took an oath."

"Doctor will be available in the morning," she said. "I can give you an emergency appointment at noon."

I put my hand on a nearby chair to steady myself.

"By noon tomorrow, I will have died of wounds," I continued, not wanting to end our pleasant repartee. "Maybe he has time to give me a Vitalis sixty-second workout."

"Mocking the war is not in good taste," she said. "You will just have to—"

"What is all the noise about?" said Hodgdon, sticking his head out of his office door. His sleeves were rolled up and he held something that looked like a roll of tape in his hand. He was gray, almost sixty-six, and hard as a tree stump. He was also the man I had never beaten at handball. He spotted me and shook his head. Everyone seemed to be shaking their heads at me this week, a pitiful specimen who should have been pickled and put on exhibition with a little sign underneath saying, "Here but for the grace of God, go you."

"Come in, come in," he said, holding the door open to his office. Then to his secretary-receptionist, "And you go home, Myra."

"Office hours are over," she said, giving me a dirty look as I eased my way across the room and into his office.

"Mr. Peters is not a patient," he said, making way for me. "He is a curio, a specimen, a phenomenon always worth another look."

With that he closed the door and helped me to his examining table.

"The back," he said.

"Ribs too," I added.

He helped me get my shirt off, touched the back, and felt the ribs. None of it made me grin.

"Nothing's broken this time," he said. "Now I'm going to tape you up and give you something for the pain."

"I've got something good," I said.

"What I give you will be less likely to destroy your organs," he said, selecting the proper tape. "Then, when I finish taping, I'm going to tell you to go home, get in bed, do nothing for three or four days, and come back to see me. Knowing you, you will neither go to bed nor come back and see me unless the pain becomes unbearable or you have some other task you feel has to be performed."

"I'm trying to save the president's dog," I explained as he plastered a thick slab of tape around my chest.

"Noble," he muttered, working away and clearly not believing me. "If you'd take better care of yourself, we'd be playing more handball. Someday my bones are not going to be able to support my musculature. I'll start the process of rapid aging, brittleness. Might even have further eye trouble. Then you might stand a chance of winning a game if you're still capable of normal speech and movement. It is, by the way, difficult though not impossible to apply this tape around a pistol."

I apologized and took off the gun, and he went on working.

"There," he said, standing back to examine me and rolling up his sleeves.

"Thanks," I said, putting my shirt back on. The soreness was there, but it wasn't bad and I knew I could move. Hodgdon went to his glass cabinet, opened it, found a bottle and took some pills from it and put them into a smaller bottle, which he handed to me.

"Take one now and then every four hours," he said. "Since you are not going to go home, but will be out looking for stray dogs, how'd you like to share dinner with me? I've got a leftover meatloaf and a bottle of Burgundy."

"Any beer?" I said.

"There is beer," he said.

We ate a meatloaf dinner with a sliced tomato and a lot of Italian bread washed down by a couple of cans of Falstaff. I found out for the first time that Hodgdon had a son who was a doctor back in Indianapolis and a daughter who had married an insurance salesman in Chicago. I already knew that Hodgdon's wife had died almost ten years earlier.

"Toby," he said after dinner, "no joke this time. Your body can't hold up under all the abuse you give it."

"Doc," I said, "I've tried to stop, but there's a not too bright rabbit inside me who won't stay still."

"And he can wind up getting you crippled, or worse; let him out," said Hodgdon, starting to pile the nonmatching china dishes in the sink. The kitchen, like the house and the man, was getting old.

"Time to go," I said. "Thanks for dinner. Have Edna Mae Oliver send me the bill."

The sun was down by the time I left Doc Hodgdon's house. We had talked longer than I had planned, but the tape, food, pills, and beer had taken away the pain, at least enough for me to get back in the Ford and head for Olson's clinic.

I got there three hours early, parked two blocks away, and went in through the same window I'd gone in before. Then I made a phone call and settled down, not in the animal room, but in Olson's operating room, the one where Anne Lyle and I had operated two days earlier.

After checking my .38, I sat down on the single straight-back chair, listened to the animals sending out bleats, barks, shrieks, and murmurs of fear, and wondered who had been taking care of them.

10

When I turned off the water after taking the second pill Doc Hodgdon had given me, I heard the metal sound. It was, I was sure, a key in a door. After some fumbling, the door, probably the front door of the clinic, opened. I was tempted to walk to the window to look at my watch to see what time it was, but my watch wouldn't really be of much help. There was a clock on Olson's desk. I turned it to the window to catch the faint night light of a clouded moon.

Footsteps were coming down the hall, heavy and slow. I gave the clock a pull to bring it closer to the window and it popped out of the wall socket. The cord scurried across the floor like an electric snake. It was ten o'clock. The dognapper had decided to come an hour early, which was probably why he or she was not particularly concerned about making noise. I, on the other hand, was definitely concerned. I stood holding the stopped clock, and the footsteps stopped too.

The animals had begun rumbling when the dognapper opened the door, and that was probably enough to cover the sound of the dangling cord. Maybe he or she had stopped for something else. Then the footsteps began again and went past the door of the room I was standing in.

The early arrival created a problem. I could wait till the right time and walk in. The surprise might then be on me. The logical thing for him to do, if I had the money, would be to blow my head off, blow the dog's head off, take the money and walk. Logic, as I have learned through painful experience, does not always govern our actions. I've known people the size of gorillas who took a slap in the face and let it pass because the slapper looked like their second-grade arithmetic teacher. I did, however, have two things that might overcome logic. First, I had the possibility of surprise if I moved soon. Second, I had a .38 automatic.

I gave the visitor about three or four minutes to get settled in the animal room and for the disturbed menagerie to get their emotions down to a rolling, frightened, and angry purr. Then I moved to the door. The tension in my chest was making it hard to breathe. It was about one-third fear, one-third excitement, and one-third pain from Hodgdon's tape. The door didn't creak much when I opened it very, very slowly.

There was no light in the hall except for that of the dim moon through the partially opened door through which I stepped. I closed the door so that I wouldn't make a tempting target and then began to inch my way along the wall toward the rear of the clinic. I tried not to, but couldn't help imagining my outstretched fingers touching flesh. That didn't stop me from moving. If anything, the fear of contact made me move more quickly.

When I reached the end of the hallway, I put out a hand, seeking the door. It was closed. Since I wanted some shot at surprise, I took my time finding the knob and then took as long to position myself in front of the door for a quick turn of the knob, flick of the switch, and confrontation with the surprised dognapper. The light switch, if I remembered correctly, was just to the left of the door. I dried my hands on my jacket, took out my .38, grabbed the knob, took a breath, and turned.

There was good news and bad news. The good news was that I got the door open in a single turn and push, and that my hand hit the switch, filling the room with light. My gun was out, level, and pointed into the room. The bad news was that the dognapper wasn't standing in the middle of the room or in a far corner. He was to my right and by the time I saw him, the animals were going nuts and I had cracked my hand against the nearest cage. My gun fell to the floor and I yelled something. My yell, the lights, and the clatter of the gun were enough to throw him off. He let out a return yell and almost dropped the dog in his arm.

It was a dead heat. He came out with his gun at the same moment I recovered mine from the floor. The trouble was, I was sitting there looking up with the one-eared shepherd doing his damnedest to get at me through the bars of his cage. From the corner of my eye I could see that someone had neatly bandaged the dog's ear stump.

"Don't shoot," I shouted, leveling my gun at Bass.

"Don't you shoot," he said, trying to get a firmer grip on the black furry bundle under his left arm. Somewhere in the corner a dog began to howl like a coyote in a Republic Western.

"I'm not shooting," I assured him, getting to my knees.

"I'm not shooting," Bass said, taking a step forward.

"And you're not coming any closer, either," I said.

"I'm not coming any closer," he said. "You got the money?"

"How do I know that's the right dog?" I said, avoiding the question.

"It's the right dog," Bass said, glancing down at the dog in case someone had switched dogs on him in the last few seconds. "You can believe me."

"Thanks," I said, getting up without touching any of the nearby cages, which might have given me stability but resulted in the loss of a finger or three.

"The money," he repeated.

"The dog first," I said.

The howling dog in the corner paused. The shepherd showed his teeth and an orange cat in a cage behind Bass circled and circled and circled. The little black dog under Bass's arm looked at me with his mouth open.

"He said I had to see the money first," Bass said, holding the gun up about level with my neck.

"He?" I said.

"The money," he shouted. "I'm getting mad here."

"Bass," I said. "Someone has set you up. You're the one who can be identified, the one who has the dog. He's likely to deflate your head and walk away free with the bundle."

"He wouldn't do that," Bass said, tossing his head to clear the blond strands of hair dangling across his eyes. "Look, I don't want to hold this dog any more. I'm afraid he'll want to poopie or something."

"Poopie?" I said. "Figures. You'd be holding the dog and the crap."

"The money," he said again, shifting the dog higher under his arm.

"I didn't bring it," I said, holding my .38 level and hoping he didn't start shooting. I should have leveled the gun at his head and fired. It was a risk. I was about ten feet from him and might have hit the dog or the wall or just about anything. The pistol is not my best weapon. I'm not sure what my best weapon is, probably the ability to tire out an arm-weary opponent. "I've got it out in my car and I don't tell you where my car is until I have the dog. You might just take the money and shoot me."

"I wouldn't do that," Bass said, a tiny trickle of sweat dribbling down his smooth forehead. "I want to get you in my hands. You know the Australian clutch? I tore Butch Feifer's right arm almost off with it in '37. That's what I want to do to you. You made me look dumb with that guy in the warehouse."

"That was Buster Keaton, and he made you look like a cross-eyed nun. We can't stand here all night. One of us will get cramps and start shooting and you can't keep holding that dog."

"I could hold the dog all night," he said with pride. "I

could hold the dog and the gun and never blink my eyes, not once. I could stand here till you get tired and blink, and then I could get you.''

"Well, pal," I said. "I'd like to keep this conversation going for a while. I really would. It's not often I get a chance to talk to someone like you or Clifton Fadiman, but that's not going to get things taken care of. Can I make a suggestion?''

"No," he said. I thought I could sense or see his finger tightening on the trigger.

"You win," I said. "I'll tell you where the car is. We can go together, down the street, guns on each other, dog under your arm, and make some excuse to the crowds who gather on Sherman Way to watch us.''

"I'm not good at excuses," Bass said reasonably. "I'm not good at anything but hurting.''

"And that's something to be proud of," I said, watching more beads of sweat come down his brow. "And stop inching forward or I'll shoot a hole through your shoes.''

He stopped but I could see that his attention span was not long, and rather than struggle to keep up the conversation, he would probably start shooting even if it meant the death of both of us.

"You got a family, Elmo?" I said, shifting the .38 to my left hand.

The question puzzled him. "Family?" he asked, glancing down at the dog in his arm as if it could answer this tough one.

"You know, father, mother, sisters, brothers, aunts, uncles, cousins, things like that?" As I asked the question I pretended to take a deep breath and moved my right leg a step toward the door.

"Everybody has a mother," he said suspiciously. "You don't get born without a mother. You making fun of my mother too?''

"I'm not making fun," I said, calculating my chances of getting back to the hall. The howling dog behind me was going wild. "I'm trying to get to know you. Your mother ever see you wrestle?''

"My mother's a Methodist," he said threateningly.

"Fine with me," I said. The gun had dropped a fraction and was aimed at the right side of my chest and not the middle. "And your father?"

"My father's . . ." he began, but I never found out what his father was because I went out the door.

Bass was fine on his feet but he left a hell of a lot to be desired with a pistol. By the time he got off a shot I was in the dark hall. The animals behind me were going mad, and as I turned to aim at the door in case he followed me, I lost my .38 again. I had been fascinated by the sweat on Bass's brow as he looked down at my pistol. But I hadn't noticed my own body fluids. The gun had flown out of my sweating hand as I went through the door.

Light from the animal room cut far down the hall. I scrambled for Olson's office. I'd go for the window, hide in the dark, and fight another day. I could hear Bass coming for me when I found the right door and pushed through. A bullet crackled into the hall behind me, and I stumbled forward for the window. My hand hit something on the desk, and I tripped forward to the sound of classical music filling the room. I almost made it to the window, would have, too, if I hadn't hit my leg on the corner of the one chair in the room. Pain from my sore rib shot through me as the light came on.

"No," Bass shouted.

I stopped and turned around slowly.

"I'll get the money," I said over the sound of a happy flute and violin.

"I don't believe it," Bass said, advancing on me, the confused black Scottie still under his arm. "I don't believe someone who laughs at a person's mother."

"I never . . ." I began, my back against the window, but he wasn't listening. He put the black dog down. Then he put his gun away and took a step toward me.

"You do something to me, and you'll never get the money," I warned, one hand out to stop him.

"I never wanted the money," he said. The violins went mad behind us and the little black dog decided to leap into my arms instead of running for cover. I caught him and considered throwing him at the advancing Bass, whose gray eyes danced with joy at the prospect of hurting.

"I'm going to do you," he said.

The dog licked my face. I dropped him gently to the ground, turned slowly to Bass and said, "You're giving . . ."

The idea was reasonably good. I'd used it before, in fact a few seconds earlier in the animal room. It worked this time too. Bass never knew the punch was coming. It was perfect; a hard, short right to the solar plexus followed by a left to the side of his head. I can't say the punches had no effect on Bass—after all he was almost human—but the effect registered very low on his Richter scale. My left hand hurt like hell.

"Okay," I said, breathing heavily as his hand found my neck. "Now you know I mean business."

"I'm going to turn your head around," he said happily. "I can do it. I did it once."

"I believe you," I said, preparing my last move, a knee to the groin, which I was afraid would either have no effect or be stopped by the former pro. I never had the chance to find out.

"Bass," came a gentle voice over his shoulder.

Bass turned to the door and found Jeremy Butler looking comfortingly massive in black pants and a black long-sleeved turtle-neck sweater. Before I left for the clinic, I had called Jeremy for backup. He was right on time.

No one can move as fast as Bass then did, certainly no one his size and bulk, but Jeremy had told me he was fast. I had seen Keaton play with him, but this was a small room and there was no place to hide. Jeremy was ready for him, but the rush sent the two of them thundering out of the room into the hallway. The building shook and I jumped forward, going for the gun Bass had dropped. I couldn't find it, but I was on my hands and knees accompanied by the violin and flute as I looked and heard the two men in the hall bang off the walls.

I found the gun under the desk along with the dog. I gave the dog a pat on the head, took the gun, and scrambled, breathing hard, into the hall. They weren't there, but I could see where they had taken their battle. I picked up my own .38 in the hall and, a gun in each hand, went into the room full of cages.

By the time I got there, they had crushed two cages, releasing one cat that came flying past me, and they had done serious damage to the front of the cage with the one-eared shepherd.

Jeremy and Bass were grunting, hands clasped and held high like two grotesque ballet dancers.

"Stop right there," I said, holding out my guns like Bill Hart in *Hell's Hinges*. When Bill Hart did it, the whole town full of bad guys put up their hands and backed away. Bass and Jeremy paid no attention.

"I've got the guns," I said as they disappeared behind a row of cages. "Are you two listening to me? I've got the guns and they shoot bullets that make holes in people and things."

To prove my point I fired Bass's pistol, a .45, into the ceiling. It recoiled in my hand. I didn't want to get my .38 dirty. I hated to clean the damn thing. My shooting had no effect on the two lumbering figures, who came crashing around the cages and would have rolled over me if I hadn't jumped out of the way. The one-eared dog went crazy and threw himself against the door. The door cracked open and the dog, surprised, came out awkwardly. He was full of anger, but the dog never thought he'd have his bluff called. Now he had to decide who to bite. He looked at me and I aimed the .38 his way.

"I don't know if you know what this is, Vincent," I said, "but one of them blew your ear off. One more step and you're going to have to learn sign language."

Sure, I knew he couldn't understand the words, but I hoped the heartfelt sympathy would make an impression. It didn't. He snarled once and, white-bandaged ear flashing, leaped out of the door and into the hall.

I went for the hall and saw him attached to Bass's arm. From where I stood, Jeremy needed the help. Bass had managed to get behind him and was trying to do something to

Jeremy's right arm, probably the Australian double clutch. Jeremy was straining to keep his arm from bending.

The dog's teeth went deep into Bass's arm, but Bass didn't seem to notice. Bass didn't let go of Jeremy or let out a yell. His teeth were clenched as he brought his head down hard so his skull cracked into that of the dog. The dog let go, fell on his behind, and began to yelp in pain. He scooted past me, back to his cage, and huddled in the corner.

The attack had given Jeremy enough help to break away from Bass. He turned, reached down between his legs, and pulled Bass's right leg forward. Bass hit the floor hard enough to send shock waves to Tarzana.

Bass's arm was bleeding, but the look on his face indicated a frantic joy as he scrambled up. He was panting like the animals behind me as he got a fresh grip on Jeremy's head and tried to bring his skull against Jeremy's as he had done with the dog, but Jeremy pulled away, hit the wall with his shoulder, and threw his full weight into the bleeding Bass, who fell backward.

Something broke—I heard it snap like a loud Rice Krispy. The snap came just as the flute recording ended. Jeremy got to his knees. Both of the massive figures were breathing hard, but no harder than I was.

"My arm is broken," Bass observed without surprise or apparent pain.

"You kill women," Jeremy said, getting up. "You kill people, animals." He helped Bass up and went past me into the examining room.

"Who set this up?" I said, waving my guns around to no effect. "Where is Jane Poslik?"

Bass looked at me blankly as Jeremy tried to stop the bleeding from the dog bite.

"I don't talk," Bass said, looking at me calmly.

"I can get you to a hospital or I can reset it," Jeremy said to Bass.

"Reset it," he said.

Jeremy did and Bass looked at me without expression through what must have been a hell of a lot of pain.

As he fixed the splint, Jeremy repeated my question.

"Where is Jane Poslik?"

Bass's eyes were closed. I assumed he was being stubborn, but Jeremy stood up and announced that he had passed out from the pain.

"You can hide it, mask it, but stopping the pain is something few can do. It creeps in, won't go away. There are Yoga techniques, but Bass never had the intellect or the spirit for such things. He is a monster, Toby, but he is a monster with pride. You will not get your answer from him."

I took Jeremy's word for it and suggested that he take Bass to his place and keep him secure until I figured out what to do with him. I couldn't turn him over to Phil, not without some evidence, not without a confession, which it didn't look as if I would get. Jeremy lifted the unconscious Bass onto his shoulders, refused the gun I offered him, and went to the door.

"That music playing when I came in," he said. "Mozart's Sonata Eleven in A. Please check the record for me."

As he stood in the door under Bass's weight, I went to the turntable and checked the record. He was right.

"In music Olson had some taste I guess, but not in friends," I said. "Some of us do better than others that way."

"You are a sentimentalist, Toby," he said and went down the hall with his burden.

Finding the missing Fala was a slight problem. I put my .38 in my cracked leather holster, removed the bullet clip from Bass's .45, and went to the room of cages. The animals wanted no part of me. They had had enough. The dog I was looking for wasn't there.

I went through the hall and into rooms one at a time, coaxing and calling. I found the big cat on a shelf, his green eyes glowing at me. He hissed and I stayed away. It took me about five more minutes to find the dog squeezed under a cabinet. I pulled him out whimpering, held him, petted him, and told him everything was going to be just great, that huge cans of Strongheart were waiting for him, that he'd soon be back standing up and breathing dog breath on the president. It helped a little.

I started down the hall for the front door, the dog cradled

in my arms, and almost ran into the beam of a flashlight through the window. I pulled back against the wall and heard voices outside.

"I don't hear anything," said a man.

"Maybe they're just hearing things, a dog or something going screwy," came a second male voice, younger.

"Dogs don't sound like guns," came the first voice impatiently. "The guy over there said it was a gun."

"So," said the other guy, "do we go in or what?"

"We go in," sighed the first cop. I eased back down the corridor, trying not to trip over the debris of the battle. I wished I had turned the lights out in the animal room, but I didn't have time to do it now. Balancing the dog, I turned off the light in Olson's office and went for the window. Behind me I could hear the door to the clinic open. I eased the window open with one hand.

"You hear that?" I heard the young voice coming down the hall.

"I heard," came the other voice as I put one leg through the window. The tape pulled against my chest as I bent over and got out, trying to keep the dog from getting hurt.

A breeze caught me, and a wet chill ran down my back. I was sweating again. The light went on in the room a few feet behind me, and I ran like hell.

I was about thirty feet away and slowed down by two guns and a dog, when the voice called, "Hold it, police."

Maybe I could have stopped and explained. Maybe I would have wound up back in Phil's office with the dog but no murderer and some very bad headlines for the Roosevelts. So I kept running. The cop fired, but I could tell from the sound that he wasn't shooting at me. Given another few hundred thousand miles of push, he might have hit the moon. My chest was burning like dry ice had been pressed against it. I don't know if they followed me. Maybe they did. I was back on the street and ducked into the nearest clump of bushes. I gave it a full twenty seconds, was sure no one was behind me, and in spite of the pain and the dog licking my face, I ran for the corner, rounded it, and got to my car. It would have been nice if the night were over, but I knew it was just starting.

Getting the front door open when I got to Mrs. Plaut's rooming house was a minor but distinct problem. I was afraid to put the dog down, afraid that he'd make a run for it. So I used my key and kept saying "Good boy," as I let myself in. The house was dark. The time was after eleven. By the glow of the forty-watt night light at the top of the stairs, the dog and I moved without a fall, bark, or comment from a resident.

I was almost at the top step when the dog began to whine. It started low and then rose.

"Cut it out," I whispered, but he didn't cut it out. I had two choices. I could either run for my room and try to keep him quiet or I could recognize what he wanted and go back outside. I went back down the stairs and let us out quietly. The dog whined all the way.

When I got him down the porch steps, I held on to him tightly while I got my belt off and looped it around his neck. With one hand on my pants and another on my belt serving as a leash, I let him lead me to the curb. I was on the way back to the porch when the front door opened and I started working on a lie, but it wasn't needed.

"Toby," whispered Gunther. He was in total disarray, at least for Gunther he was. He wore pants, shirt, tie, vest, but no jacket. "I heard you coming up and then going down."

"I had to walk the dog," I explained, whispering back.

He looked at the dog and the dog looked at him curiously. On his hind legs, the dog would have been about Gunther's size. We could have saddled the animal for him.

"This, then, is the dog of the president of the United States?" he whispered.

"Looks that way," I said.

"Why are you bringing him here instead of to the police or the president?" he asked reasonably.

I came up on the porch and sat on the bottom step. Gunther moved closer. We were about eye level.

"I think the people who took the dog have a woman named

Jane Poslik," I explained. "I might have to make a trade or something. I'll just have to wait till they contact me and try to stay out of the way of the police, who I promised to give the killer to."

I sat on the porch talking and the animal kept his eyes riveted on Gunther. Gunther stood erect the entire time while I went over the events of the past two days. Gunther touched a spot just under his lip, a sure sign that he had an idea.

"In my mind," he said, "I have gone over the listing of suspects, events. Perhaps it is a problem in logical or even literary formalism."

"Maybe," I said with no great hope as I reached over to pet the dog. "I've got a plan."

"What might that be?" asked Gunther seriously. A slight night breeze ruffled his neat hair and a tiny hand went up immediately to put it back in place.

"I'll find Lyle and threaten to kick his face in if he doesn't confess and tell me where Jane Poslik is," I explained. "It's direct, simple, and inexpensive."

"And not likely to yield results," he said pensively. "May I suggest an alternative procedure?"

"If it's not one that requires a lot of thought on my part," I said wearily. "I've had a long hard day. Hell, a long hard lifetime."

Thunder rumbled somewhere far over the hills near Santa Monica as Gunther went through his chain of logic. It made sense to me but it would take time to set up. It also involved the possibility that I had made a big mistake.

When he was done talking and I agreed, as much out of pain and tiredness as out of conviction, I picked up the dog, did an awkward dance as I put my belt back on, and followed Gunther into the house and up the stairs.

When we got in front of my room, I whispered to Gunther, "I'll set it up for tomorrow night, in my office."

"That," said Gunther, "will be sufficient."

When I got into my room, I considered removing the itching tape on my chest, but that would have proven foolish. Instead, I took off my clothes, put on fresh underwear, took one of the pills Doc Hodgdon had given me, and shared the last of a bottle of milk with the dog.

"You want Wheaties?" I asked. He looked like the answer was yes, so I gave him a bowl of Wheaties, which he ate dry.

Sleeping was a little problem. I'm not used to a warm body near mine through the night. Even if it's a dog, it brings back memories, but I finally fell asleep on my mattress on the floor. Once during the night I started to turn over. The pain woke me, and the dog, in the moonlight, wept for me. I gave him a pat and went back to a careful sleep.

"Mr. Peelers," came the distinct, thin, and insistent morning voice of Mrs. Plaut.

"Huh?" I answered alertly, glancing around the room for something I couldn't remember but knew would be familiar when it came before my eyes. The dog was sitting on the sofa looking at me, his pink tongue out. I rolled over, felt the pain in my chest, and let myself fall back on the mattress on the floor as Mrs. Plaut stepped in.

"Come in," I said with what I thought was good-natured sarcasm.

"I'm already in," she replied, hands on her hips. She didn't seem to notice a dog panting and looking at her from the depths of the sofa.

"What can I do for you, Mrs. Plaut?" I asked, forcing myself up on one elbow.

"Pensecola cookies," she replied.

My first thought was that this was one of the colorful near-curses of her family. I immediately learned the truth.

"I would like to make my recipe for Pensecola cookies," she explained. "But I can't."

I looked at her and she looked back at me.

"Go on," she finally said.

"Where am I going?" I asked, coming to a sitting position and rubbing the stubble on my chin.

"Aren't you going to ask me why I can't make Pensecola cookies?" she said with exasperation.

"Why can't you make Pensecola cookies?" I asked, feeling something like George Burns.

"No sugar—or not enough sugar—calls for a lot of sugar," she said, looking around the room to see if there was some doily or knick-knack she could straighten. "The recipe was developed in the old country by my Uncle Fabian's wife."

"The old country?" I asked, knowing from Mrs. Plaut's massive family biography that the Plaut's, Cornell's, Lamphrets, and all the other ilk of my landlady had been in on the first invasions of the American shores. Some of them had predated the Indians.

"Ohio," Mrs. Plaut explained. "We can pick up sugar rationing books at the elementary school. As a resident of this home, I think you should allow me some of your sugar ration in exchange for which I will give you a generous dose of Pensecola cookies."

I wrapped the blanket around my waist and stood up.

"I'll pick my sugar stamps up this afternoon," I promised, reaching for my pants, which were on the sofa and covered with a fine layer of dark dog hair.

"This morning will be essential," she said. "I'm working on the cookies this morning."

"I've got a killer to catch," I appealed to her.

"Your train can wait," she replied firmly. "Do you know what Uncle Fabian's wife went through to perfect this recipe?"

I neither knew nor cared, but I could think of only one way to stop from being told.

"I'll do it," I said awkwardly, scrambling into my pants under the blanket. Mrs. Plaut looked satisfied.

"We will drive in your automobile," she said. "I don't think you can walk the three streets over with that injury." She pointed to my chest, which I was trying to cover with a semi-soiled white shirt from the closet. "Have you killed someone again?"

She looked around the room suspiciously for a possible body and then turned to me. I hadn't bothered to answer her question. Satisfied that I had stashed no corpses in the quite visible corners, Mrs. Plaut instructed me to meet her downstairs in five minutes, and parted with: "Shave your scratchy face, Mr. Peelers, and bring the president's dog with you."

I left the dog in my room wagging his tail and scratching at the door while I hurried down the hall to shave as quickly as my chest tape would allow. I was dropping a nickel into the hall phone when Mrs. Plaut called up for me to hurry.

There were four or five calls I had to make, but at the moment I only had time for one, to the number Eleanor Roosevelt had given me. She was in and came to the phone.

"I've got the dog," I said.

"Mr. Peters, you have my gratitude. I'll pick him up personally," she answered.

"I'd like to hold on to him today," I said, and then I explained why. She listened quietly, politely, and asked me a few questions.

"And you believe this scheme will work?" she said finally. "You believe it is worth risking both your life and that of Fala?"

There was something about Fala that I didn't want to tell her, but I held back and assured her that I thought it was worth it. We didn't have a long discussion of my assessment of the value of my own life. Many was the night I spent lying on the floor on my mattress when Time and I had discussions in which I tried to argue that my life was of cosmic import; but Time just wouldn't buy it and kept proving from the history of my own behavior that I didn't buy it either.

"It's a shot," I finally said.

"Mr. Peters, please be careful. It is important that Franklin have the comfort of his dog. The war news has not been good today. Corregidor has fallen. But I think a human life is worth more than the risk involved."

"Mr. Peelers," Mrs. Plaut shouted from the bottom of the stairs.

"I've got to go now," I said. "I've got to pick up some sugar for Pensecola cookies."

"My aunt's maid baked them when I was a child in New York," Eleanor Roosevelt said.

"I'll save some for you."

Before she hung up she told me that she could stay till the night with some stalling, but she would have to travel all night on the plane to get back to Washington for the reception.

I went back to my room, removed the hunk of rope I was using to hold together one of my four wooden kitchen chairs, and tied it around the dog for a leash. Downstairs Mrs. Plaut was waiting impatiently, a little black hat on her little white-haired head, with a black coat and black purse.

"And remember," she said as the dog pulled me through the front door, "let no one push you around in the line. It's—"

"I remember," I said as the dog pulled me down the wooden steps and made for the curb. "It's a doggie dog world out there."

As it turned out, Mrs. Plaut was right. The elementary school was filled with people making deals, pushing, pleading, lying about the size of their family to get more sugar than they were allotted.

A small man wearing a wool cap down to his ears, his teeth clenched, hit me in the sore ribs with an elbow, claiming I was trying to get in front of him. A crony of Mrs. Plaut named Evelyn Barkmer informed us that there was a man of unsavory demeanor in a De Soto behind the school who was buying and selling ration books. A harassed man who sounded like Raymond on the "Inner Sanctum," and possibly was, stood up from behind the desk where he was helping to issue ration books to shout, "Ladies and gentlemen, you do not have to pick up a ration book if you don't want or need one. If you don't want or need one, you can simply go home. Go home."

"You mean," came a woman's shout, "if I don't want no sugar stamps, I don't have to stay here?"

"That's what I said," shouted the man.

"Why didn't someone say so?" The woman sighed and turned for the door. She didn't get far, however. She was surrounded almost instantly in an Apache-style attack by a party of people who had offers for her unwanted ration.

One woman who reminded me of my mother's sister Bess

told me that my dog looked like Fala but that she, herself, preferred a dog with size and meat on its bones.

I kept enough stamps for my coffee and cereal and turned the rest over to the waiting Mrs. Plaut, who did a recount to be sure that the guy who sounded like Raymond and I hadn't short-changed her. Satisfied, she stuffed the coupon book into her black purse, snapped it closed, and looked around to see if anyone was going to challenge her for them.

"Like *One Million B.C.*," I said. "Cave men protecting their food from each other."

"How would you know what it was like way back then?" she said, leading the way through the crowd with me and the dog following.

"I meant the movie," I explained. "You know, Victor Mature, Carole Landis."

"Next time we come earlier," Mrs. Plaut said and went directly to my car. Having already gone through an explanation of the broken car door to her on the way to the school, I said nothing and watched her slide in the driver's side and over, and then slowly followed her, putting the dog in the small back seat.

Dropping Mrs. Plaut off, I headed for the Farraday. Mrs. Roosevelt would, I was sure, pay her bill fast and probably in cash to keep any records from turning up in the future. So I drove to No-Neck Arnie's and told him to fix the car door.

"Nice dog," Arnie said. He had a black dot of grease on his nose like a clown and was wearing his gray overalls.

"Right," I agreed.

"Make a deal," Arnie said, putting an arm on my shoulder and breathing a dreaded combination into my face. "You give me the dog. I fix the door for ten bucks."

"Not my dog," I said.

Arnie shrugged, touched his nose to make the spot worse, fished in the pocket of his overalls for a used cigar, and said, "That's a genuine Scottie. Like FDR's."

"That a fact?" I said, leading the dog to the door.

"A fact," said Arnie, following my progress by turning his entire body.

The dog's legs moved double-time to keep up with me. In spite of the tightness in my chest, I had things to wrap up. My stomach rumbled when I hit Ninth and I considered stopping in one of the restaurants for a quick bite, but I didn't think any of them would welcome the dog, any except one and that one was Manny's Tacos.

Since it was before eleven, there weren't many people in Manny's. I got up on one of the red leather swivel stools at the counter and helped the dog up onto the one next to me. A man made out of old leather a few stools down took the cigarette out of his mouth and turned to look at us, but we weren't all that interesting to him.

"What'll it be, the usual?" asked Manny. Manny was Emanuel Perez, dark, tired, thirty, and hard-working.

"The usual," I said. "Same for the dog. Bring a bowl for the dog."

Manny didn't blink an eye, just nodded and said, "Check," and went off to bring us each a taco and a Pepsi.

"Chili be better for a dog," said the leather man at the end of the counter in a raspy voice.

"If he survives the taco," I said amiably, "he can order the chili."

"I know dogs," the leather man said with a shrug.

The dog liked the tacos though I can't say he was the neatest eater I had dined with, but then again I had been told that my own eating habits left a little to be desired. After he noisily lapped the Pepsi up, I refilled his bowl. He still looked hungry but not chili hungry.

"Manny," I said, "you got some crackers I can give him?"

"Check," called Manny and brought some little oyster crackers which I added to the bowl of Pepsi.

"Crackers is for pollies, not dogs," said the leather man.

"He likes them," I countered.

"He ain't no gor-met," said the leather man, wisely returning to his own bowl of Carumba super hot chili.

Fed and fat, I led the dog to the Farraday and made my way slowly up the stairs to Jeremy's office. Jeremy was sitting opposite Bass and reading a book. Bass gave me and the dog, in that order, dirty looks, but there wasn't much he could do beyond that. He was firmly tied where he sat.

"Toby," said Jeremy, rising from his chair, inserting a blue felt bookmark in his book of Frost poems and putting it neatly on the small table nearby. "I have been endeavoring to convince our guest that he should tell us the location of Miss Poslik and the identity of his accomplice or accomplices, but he remains mute. His arm seems, at this point, to be uninfected, but his soul, his very essence, is so corrupted that I doubt if much can be done."

Bass looked up at Jeremy with a hatred that outdid the blast he had fired at me and the dog.

"When I get out," Bass said, "I'll do you."

"Bass, you are not getting out," I explained while the dog sniffed at his right foot and just managed to escape the kick Bass threw. "You killed Mrs. Olson, kidnapped the dog and Jane Poslik, and, in general I'm sure, have been less than charming. You are going to trial and jail, maybe to the chair. Can you follow all that?"

Bass shook his head and looked bored. "He won't let that happen," he said. "He's got connections, big connections. When things change in this country, I'm gonna be running the jails."

"That's a comforting vision of the future," I said. "I'll pass it on to my friends. Should give them added reason for surviving the war."

"You can laugh," Bass said. "People laugh at me sometimes when I can't touch them, but they can't stay away forever."

"I can't laugh," I said. "You bruised a few of my ribs, but we'll let bygones be bygones. Maybe I'll even vote Whig in the next election in Oz if you—"

"No," Bass said.

I looked at Jeremy, who closed his eyes and opened them slowly to show that communication with Bass was hopeless.

"I got loyalty," Bass said, his fingers turning white as he gripped the wooden arms of the chair to which he was strapped. "I know I've got loyalty. Even when I was wrestling and all those people were out there eating those hot dogs and booing me. I knew people who were my friends could count on me. My word means something.''

He was sounding too much like me, and I didn't like that at all, so I told Jeremy to keep him tied till tonight. Jeremy followed me to the door and I whispered the plan to him while Bass pretended to be looking at a row of books but strained without success to hear.

"Toby," Jeremy said after I had explained things to him, "please do not be offended by this, but your plans in such situations tend to be precarious and fraught with danger for you."

"I've noticed that," I agreed.

"*Ulysses*," said Jeremy.

> *"I cannot rest from travel; I will drink*
> *Life to the lees' all times I have enjoyed*
> *Greatly, have suffered greatly, both with those*
> *That loved me, and alone; on shores, and when*
> *Through scudding drifts the rainy Haydes*
> *Vexed the dim sea: I am become a name;*
> *For always roaming with a hungry heart*
> *Much have I seen and know."*

"If you say so, Jeremy," I whispered, touched his solid arm, and went into the hall with the dog waddling behind me.

The late-morning sounds of the Farraday accompanied me back to and up the stairs. Arguments coming through closed office doors, a machine whirring, a shout of laughter, some male voice echoing from below, "Then you just come back tomorrow at the same time, and we'll see what can be done about it."

I had some time to kill, and possibly to be killed, and some phone calls to make. The game was set for eight that night. It had to be to get it all wrapped up so Eleanor Roosevelt could head back to Washington with her mystery solved and, hopefully, a bill for services, and I could pick Carmen up and get to the Armstrong fight.

My wardrobe was down to rock-bottom pitiful. The wind-breaker I was wearing didn't even have a zipper. Fortune may have been laughing at me but I had a joke or two ready myself.

As it turned out, my phone calls were delayed. When I opened the door of the outer office of Minck and Peters, specialists in finding lost grandfathers and filling teeth, I heard voices—three voices, one female, two male—in Shelly's office. I considered turning around and heading the dog back to the street. We could find a park and take in the threatening rainstorm.

Instead I made the move, opened the inner door, and stepped into Shelly's office.

11

The scene: Shelly's spick and span, squeaky clean, falsely antiseptic office. In it, behind the dental chair that occupies the position of power in the room—the electric chair, the throne—stands Shelly in a clean white dental smock buttoned at the collar, cigar nowhere in evidence. Next to Shelly, flanking him, are a man and a woman. The woman, about sixty, is dressed in a dark blue dress with big white flowers on it. She looks like Marjorie Main wrapped in wallpaper designed for the women's room of a Dolly Dainty restaurant. The man is small, mustached, with a determined little chin, and losing his hair. He is like Porter Hall, the actor who snivels and makes a living by betraying Gary Cooper.

All three of them look at me and the dog, who wags his tail. Shelly looks bewildered, confused, and then an idea comes into his eyes. I can see it from where I stand and decide to break for my door, but the demon has taken over and the drama begins.

"Mr. Peters," Shelly said, holding out an arm and grin-

ning. The sweat was trickling down his nose and giving him
a hell of a time keeping his glasses from falling to the floor.
"You are a bit late for your appointment."

"Wait a minute," I said, holding up my own hand as
Shelly advanced.

"Sorry," Shelly chuckled, taking my arm. "But I'm afraid
you'll have to use the washroom later, Mr. Peters. Drs. Ferzetti and Vaughan are from the Dental Association and they
would like to observe me with a patient."

"Look," I said, but Shelly whispered quickly, his back to
the stony inspectors: "You can't go in your office and give
it away. You can't, for chrissake, bring a dog in here. You
can't let me down on this, Toby."

I grinned over Shelly's shoulder at the two dentists, who
did not grin back, and I talked to Shelly through my teeth
like a third-rate ventriloquist.

"You are not getting me in that chair," I said. "You are
not working on my mouth, Minck. I've seen too many disas-
ters crawl out of this office never to be heard from again, at
least among the living."

"Be with you in just a moment," Shelly said to the two
dentists. "Mr. Peters is just a bit shy about having people
observe." And then, whispering back to me, "That's just
what I'm telling you. They have complaints, for God's sake.
You know what kind of trouble I can be in if I don't prove
something here?"

"No more than you deserve to be in," I said, tugging at
the rope around the dog's collar to keep him from sniffing
Marjorie Main.

"My career," Shelly said, putting a fat hand to his heart.
"My life." He was close enough for me to smell his cigar
breath and sweat. The tears in his eyes were fogging his
glasses.

"Our names go on the door the same size," I said.

"Never," said Shelly.

"Dr. Minck," Porter Hall said, looking at his watch impatiently.

"Same size," Shelly whispered to me.

"And—" I began.

"No ands, no ands here, Toby, this is blackmail," Shelly said, almost weeping.

"You think I don't know blackmail when I'm engaged in it?" I said. "I'm a detective. And . . . you keep the sink clean."

"Dr. Minck," the man said again. "We really must . . ."

"Here we come," said Shelly, taking my arm and hissing to me. "All right."

I should have asked for more. I knew it when I sat in the chair and watched Shelly lead the dog to my office door, open it, close the dog inside, and turn to me with a grin like Karloff as Fu Manchu.

"Now just what kind of dental work does this man need?" said Marjorie Main, looking down at me as if I were a fraud.

Shelly was pinning a clean sheet around my neck. I felt as if I were in a barber shop with W. C. Fields about to drop a scalding towel on my face to keep his own hands from burning.

"A great deal," said Shelly, touching his chin and selecting an instrument to begin with.

"Doctor," I said ominously.

"But," Shelly went on, "today we are simply going to begin. We've got to take the X rays first."

Before I could protest, Shelly had rolled out his X ray machine and placed a black metal cone from it against my cheek, then turned out the lights and filled my mouth with film. I tried with little success to breathe while three of us watched Shelly put on his dark goggles and heavy lead coat and unreel the extra long electrical cord.

"We'll go behind the barricade in the corner," he told the other doctors and headed over, looking like a field colonel directing his adjutants to safety during an attack.

"Hold it," I said, pulling the boards out of my mouth. Shelly flicked the lights back on.

"Mr. Peters," he said, removing his goggles. "You've exposed the goddamn film."

"Better the film than me, Minck," I said threateningly.

"Dr. Minck," Marjorie Main stepped in. "We haven't time to wait while you get the X rays developed. Can't you simply do a visual examination now and some preliminary work so we can observe your procedures?"

"Dr. Ferzetti is right," said the man. "We have other stops to make."

Reluctantly, Shelly took off the lead coat and hung it, along with the goggles, in the closet. Then he turned to me.

"Open wide, Mr. Peters," he said, leaning over, a recently cleaned mirror in his hand. He was breathing heavily as he put his weight on my chest and explored my mouth with a series of "Ah-ha's" and "Well, well, wells."

When he stepped back, he had a satisfied look on his face. Shelly cleaned the mirror on his smock, put it down on the clean white towel on his work tray, and asked me, "Do you brush your teeth regularly, Mr. Peters?"

"Regularly," I said. "With Teel, or Dr. Lyon's."

"You've got some cavities," Shelly said, picking up something with a sharp point and tapping it against his palm. "Let's take care of one or two of them now."

"Let's," sighed Porter Hall with more than a touch of impatience.

As soon as he had my mouth propped open and little blocks put in, Shelly turned to the two inspectors and said, "Mr. Peters is a well-known radio personality, aren't you, Mr. Peters?"

I gargled and almost choked.

"Yes?" said the woman with some incredulity.

"Mr. Peters is the voice of Captain Midnight," Shelly said, leaning over on the drill, which began to spin evilly just beyond the range of my right eye, which was straining toward it.

Shelly worked quickly, dripping sweat on me and singing a medley of Cole Porter tunes. He paused during "Anything Goes" to smile grimly and shrug. "Stubborn little yentz, but we'll get him."

Pain and I are not strangers, but even so, Shelly redefined it for me. It wasn't the intensity but the duration. Shelly had the touch of a blind hippo and a tastefully matching manner and odor. But he was on his best behavior, which resulted in his failing to maim or kill me in the chair.

"That should do it," he said, packing the silver filling into the two holes he had excavated in my teeth. "Have a look, colleagues."

Shelly stepped back, and the two unfamiliar faces leaned forward to examine my mouth.

"Captain Midnight," the woman said, after pursing her lips with doubt. "Can I have your autograph for my grandson?"

Shelly stuck a piece of paper and a pencil in my hand. I felt my tingling teeth with my torpid tongue and signed Tobias Leo Pevsner, parent-given name, adding, "With good wishes from your pal, Captain Midnight."

"Okay, so what do you think?" Shelly said, turning to the two inspectors, his hands wringing.

"Well," said the man. "You seem minimally competent."

"Your office is clean if not modern," the woman added.

"Your technique is very old-fashioned," the man went on, taking out a notebook to write something. Shelly craned his neck to try to see what the man was carefully noting, but had no success.

"Frankly, Dr. Minck," the woman said, looking at me and back at Shelly, "our primary complaints seem at odds with what we have seen here, though I have the impression that you've cleaned this office up very recently."

"Not so," said Shelly, actually crossing his heart. "Ask Mr. Peters. Did the office look like this the last time you were here?"

I nodded my head in agreement, trying to get my stiff jaws working again.

In my office, the little dog was whining and scratching at the door. The woman wandered about the room touching, examining, and the man kept jotting notes.

"What are you writing there, what?" Shelly said, unable to restrain himself.

"Notes," said Porter Hall.

"I know notes," sighed Shelly, "but what kind of notes? Are you writing bad things or good things?"

"Just notes," the man said cryptically.

"I think we have seen quite enough, Dr. Minck," came the voice of the woman, who was returning to our line of vision. The flowers were in bloom on her dress, and her smile was without committment.

"So," said Shelly too eagerly, "do I pass?"

"Dr. Minck," the man said, following the woman to the door, "this is not a grade school mathematics test. This is a professional assessment."

"You got the autograph," Shelly reminded the woman, pushing his glasses back on his nose.

"That's not really relevant to your competency," she said.

"I know, I know," said Shelly, "but it was a nice thing, wasn't it?"

She didn't answer, but the man put his notebook away and held out his hand to Shelly, who shook it.

"You'll be hearing from our office soon," the man said with a polite little grin. "Good-bye, doctor, and to you, Captain."

"Good-bye," I said, reaching back to remove the sheet pinned around my neck as the two inspectors went out into the reception room. We waited till they were in the hall, then Shelly turned to me.

"He shook my hand," he said, walking over to me cradling his face in his hands. "He wouldn't do that if they were planning to impale me, would he?"

"Probably not," I said, pushing out of the chair and trying to get a decent breath, no easy task with sore ribs and in the aftermath of Shelly's work.

Shelly got into the chair I had just vacated, fished a cigar out of his pants pocket, and lit it pensively.

"I did a good job on your teeth," he puffed. "I'm only gonna charge you half price out of gratitude for helping me out."

"You're going to charge me nothing," I said, stepping toward him with heartfelt malice.

"A joke," he said. "A joke. I'm trying to relieve the tension here. I've been under a lot of tension here."

The dog was scratching away, and we didn't hear the hall door open. Our first sense of it was the voice of Marjorie

Main saying, "You should be hearing from us by the end of the week. I wouldn't worry about it if I were you." And she was off.

I turned back to Shelly, who gave me a look of agony instead of relief. He had almost swallowed his cigar in an attempt to hide it in his mouth. He spat out the butt in his sink and choked away while I got him a glass of water, which he downed in one long gulp.

"The pressures of this job," he gasped. "You wouldn't know. You've got all the fun and what do I get?"

"Older," I answered. "Remember to make those name changes on the door."

Shelly's fit of choking was passing. He leaned back in the dental chair and closed his eyes, the calm after battle. "We'll see," he said.

"We'll see it the way we agreed," I went on, moving to my office door, "or I call Miss Ferzetti at the State Dental Office and tell her I am not Captain Midnight and that you are a menace to home-front hygiene."

"Where has compassion gone?" Shelly sobbed, his eyes still closed. "Where is friendship?"

"It sat down in that chair of yours and let itself get drilled and filled," I said. "Now I've got some work to do."

"Almost forgot," Shelly said, opening his eyes without sitting up. "You had a guy looking for you."

"A guy?"

"Right."

"Did he leave his name? Number?"

"No," said Shelly sheepishly. "He didn't have to. He looked kind of sick when he came in. I sent him into your office and then the inspectors came."

"You mean I've got a client in my office right now?"

"I forgot," Shelly said with a shrug.

"You always forget," I said, opening my office door. Fala came running out.

"That dog doesn't stay around here," Shelly said with all the authority he could put into it. "I'm in a good mood and everything, but I can't have a dog here."

I coaxed Fala to me, but he didn't seem to want to meet

my visitor. He whimpered as I picked him up, put him under my arm, and opened the door.

When I closed the door to my cubbyhole, I spotted Martin Lyle seated in the chair in the corner. He was looking out the window at a darkening sky.

This wasn't quite the way I had planned to settle the whole thing, but I was willing to wrap it up any way I could.

I put the whining dog on the floor, went around my desk, sat down with satisfaction, and said, "Okay, Lyle, we talk, but we don't leave this office till I have a murderer to hand over to the cops. Do we understand each other?"

It was at that point that I realized Martin Lyle was beyond understanding. His dead stare behind his Ben Franklin glasses went right through me and beyond. No more New Whigs, memories of Henry Clay, and wacky speeches about the future. There was no more future on earth for Martin Lyle.

I sat looking at him for a minute or two and watched him looking at me. The hole in his chest had stopped bleeding long before I arrived. There was no final pulsing of the thin chest under his white shirt. I looked at him and silently asked him some questions I had to answer myself.

He couldn't have traveled far with a bullet in his chest, which meant that he had probably been shot in the building, on his way to see me. While it didn't rule him out as the killer of Olson or his wife, it did eliminate him as a suspect for one murder, his own. Since Bass was firmly tied to Jeremy's chair and probably listening to Byron's poetry, he was safe on this one.

"So who punctuated you?" I asked Lyle.

Since he had no answers, I got up, walked over to him, and closed his eyes.

I folded my hands, exercised my jaw, unfolded my hands, and went through my mail. There was nothing much in it. I looked at Lyle again and made my decision.

I would feed the dog, make my phone calls, and come back to wait it out with Lyle's corpse. I could see that the dog didn't think very much of the plan. He went to the door and looked back at me, tail wagging in hope.

I went over to him, let us out, locked the office door behind me, and turned to Shelly.

"Mr. Lyle is going to wait for me," I said. "We've got a lot of work to do. Big case. I'll be back in a little while."

Shelly nodded. "How's the tooth?" he asked.

"Okay," I admitted.

"Professionalism," he sighed. "It'll show everytime."

There is not much you can do with a dog outdoors in Los Angeles after you've fed him a decent taco lunch and walked him in the park, but we had some hours to kill and no place to go. I drove up Wilshire to Westlake Park, parked near the eastern Wilshire Boulevard entrance, and got out to let the dog sniff around the eight-foot-high black cement nude of Prometheus holding a torch and a globe. Jeremy had once told me that if Los Angeles had a patron saint, it was Prometheus. Jeremy's favorite Prometheus was in a painting up at Pomona College in Claremont by a Mexican named Orozco. He had driven me out to see it a year earlier, and the damned thing depressed me. Prometheus had looked miserable, a big naked giant trying to keep the roof from falling on the heads of a whole bunch of bald guys who looked like zombies.

Jeremy also called me the poor man's Prometheus when he was feeling particularly fatherly. He had even given me a book of Greek myths to read, but I had put it aside before getting to Prometheus because a walnut farmer from the San Jose Valley hired me to find his son who had run away with the daughter of one of his walnut sorters. I found the two kids in Fresno, married and working in an Arthur Murray dance studio as instructors. The kid was eighteen but looked a lot older. The girl was twenty and looked a lot younger. They both smiled a lot and I told the walnut grower I couldn't find them. Someday I'll get back to reading about Prometheus.

We spent an hour on and near a park bench watching some kids in the playground and talking to an old guy in a gray cardigan sweater who seemed to live on the bench. He knew a lot about dogs and was willing to tell me. I knew nothing about dogs and wasn't very interested, but I had nothing better to do so I watched the kids, heard about short-hairs, and kept asking him for the time.

"Good dog you got there," the old guy said, pointing the stem of his pipe.

"Man's best friend," I agreed, while the dog lay on the bench next to us, following the conversation.

"Like hell," said the old man, leaning toward me. "People always say that. Dogs are something special in God's world. That's a fact, but they are dumb sons of bitches, and I mean that literally. They do what you teach them and if you treat them good they lick your hand and stay out of trouble if something doesn't itch away at them. But you ask me, I'd rather have a friend who can talk back and have his own ideas. Dogs are just yes-men or no-men. You want a friend who just licks your mitt and tells you you're right all the time? Hell, that's no friend, that's a dumb dog."

The old guy spat, nodded his head, and put his pipe back in his mouth as he crossed his legs and looked out at the kids in the playground. "And," he added, remembering an important point, "you've got to walk them, clean them, and feed them."

"A lot of trouble," I agreed, reaching down to pet the dog looking up at me.

"And there's worse," the old man said, looking away from me. "They don't live long. Slobber all over you, trick you into investing some feeling in them, and their goddamn life span catches up with them."

"You've had a dog or two," I said.

"A few," he said, still not turning to me. "A few."

He told me some interesting things about the dog I was petting and I got up.

The dog and I said good-bye to the old guy and he waved, puffed on his pipe, and didn't turn to watch us as we made our way back to Wilshire.

I found a small hot dog stand shaped like a hot dog bun with a fake hot dog coming out of each end and bought a sack with fries and a pair of Pepsis. On the way back to the Farraday, the dog kept sniffing at the bag and I had to protect it with my right hand while driving with my left. I had to

ease my defense when I shifted gears, but I managed to keep
the pooch at bay.

It was a few minutes after five when I hit Hoover. Traffic
was leaving downtown and not coming in. I found a parking
space on the street without too much trouble, locked up, and
made my way through the going-home crowd with the sack
under one arm and the dog under the other.

A chunky woman in a gray coat was coming out of the
Farraday and held the door open for me.

"Thanks," I said, easing past.

"You're Peters," she said.

"Right." I looked at her dark, heavily made-up face and
didn't place her for a second.

"You're the new mind reader," I said.

"Tante Kuble," she said. "Moved in last week. On the
third right below you."

"Right," I said, shifting my load. "Didn't recognize you
without the gypsy suit. How's it going?"

"Could be better, could be worse," she said. "Mostly I'm
getting the kids—soldiers, sailors—wanting to know what's
going to happen to them."

"What do you tell them?"

"I tell them they're all going to be all right, that they're
going to live forever or close to it," she said, looking hard
into my eyes. "Some of them I can see things I don't want
to tell them."

"See you around," I said, feeling uncomfortable under
her hard look.

"Peters," she said as I turned my back. "Don't eat with
the dead and get the dog to the one who wants it as fast as
you can. You know what I'm talking about?"

"I know," I said, walking into the dark echo of the Farraday. "Good talking to you."

"See you around," she shouted. "Damn it looks like
rain."

Then she was gone.

Some days are definitely not the ones you want to remember when you take a hot bath and plan your future. This one
had found me in Shelly's dental chair for the first time and

brought me face to face with an old man in the park who lost his dogs and a fortune teller who saw death. I let the dog down, and he trotted up the stairs behind me, his stubby claws scratching against the marble and metal.

My big fear was that Shelly might still be in the office, but the door was locked. No one had put my name back on it yet in the terms that Shelly and I had agreed on, but I'd given him a week to get it done. I opened the door and left it open as I went in. There was enough light coming through the windows so that I didn't have to use any electricity.

I unlocked the door to my inner office, but I didn't go in. Tante Koble might have hit on something. Instead, I tore open the sack, took out a couple of hot dogs for the dog, put them on a towel on the floor, and poured him a cup of Pepsi. He went to work on them in a manner unbecoming to the dog of a president. I should have cut the hot dogs up but it was too late now. If I tried anything I might lose a finger or two.

Climbing into Shelly's dental chair, I took my time eating and reached over to flip on Shelly's radio. Captain Midnight was on. I didn't sound anything like him—or the guy who played Ichabod Mudd or the guy who played Ivan Shark, for that matter.

After our dinner I cleaned up and went into my office. Martin Lyle was sitting there as I had left him, eyes closed, a lot more pale than he had been before. I wanted to turn on the lights because the sun was dropping down fast and the sky was cloudy, but I resisted.

So in I went and got behind my desk, checked my .38 and waited, and that, my friends, brought me to the moment at which I started this story, just before the killer walked in and I promised to tell a tale.

12

I considered offering the killer a chair, but there was none available unless we threw Lyle's body on the floor or out the window or I stood up. So the killer stood while I talked.

"You fooled me," I admitted. "I was hot on the trail of Bass and Lyle, just where you put me. The way I figure it, you planned to put Lyle away from the start, and if Bass got me at Olson's, you'd get rid of him too."

"So far," said the killer, "there's nothing very interesting in this."

"You wanted the fifty thousand and the dog to make another pitch for more money," I said.

The dog watched the gun on my midsection and whimpered, head down in his paws. I reached over very slowly and patted his head.

"Accurate," said the killer, "but . . ."

"I'm coming to it," I said. "But it's got to be a trade. I'll tell you something you need to know if you tell me why you killed Olson and Lyle."

The killer considered the request, decided there was nothing to lose, and said, "I only killed Lyle. He was on his way here to talk to you. We had tried to make a deal with him, but Lyle was a fanatic, all politics, and the money didn't mean a thing. The kidnapping of the dog had been his idea, not for money, but in the hope that it would be used to force Roosevelt into some kind of deal. He forced Olson to go along with it. We brought Bass in to keep an eye on things, watch, wait, see if there was some way to profit from it. Mrs. Olson found out. We didn't want to kill her, but Bass got carried away with loyalty."

"He's just a big, loyal, dumb dog, is that it?" I asked.

"Something like that," the killer agreed.

"Fifty thousand isn't all that much for a possible murder rap," I said.

"It wasn't supposed to turn out like this," the killer said. "There weren't supposed to be any killings. Bass started it."

"And Anne Lyle?" I asked, trying to think of something I could use to stall for the thirty minutes I needed before help arrived.

"We were waiting for Olson," the killer explained, "when he came to the house with her. We didn't want her to see us so we went upstairs and hid while he got ready for his bath. Then we heard you come and Anne Lyle go into her story. That didn't give us much time. The idea was to scare Olson, but Bass panicked and Olson started to yell. You know the rest."

Maybe my hearing was better than that of my visitor, but I knew someone was coming down the hall outside. I started to talk and talk fast.

"Stupid," I said, hitting the desk with the palm of my hand. "All this for—"

"Enough, Peters," said the killer, pulling back the hammer of the pistol. "What is the information you have that's kept you alive an extra few minutes?"

"The information," I said with satisfaction as I saw the doorknob turn slowly, "is that you are about to take a trip downtown to explain all this to the police."

The room was nearly dark, but a band of moonlight through the clouds showed the determined jaw of the killer. The door opened and the pistol turned from me to the new arrival.

"Look out," I shouted, standing, bad ribs or no, to take a leap at the killer with the gun. But the surprise was mine and I stopped.

"Sit down, Peters," Academy Dolmitz said, stepping into the small office and closing the door. "After what you've been through, you think you can just go jumping over desks and grabbing guns like the Cisco Kid? You know, Warner Baxter in *Old Arizona*, best actor 1929? Overrated performance, but what the hell, sound was just coming in and he yelled and whooped and had that farcockta accent.''

"Dad," said the killer impatiently, "why did you come up here? I told you I'd take care of it.''

"That's the kind of father you think I am?'' he said, pointing to his chest. "I'd let my daughter come in here and shoot a man who might get violent back. You got kids, Peters?''

"No," I said. "Not married, not any more.''

"Too bad," sighed Dolmitz. "It's good to have kids, you know what I'm talking about here? Your brother the cop, he would know. But it's not so good sometimes to let the kids in on your business. You want to, but it doesn't always work out.''

"Dad," Jane Poslik pleaded, her gun back on me. "Let's just get this over and get out.''

"A minute more," I said. "I just want to get this straight. Lyle came to you looking for someone to keep an eye on Olson, some muscle, so you gave him Bass and decided to see if you could make a few bucks on the deal.''

"You blame a guy?'' asked Dolmitz, scratching his scalp through his mop of hair.

"And you had your daughter go to work for Olson to find out what profits you could make from the deal. After all, Lyle had a lot of money and he must have had some reason for wanting to keep an eye on Olson.''

"I didn't send her," Dolmitz said. "On that I could cross my heart. It was her idea. She was between jobs. More like a regular job it was.''

"And then," I went on, "when she found out and people, the FBI, others, started asking questions, she decided to cover herself by writing the letters, claiming that Olson had kidnapped the president's dog.''

"We figured they were going to check anyway.'' Dolmitz shrugged. "So she might as well push a little and sit back and see how far they took it. What the hell, if the FBI or the cops moved in and took the dog then we were out a little time. Jane collected her salary. I got paid a commission for

Bass's services. You lose once in a while on an investment, but let me tell you, you cover yourself. Right? Is it a bad idea to cover yourself? That was Walter Brennan's mistake in *The Westerner*, you know, Judge Roy Bean, best supporting actor. He walked into that theater where Gary Cooper could get him. You gotta learn from a good performance like that."

"But things went bad?" I asked.

"Bad?" he asked, looking around the room. "What are you, the crown prince of understatement? Bad? If my daughter weren't here, I'd use a word to tell you how bad it got. Killing, shooting. Let me tell you, I thought I got out of all that many years ago back East. You think I want my daughter involved in this dreck?"

"She's up to her neck in it," I said, as the dog leaped off the table and went to the door.

"It was all accidents," Dolmitz said. "Bass got carried away with the Olsons. I, I must admit, got a little nervous when I saw Lyle coming in here. Bass hadn't come back last night with the pooch or the fifty grand, so Janey and me came looking for you and who should we see prancing in the doorway downstairs like the best supporting actress of 1936, who was?"

"Gale Sondergaard for *Anthony Adverse*," I answered. He had picked another Warner Brothers production.

"He's good," Dolmitz said to his daughter. "You are very good. You know how hard it's going to be to shoot you?"

"Very hard I hope," I said.

"Pa," Jane sighed in little girl exasperation.

"Lyle came prancing into the Farraday like Gale Sondergaard," I jumped in.

"Right," said Dolmitz. "We stopped him, asked him where he was going and he tells us he is going to see you, tell you what he knows, which is not all that much, but enough to get me in trouble maybe, especially with you knowing Bass is connected to me. We follow him up the elevator trying to talk him out of it but he's not listening, just goes on like a meshuganeh about generals and presidents. So I shot him when we got to the fourth floor, which, by the way, took forever. Our mistake was we left him there and didn't make sure he was dead, but it was morning, people might come. You know how it is. Listen, in my imagination I may be a Spencer Tracy, a two-time winner, but when it comes to shooting real people, I'll confess to you, I'm not such a brave character.''

''That's enough, Pa,'' Jane interjected.

Dolmitz held up his hands as if to say, What are you going to do with kids? I wasn't sure how much time I had to stall. I'd have to use my last trick, which would give me perhaps a minute or two extra.

''Has any animal ever won an Oscar?'' I asked.

''No animal,'' Dolmitz said, ''but you may remember in '37 Charlie McCarthy was given a special wooden Oscar. What's with the animal question?''

''The dog over there deserves a nomination,'' I said.

Dolmitz scratched his chin, looked at his daughter, and then back at the dog.

''Pa,'' Jane said. ''How long do you think I can hold this gun up like this?''

''What's the cryptic comment on the dog?'' Dolmitz asked. ''You've got a point here or just making conversation? That's the way you want to die, saying something stupid about a dog?''

''That's not Fala,'' I said.

''It's Fala,'' Jane said.

''No Fala, no fifty thousand bucks,'' I said. ''You did a lot of killing for nothing. Any performance ever been good enough to get people to kill themselves over it?''

''No,'' said Dolmitz suspiciously, ''but a few years ago when Gable took his shirt off in *It Happened One Night* and wasn't wearing a T-shirt, the undershirt business went to hell. I think, Mr. Private Detective, you are lying to us.''

''I put it together this way,'' I said, ignoring his insult. ''Olson was told by Lyle to snatch the dog in Washington, but Olson was too scared or smart to do it. He switched dogs. He did something to the real Fala, prescribed some medicine, vitamin, gave him some spiked food, who knows, but enough to make the real Fala act strange so there might be some concern about it, some doubt if and when Lyle followed through with his threat to use the dog to get some political foothold.''

"So you are telling us that the real Fala is in Washington right now?" said Jane, putting the gun into her other hand.

"In the White House where he's always been," I said.

"I don't believe you," Jane said.

"It's hard, Peters," Dolmitz agreed. "Put yourself in my place."

"Even with the gun on me," I said. "I think I'd rather be in mine. No one, Lyle, you, Jane here, bothered to take a good look at this dog. You didn't have to. You thought it was Fala, but a friend of mine went to the library and looked up the pictures in the *Times*, even got a print made from a negative and blown up, and an old guy in the park gave me a dog lecture. Our friend shivering in the corner—not Lyle, the black furry one—is bigger, curlier, has longer legs.''

"Dogs like this look alike," said Dolmitz. "A cocker's a cocker.''

"I don't know anything about dogs, but it doesn't take an expert to check," I said. "Face it, Academy, you got taken by a second-rate performance.''

"The dog's?" he said, shaking his head.

"Not just his," I said, getting up slowly and nodding toward the door. "Mine."

The door shot open, this time hitting Dolmitz. The dog let out a yowl and ran under the desk as Jane let go with a shot that went through Lyle's corpse, giving him an extra bullet he did not need.

Bass, still tied, lurched into the room and against the wall with Jeremy behind him. My office was now three people beyond its maximum occupancy. Jane's gun came up, leveled at Jeremy's massive chest, and Dolmitz staggered away from the door, kicking it shut and moaning.

"Don't move, anyone," Jane said, now holding the pistol in two hands. "Pa, are you all right?"

"No," groaned Dolmitz, holding his right hand to his face. "Do I go around groaning like Lionel Barrymore when I'm feeling all right? I'll survive, but I'm not all right.''

"Toby, they haven't——" Jeremy began.

"I'm fine," I said.

"Cut me loose," said Bass. "I've got things to do to these two."

He looked first at Jeremy and then at me.

Dolmitz examined his hand to see if there was any blood on it from his nose and said, "More killing, putz? You know why we're all crowded in here instead of reading a book or off at Loew's? Because you kill. You are the last person in California I would untie."

"Mr. Dolmitz," Bass whined.

Dolmitz held up a finger and said, "Shah, still."

"So," I said. "You going to shoot me, Jeremy, Bass, and the dog? You up for mass murder, Academy?"

"You've got a point, Peters, but I tell you, what am I going to do? I shot the poor yetz in the corner. Now Janey's shot him. I don't want to see my only daughter get, God forbid, the gas chamber, and I don't want it to happen to me."

"You can make a deal," I said. "My brother's a cop, a captain, you know that. You give him Bass and the two of you get a few years. It's that or you start shooting and I can tell you that as soon as that gun in Jane's hand goes off, the person it doesn't hit is going to be all over her. The way she shoots, even in this little box she might wind up hitting you or nothing. Now I don't want to risk that, but it's better than just sitting and waiting to let her take aim."

"Pa?" Jane said, backing into Lyle's body as Jeremy took a short step toward her. The body, already off balance, toppled over and into her. She let out a scream and another bullet. This one went through my window, shattering glass into the dark alley.

Dolmitz took the pistol from her and the door opened again. This time Gunther walked in.

"Toby," he began, finding a small spot of floor in the corner under the photograph of me, my old man, Phil, and our dog. "I know I wasn't supposed to but I heard the shots."

"Who's this?" Dolmitz demanded.

"Another person you'll have to shoot," I said.

"Mr. Dolmitz," Bass pleaded. "Let me go and I'll just step on him, squash him."

"Did you get it?" I asked Gunther.

"I've got it," he said, "but I—"

"Got what?" said Dolmitz. "What's this, got it? You got a gun, dwarf?"

"Gunther's not a dwarf," Jeremy corrected. "He is perfectly formed, better, in fact, than you. He's a little person."

"Look," Dolmitz said, "I'm not in the business here of insulting people or being polite. What is this thing he's got?"

"Transcription," I said, easing over so Bass could have a little more space in the corner.

"I see," said Dolmitz. "You're going to let us hear the real president's dog and I'm supposed to compare it to the little cocker here."

"Better," I said. "Gunther's an electronics wizard. I'm going to show you something, so don't shoot." I opened the drawer to my desk slowly.

"Pa," shouted Jane. "Don't let him."

My hand came out slowly with the microphone and I said, "Gunther was in an office recording everything we've been saying in here. Now you've got another problem. First, you've got three people to shoot and only four bullets left in that gun."

"I shoot the little guy last," Dolmitz said.

"Second," I went on, trying to ignore the offense to Gunther's dignity, "you have a record to find in a very big building. There's no percentage in it. Make a deal, put the gun down."

The lights suddenly went on in the outer office and light trickled in under the door.

"Toby, is that you in there?" screamed Shelly. "This place smells like someone's been eating hot dogs on the floor. What're you—"

Shelly opened the door, reached in, turned on the single overhead light and, mouth open, looked around the room. He took in Bass, Jeremy, Gunther, Jane, Dolmitz with the gun, me, and the corpse on the floor.

"You're busy now," he said politely. "We can talk about this tomorrow."

"Get in here," Dolmitz shouted.

"There's no place for him to get," I observed. "What do you want him to do, stand on the corpse?"

"I'd rather not," Shelly said, forcing himself in. "Look, I just stopped by to pick up those tickets for the show. I left them—"

"Shut up," shouted Jane, running her hand through her hair. "Shut up."

Shelly shut up.

"Mr. Dolmitz," Bass whispered, but Dolmitz didn't answer.

"This is enough," Jeremy said after a few beats. "Give me the gun." He stepped forward one pace, which was all he had room for, his hand out.

"Take it easy, Jeremy," I said, ready, ribs or no ribs, to go over the desk and for Dolmitz's gun.

Academy looked at me and took a step back away from the huge poet. When he too tripped over Lyle, hell broke loose again. A shot went off, hitting the light bulb, as Jeremy lunged for the fallen Dolmitz and Jane kicked out at Jeremy. Then there was a second shot, which brought an "Oh my god" from Shelly.

It brought something else too. Something filled the space of the broken window behind me and went through, taking the remaining glass with it. I went around the desk, pulled Jane off of Jeremy, and told Jeremy that he had better get up off of both Dolmitz and Lyle. His bulk would mean nothing to the corpse of Lyle but a few seconds of it would mean the end for Dolmitz.

Gunther opened the door to let in light, and Jeremy stood up, holding Dolmitz by the neck with one hand and the gun with the other. He handed the gun to me and we looked around the room. Bass was missing. I knew where he was, but I didn't want to look out the window and down to the alley below. Instead, I reached under the desk, pulled the pooch out, and petted him reassuringly.

We filed into Shelly's office, leaving Lyle behind. I had

also left the gun on my desk. I'd retrieve my .38 some other time. I wasn't worried about Jane and Academy while Jeremy was in the room.

"Shel," I said, "call the cops."

"Me?" said Shelly, his hand to his chest. He was wearing his best suit. "Why don't I just walk out of here and pretend I never came back? Who would that hurt? I ask you?" He looked around the room for sympathy, but got none.

"I will make the call," said Gunther, going back into my office.

Jeremy placed Dolmitz in the dental chair and motioned for Jane to back up.

"He's not bleeding, is he?" Shelly said, stepping forward. "I don't want him bleeding on that chair. I just cleaned it." Then to me: "Toby, this is it. Our deal is off. No dishes, no equal billing on the door. You've violated our agreement here with killers, shooting . . . Wait a minute. Where's the big guy, the one what was all tied up. He . . ." And then it struck Shelly. He sat back against the wall and moaned, "Mildred. Mildred's downstairs waiting for me in the car."

"Just go down and tell her to go to the play alone," I said gently. "I'll drive you home later."

Gunther came out, said he had called the police, and went downstairs with Shelly to be sure he'd be back and to help him talk to Mildred.

Jane looked dazed, beaten. I held the dog in my arms and petted it while I walked over to her. Her thin blond hair dangled down her forehead.

"You'll probably be out on the streets before the war is over," I said. "Your father'll take the big rap. The two of you might even be able to pin it all on Bass, except the Lyle shooting. Bass was tied up downstairs when that happened."

"The record," she said looking up. "The little man made a record."

"No," I said. "Microphone's not attached to anything. We just made it up."

Dolmitz, sitting in the dental chair, groaned. He had heard my nearby whisper. "Taken in by the performance of fools," he said.

"I think Preston Foster said that in *The Informer*," I said. "Who gives a crap," said Dolmitz.

13

We were the main attraction at the Wilshire station, the big act. The six of us were interviewed individually after an unsuccessful attempt by Phil to talk to us as a group.

When I was led into Phil's new office, he was rubbing his forehead and looking deeply into a metal cup filled with steaming coffee.

"You know," he said, looking up, "it's going to take us half the night to get this all straightened out."

His jacket was off and his tie was loose. Somewhere in other rooms the ailing Seidman was talking to Dolmitz, Cawelti was dealing with Jane and Jeremy, and Gunther and Shelly were waiting to give their pieces of the tale.

"Phil, I've got a date tonight and I'd really—"

His hand came down on the desk. Unfortunately, it still held the cup and even more unfortunately, the cup still had some coffee in it. The brown liquid dotted Phil's shirt and soaked his hand. He pulled out a handkerchief, wiped his palms, and threw the sopping piece of cloth in the wastebasket.

"Ruth can clean that," I volunteered, standing close to the door for a quick getaway.

"Toby," Phil said, looking up at me but not moving forward. "You were supposed to hand-deliver a killer, to make this all nice, quiet, neat. And what do I get? Two more corpses and a screwed-up case with too many witnesses. And you want to go off somewhere on a date?"

He moved toward me and I said quickly, "I'll stay awhile."

He was a foot from me and ready to go to work.

"I'm going to stay calm," he said after running his right hand over his bristly head of hair. His left fist was clenched.

"That's a good idea," I agreed.

"Eleanor Roosevelt," he said. "How the hell am I supposed to keep her out of this? You know what this is going to do?"

"You're a Democrat," I said.

"I'm a cop," he said, holding his left fist up to my face.

"Captain," I said, "this has nothing to do with Eleanor Roosevelt. Some confused political loonies got together and convinced themselves they had the president's dog. Before they could do anything about it, they started bumping each other off and got themselves caught."

"That's simple, huh?" said Phil. "You think that football team out there is going to go along with that story?"

"Why not? Shelly just wants to go home. Jeremy and Gunther are patriotic, Dolmitz and his daughter will be happy to put most of it on Bass and Lyle, and I've got a date."

He reached out a hand and shoved me against the wall.

"I've got some bruised ribs," I said, holding out a hand to keep him back.

"You think the newspapers are going to drop it that easy?" he said, shaking his head.

"How do they find out?"

"Two bodies," he screamed. "Two bodies. One in your office with two bullets put into it eight hours apart and a tied-up giant with a broken arm who flew out of your office window. You think they might be just a tiny bit curious about that?"

"You'll think of something," I said.

"The only thing I can think of right now is to smash your face," he went on.

"That'll make you feel better?"

I reached for the door. Hell, he would probably catch me before I hit the stairway, but I wasn't going to take a session with Phil without giving escape a fair chance. Then the phone rang, a bell announcing the end of round one.

Phil picked it up and said, "What is it?"

Then someone on the other end said something to change his face from rage to bewilderment.

"Captain Pevsner, sir," he said. "Yes sir, I recognize your voice. Of course. Yes, I understand."

Then he was silent for a good three minutes, just nodding his head. Finally, he looked up at me.

"Someone wants to talk to you," he said, holding out the phone.

I took it and said, "Hello."

"Mr. Peters," said Eleanor Roosevelt. "I'm back in Washington. I have definite proof that Fala is right here and that the dog you retrieved was quite another animal."

"I know," I said.

"I understand that you have been through a great deal of discomfort over this and under the circumstances I've had to inform Franklin. He has just spoken to the officer in charge, and I hope your difficulties are now over. You have my thanks for your efforts and please send me your bill. We must get back to the Peruvian reception now. Good-bye."

I was about to say good-bye on my end when the voice of the president came over the phone as clear as if it were a fireside chat.

"Thank you, Mr. Peters."

"You're welcome, sir," I said, and he hung up, but a demon took me and I went on talking. "No sir. . . . Yes . . . I understand. . . . If it's absolutely essential for national morale of course I will, but I don't know if I'm really qualified to be Mr. Hoover's assistant. . . . No, I'm flattered but . . ."

Phil pulled the phone out of my hand, put it to his ear and heard nothing.

"He just hung up," I said, grinning.

"Get out," Phil said, giving me an extra shove across the room. "Just pack your jokes and get out, leave the bodies for me, for the adults to take care of."

"Come on, Phil," I said, adjusting my windbreaker. "We caught the bad guys."

"And you're going on a date while I put my career on the line to cover all this up," he said, getting behind his desk. "What are you risking, junior G-man?"

"Nothing," I said.

"Nothing," he agreed. "Because you've got nothing to lose. Because you haven't invested in anything."

"That's the way I wanted it, Phil," I said, waiting for him to get up and go for me again. He didn't get up.

"I'm going, Phil," I went on. No answer. He picked up the phone, pushed a button, told Seidman and Cawelti to come in, and waved me away as if I were a fly on a hot day.

Cawelti and Seidman passed me in the hall, the former giving me a look of hatred, the latter ignoring me. I found Shelly, Jeremy, and Gunther in the squadroom, told them to follow me, and we made a package exit that would have been pointed out by tourists if we were on the street. But in the Wilshire station we were part of an average day.

"And we are free?" said Gunther. "No more questions?"

"No more questions," I said. "The president thanked us and closed the case."

"Dolmitz and Jane," said Jeremy, trying to hail a cab. One slowed down, looked us over, and sped away. "She is really a very good illustrator. Perhaps she can work on the children's book from prison. I don't know the rules."

"Maybe," I said.

Shelly was looking glumly at the sidewalk. Another cab came cruising and I stepped into the street in front of it. The cabbie had to stop or face two to five years for manslaughter. He stopped.

We piled in and I told him to take us to the Farraday. He hummed all the way to keep from dealing with us, and I watched Gunther try to maintain his dignity on the jump seat in front of me. Shelly wasn't worrying about his dignity. He bounced and talked to himself.

Back at the Farraday, I checked on the dog, which Jeremy had locked in his office. He was all right. Then I called Carmen, after thanking Gunther and asking Shelly to wait.

Carmen was angry but we still had time to get to the fights if I moved quickly.

"Shelly," I said, hanging up. "How about calling Mildred and telling her to meet us at the stadium. Tickets are on me. Gunther and Jeremy are coming too."

With a little coaxing, Shelly agreed. The idea had come to me without bidding, and as soon as it had come I knew that my chance of getting alone with Carmen for the night was down to nearly nothing. As it turned out, I was right. Alice Palice also joined us for the evening and we easily filled two cars.

By the time I dropped Carmen off and Gunther and I headed back to Mrs. Plaut's, I was flat broke.

"I would like to have offered to drive the car back here," Gunther said, "so that you might have remained to bid Carmen good night, but I am, as you know, unable to drive any automobile but my own or one—"

"Forget it, Gunther," I said, looking back at the dog curled asleep in the back seat. "I've got too many bruises for anything more tonight."

Mrs. Plaut didn't greet us. It was far too late for that. Gunther went to his room. I went to mine, talked to the dog, and shared some puffed rice with him before going to bed. When I turned the lights out I realized that I wouldn't have the dog the next night. Something threatened me with a feeling I didn't like, so I shut my eyes and went over my bill to Mrs. Roosevelt. It was like counting sheep for me. Repair of torn sleeve, two dollars; gas, two dollars; repair of Olson's (now my) pants where shepherd had bitten, eighty cents; taxi from the warehouse where I met Keaton, a buck eighty with tip; five for the manager of the Gaucho Arms; medical bill from Doc Hodgdon, five dollars; windbreaker zipper, forty cents; car door, twenty dollars; two hot dogs, two pepsis and a taco for the dog, a buck.

In the morning, the dog and I went back to my office after having coffee and some donuts at Manny's. The bodies were gone, and a man was already putting a new pane in my window. Shelly was nowhere around.

It took me about seven calls to find the person I was looking for, and I arranged to meet him in an hour. That was about how long it took me to find the place, a deserted farmhouse on the way to Santa Barbara.

When I pulled into the side road, the dog climbed up to look out the window. We drove about half a mile and then stopped. A pile of dust was moving toward us. When it got close enough, maybe fifty yards away, I could see a man running toward us, arms churning, one hand holding a little hat on his head. Behind him a truck was bouncing along the road with a movie camera mounted in the seat grinding away.

When Buster Keaton was about fifteen yards away, the man in the truck shouted, "Cut!"

Keaton stopped, leaned over, panting, and coughed. I got out of the car, leaving the dog behind, and walked over to him.

"Getting a little old for this," Keaton said.

"We'll have to do it again," the man in the truck yelled.

"Like hell we will," Keaton croaked back.

"That damn car is in the shot," the director said, pointing to my car.

"Then we'll work it in," Keaton said, catching his breath. Turning to me, he said, "We'll rent your car for an hour. Twenty bucks."

"Fifteen," shouted the director, hearing our conversation.

"Fifteen will be enough for gas and to get me through a few days till a client pays me," I agreed.

"Fifteen then," said Keaton. "Wish it could be more." He shouted back at the director. "We'll go to a point of view shot of me looking at the car parked in front of me. Then a shot of the car and Emil getting out. I'm trapped. I give it a gulp, same shot continues after a point of view. Then I start running again, right over the car. Pull the truck off the road and shoot me from the side, one take."

"Sounds good," said the director.

"It'll do," said Keaton. "Give me a day and I'll come up with better, but for this, it'll have to do. What can I do for you, Mr. Peters? I can't offer you a drink. The suitcase is back at the farmhouse. But you're not a drinking man, are you?"

"The dog," I said.

"You brought the dog? It's not Fala?"

He stood up and looked over at the car while I explained. His eyes were straining. He pulled out a pair of glasses and put them on to see the dog in the window.

"How much you want for him?" said Keaton.

"Nothing," I said. "Guy he belonged to can't take care of him anymore, and you already paid once."

"And you don't want to keep him?" Keaton said, walking with me to the car.

"No," I said. "In my business there's no room for a dog."

Keaton opened the car door and the dog jumped out and ran circles around us. I watched Keaton's face. His expression didn't change as he took off the glasses and put them under his coat.

"He'll be good in the movie," Keaton said.

"I'm sure," I agreed.

"Buster," shouted the director from the bouncing truck driving off the road.

"Okay," said Keaton.

I took the dog and moved to the side of the road, out of the frame, and let Keaton and the crew take over. I held the dog and kept him calm while he watched Keaton with fascination. Since the shot was silent, I didn't try to stop him from barking.

After the shot was over, I agreed to stay around for lunch, which consisted of sandwiches back at the farmhouse. I accepted the fifteen bucks for the use of my car and shook Keaton's hand as I got back in after reaching down to pet the dog.

"What's his name?" Keaton said, as I closed the door.

"I don't know. I thought I knew for a while, but . . ."

"Give him a name," Keaton said, watching the little black dog run back toward the farmhouse. Beyond the building, weeds and grass waved in the May wind. "I was going to call him Fella, but the honor's yours."

"Murphy or Kaiser Wilhelm," I said.

Keaton looked at me blankly. "Kaiser Wilhelm?"

I turned the key, pulled the choke, and stepped on the gas. "I once had a dog with both names."

"Then that's it," Keaton said, stepping back and waving. "Kaiser Wilhelm."

I drove down the dusty dirt road and watched Keaton in my rearview mirror turn and follow the dog toward the farmhouse. I found a gas station as fast as I could and used a few of the fifteen dollars to fill the tank. Then I headed back to Los Angeles.

I got back late in the afternoon and called the office. Shelly said he was busy, that the sign painters were coming in to put the names on the door, and that I had had a call from Anne.

I found some change and the number of Lyle's house and called. Anne Lyle answered the phone.

"This is Toby Peters," I said.

"Martin's dead," she said.

"I know. I'm sorry."

"Why, you didn't do it, did you?"

I could tell from the way she said it that if she wasn't drunk, she was as close to it as a person could be without getting credit.

"I didn't kill him," I said. The truth was that maybe I helped to get him killed, but she was in no condition and I was in no mood to go into that.

"Police won't tell me much," she said. "Ha. I'm a very rich widow, Toby. You want to come on over and be nice to a very rich widow?"

"Some other time," I said. "Anne, you didn't kill him either."

"I didn't even like him," she said. "And he knew it. Am I going to see you again?"

"Sure," I said, but I wasn't sure at all.

"Is that why you called?"

"I just returned your call," I explained.

"I didn't call you. At least I don't remember calling you. I've . . ."

"It's all right," I said. "You didn't call. I made a mistake. Take care of yourself."

I hung up and dropped another coin in the phone. I was standing in a Rexall and a man with a cap who looked like a trucker flipped a quarter nearby and looked at me to let me know he wanted the phone. I turned my back to him and told the operator the number. It was the other Anne, the real Anne, who had called me.

My palms were wet as the phone rang. I wiped them on

my pants and looked at my dark reflection in the polished wood of the phone booth.

The trucker tapped his watch. I watched him tap and waited. Finally, someone answered.

"Howard residence," said a woman's voice.

"Mrs. Howard," I said. I didn't think I would ever be able to say Mrs. Howard, but when the moment arrived, I had managed.

"Who is calling?" the woman said.

"Her husband," I said. "Her first husband."

"I'll tell her you are on the phone," the woman said, unmoved by my revelation. "And your name?"

"Toby. She won't need the last name. Her memory will almost certainly cover that period of her life."

The phone was put down gently and I waited, giving the trucker a shrug to show I couldn't help the insolence and delay of others.

"Toby," came Anne's voice.

"It's me," I said.

"How have you been?" she said.

"Fine," I told her and the trucker. "Just finished a job for Mrs. Roosevelt; the president called personally to thank me."

"Toby," she said in familiar exasperation, "I'm not up for your games. I never found them funny. Not then and certainly not now."

"I know," I agreed. "You couldn't tell the difference between my serious moments and the comic ones."

"Was there a difference?" she countered.

"Come on, buddy," said the trucker, "I've got a call to make."

"Anne," I said, "you called me, remember. And I'm calling back. You told me to stay away. Okay. You got married, okay. I didn't call to start it all again, but it comes. It just comes automatically, like a—"

"I need your help," she said. "But I don't want it unless you keep this on a business level."

"No more work for Hughes," I jumped in. "The last time I worked for him I got too little thanks, too little money, and almost killed."

"Which was just what you wanted," she said. She knew me too well. "It's not Hughes. It's Ralph, my husband. I can't talk about it on the phone. Will you come over, please?"

"Anne," I said, "I'll go wherever you want me to go."

"That's today. It wasn't always like that."

She gave me the address and I pretended to write it down. I knew where she lived in Santa Monica. I had driven by there twice at night just to see the place.

"It'll take me a while to get there," I said. "I've got to stop off and pick up a report on a client."

I hung up the phone, got out of the way of the trucker, and stood back to look down at myself while he barked at the operator.

In the next two hours, I borrowed fifty dollars from Gunther and, while Arnie worked on my car, charging me thirty for the inconvenience of having to put aside another job, I found a store and bought a new suit, shirt, and tie, and had my shoes polished.

When Arnie found I didn't have the cash to pay him and saw that I had just gotten a complete wardrobe, he upped the price by another five.

Car shined, door fixed, sun bright, and new clothes on my back, I took a Doc Hodgdon magic pill, scratched at my itching chest, and headed for Santa Monica.

The house was on the beach, separated from its nearest neighbor by a few hundred yards. A trio of gulls swooped down to greet me as I turned and let my Ford glide down the driveway. I parked next to the three-floor white wooden house and got out to look around and give my ribs one last scratch. It was then I noticed the body on the shore and the man standing over it.

I ran down the slope and through the sand, ruining the shine on my shoes. When I was about thirty yards away I recognized both the corpse and the standing man. The corpse was my ex-wife's husband, Ralph, and the bewildered man standing over him wearing only a gold bathing suit was the heavyweight champion of the world, Joe Louis.